Praise

Foul Play at the Fair

"All the charm of a Norman Rockwell painting, but with a much more colorful cast of characters!"
—Cynthia Baxter, author of the Reigning Cats & Dogs Mysteries

"Celebrate Shelley Freydont's new mystery series in Celebration Bay, a city of festivals where the event coordinator plans everything. Except solving murders."
—Janet Bolin, author of the Threadville Mysteries

"Event coordinator Liv Montgomery is doing her best to squash any obstacles to a successful Celebration Bay Harvest Festival, and when a body crops up, she's not going to let her plans be plowed under."
—Sheila Connolly, *New York Times* bestselling author of the Orchard Mysteries

"*Foul Play at the Fair* is a fun romp of a story about Liv Montgomery, who gives up her irritating life of handling bridezillas and finds the perfect job in Celebration Bay, New York, with her Westie, Whiskey. A delicious read filled with interesting characters and good times."
—Joyce Lavene, coauthor of the Missing Pieces Mysteries

"I fell in love with Liv Montgomery and the citizens of Celebration Bay from the very first page."
—Mary Kennedy, author of the Talk Radio Mysteries

continued . . .

Berkley Prime Crime titles by Shelley Freydont

FOUL PLAY AT THE FAIR
SILENT KNIFE
INDEPENDENCE SLAY

Specials

COLD TURKEY

Independence Slay

Shelley Freydont

BERKLEY PRIME CRIME, NEW YORK

THE BERKLEY PUBLISHING GROUP
Published by the Penguin Group
Penguin Group (USA) LLC
375 Hudson Street, New York, New York 10014

USA • Canada • UK • Ireland • Australia • New Zealand • India • South Africa • China

penguin.com

A Penguin Random House Company

INDEPENDENCE SLAY

A Berkley Prime Crime Book / published by arrangement with the author

Berkley Prime Crime Books are published by The Berkley Publishing Group.
BERKLEY® PRIME CRIME and the PRIME CRIME logo are trademarks of
Penguin Group (USA) LLC.

For information, address: The Berkley Publishing Group,
a division of Penguin Group (USA) LLC,
375 Hudson Street, New York, New York 10014.

ISBN: 978-0-425-25256-7

PUBLISHING HISTORY
Berkley Prime Crime mass-market edition / June 2014

PRINTED IN THE UNITED STATES OF AMERICA

10 9 8 7 6 5 4 3 2 1

Cover art by Robert Crawford.
Cover design by Lesley Worrell.
Interior text design by Tiffany Estreicher.

Chapter One

··

Liv Montgomery slapped at her cheek. "Ugh. This might be my least favorite thing about summer in Celebration Bay."

"Told you to spray on some deet," her assistant, Ted Driscoll, told her. "Not to brag, but in July upstate New York is the capital of biting bugs. The mosquitoes here are so large—"

"I get it," Liv said. "Please hand me that bug spray." She traded him her clipboard for the spray.

"And it only gets worse around sunset."

"Great." Liv spritzed the vile-smelling spray on her hands and patted it on her face. She handed it back to Ted, who slipped it in his pocket. "What about later, when it's dark? Or will we all be eaten alive while we watch the Battle of the Bay reenactment and fireworks?"

Ted shrugged. "Hopefully this will be the last of them. The county sprayed already. That got most of them, and we have volunteers whose job is to eliminate any standing water and to keep the lakeshore cleared so people can enjoy the reenactment without being constantly assaulted by the little bloodsuckers.

"They probably disturbed the last hangers-on while clearing out this underbrush." He motioned to the edge of a thick wooded area where teenagers from the local community center were hauling out underbrush.

"Do they get paid to do that?" Liv asked.

"No, they're all volunteers. Henry gives a contribution to the teen program. And they clear out debris for the reenactment and become lunch for the mosquitoes they stir up."

The two of them surveyed the wide lawn of Henry Gallantine's mansion, home to the Revolutionary War patriot as well as the current Henry Gallantine.

The original Henry had been hung as a traitor, though he was exonerated years later. The imaginative residents of Celebration Bay, New York, had gleefully appropriated the ghoulish story for its Fourth of July celebrations.

Liv had looked up the Battle of the Bay when she'd taken over as event coordinator for the quaint destination town. The closest battle she'd found was the Battle of Valcour Island, which had taken place farther north and hadn't involved any cannonading of British ships.

But heck, what was a little reinvention with your reenactments when it attracted tourists from all over the Eastern Seaboard?

Liv slapped at her face again and scratched her ankle with her other foot.

"You must have missed a place . . . or two." Ted smiled complacently, his blue eyes twinkling. He was wearing a tasteful red, white, and blue plaid sports shirt, navy slacks, and a lot of bug spray.

Ted loved his holidays. The whole town loved their holidays. Even Liv loved their holidays, but she hadn't quite perfected the art of theme dressing.

As a Manhattan event planner, Liv had worn basic black with four-inch heels; here she opted for Topsiders in fall and spring, snow boots in winter, and colorful flats in the summer. Though today she was wearing a pair of running shoes. Not that she thought she'd get any running in today or at all until the Fourth of July weekend was over.

Until then she would be running errands, running resistance, and running her committee heads crazy with last-minute checks and double checks.

She had dressed down in lightweight slacks and a boatneck T-shirt and pulled her hair—which Dolly Hunnicutt, the local baker, had once compared to the color of burnt sugar—back into a high ponytail, finished in a messy bun.

Not exactly a corporate look, but then neither was she—not anymore. Her desperate housewives, mad men, and overspent fathers of the bride had been replaced by bakers, quilters, nurserymen, and farmers, who had their moments of less-than-stellar behavior but who were, for the most part, great neighbors and friends.

She was still getting used to the theme attire that everyone seemed to favor. Today, the only thing about her that remotely resembled red, white, and blue were her eyes, which were blue and bloodshot from lack of sleep.

"There's old Jacob Rundle coming this way," Ted said. "Ignore his charming manners. He's been gardener and dogsbody for Henry Gallantine forever. He's not the friendliest man in town, but then, neither is Henry."

"But Henry lets the town use his property for the reenactment."

"Just because he's a crank and a recluse doesn't mean he isn't a good citizen. Plus he leaves town for the whole summer as soon as it's over so he won't be bothered by the tourists."

"I just met him the one or two times when we were confirming the event. He was perfectly charming."

"One-on-one with a beautiful woman."

"Why thank you, Ted. Are you saying that Henry is a womanizer?"

"Just the opposite. Women fall over themselves when he's around. Another reason he keeps to himself. He was a child star in Hollywood. Still a good-looking guy, keeps fit and well groomed."

This from a man who had to be in his sixties—though Ted had never admitted to any age—and looked pretty darn good himself.

"He has a gym and a lap pool in the house. The only people invited in are his hairstylist and personal trainer, who always come to him."

"In case of making a comeback?"

"Don't laugh. I think, for Henry, hope springs eternal."

"Anything I would have seen him in?"

"Only if you watch reruns of fifties movies or television."

Liv hardly had time for television of any decade.

While they were standing there, a slightly stooped, raw-boned man ambled toward them. He was wearing khaki pants and an old button-up shirt. Stringy hair was topped by a gimme hat bearing the logo of a local machine shop. Obviously the gardener and not the dapper Henry Gallantine.

"Ted," he said in a gravelly voice. "Ma'am." He touched the bill of his hat but didn't take it off. Which was just as well; his hair looked like it might not have been washed in a long time.

"This is Liv Montgomery, the new event coordinator," Ted said. "Liv, Jacob Rundle."

"How do you do, Mr. Rundle." Liv didn't offer her hand, since he was holding a nasty-looking pair of secateurs.

"Heard someone took Janine Tudor's job."

Ted stifled a grin. Liv gritted her teeth. She hadn't taken Janine's job. Janine had been a volunteer and not a very efficient one. The town council saw the need for hiring a professional, and Liv had applied for the job. But after nearly a year, Liv had stopped trying to explain this to people. She just smiled back at the gardener.

"How's it going?" Ted asked.

"Slow."

"Looks like you've got a good crew."

"Dang kids. That pastor over at the Presbyterian church got Mr. G to let them take over the cleanup. Half of them don't have an ounce of sense. Gotta tell them every dang thing. Faster to do it myself."

He looked around at the workers. Most of them, teenagers from the community center, carried cut branches and brush and leaf clippings out to a line of big barrels.

"You there, what the heck are you doing with those?"

The teenager, who had been carrying an armload of branches, stopped. Looked warily at Rundle, saw Liv and Ted.

"Hiya, Miss Montgomery." He raised his hand in greeting, dropping half his load of weeds. "How's Whiskey?"

Liv recognized the young man who'd entertained her Westie terrier, Whiskey, while she'd attended the Christmas *Messiah* sing-along. Leo was "a gentle soul," according to Pastor Schorr. Gentle and slow, though no one had mentioned that he had any neurological problem. "He's fine, but he's staying with Miss Ida and Miss Edna today."

"I like him."

"He likes you, too."

Rundle raised his fist. "What's the matter with your brains, boy? Look what'cha done. Now stop jawing and pick all that stuff up. And take it over to the blue barrel. Blue. You know what color blue is?"

Leo nodded and quickly knelt down to gather up the weeds again. Liv was about to go help when Roseanne Waterbury, another teenager who sometimes volunteered at the center, ran over and began to help Leo collect his bundle.

Rundle turned back to Liv and Ted. "Boy don't have good sense." He pointed to his temple.

"Well," Ted said. "We won't keep you; just came down so I could show Liv the schematic of the battle."

Rundle nodded slowly. "Seen the ghost last night."

"Did you?" Ted said. "That makes four sightings so far."

"'Cause he ain't happy."

Liv narrowed her eyes. Was he playing a part? Who actually played the ghost each year was a well-kept secret, which was nearly an impossibility in Celebration Bay. And her assistant, who was Gossip Central, had sworn for months that he didn't know, not that she believed him. Ted knew all the gossip, but he also knew how to keep a secret.

Liv figured the ghost had to be the current house occupant, Henry Gallantine. After all, it was his ancestor who'd given the signal. It was so obvious, but it had taken months to get anyone to let her in on the secret.

"Why isn't he happy?" Liv asked. Out of the corner of her eye she saw Leo stop gathering up his branches and stare at the gardener.

"Things going on."

For the first time, Ted actually looked concerned. "What kind of things?"

"Bad things. People comin' round asking questions. He was wandering down by the lake. Looking for something. The treasure maybe." Rundle shot an ominous look at Roseanne and Leo.

Leo's eyes rounded and more twigs and leaves fell to the ground.

Roseanne frowned at the gardener. Today her cinnamon-colored hair was stuck under her cap, and she was wearing a long-sleeve shirt to ward off the deer ticks. "Don't pay any attention to those stories about ghosts, Leo. It's just somebody dressed up in a costume for the reenactment. Like at Halloween."

"He was looking for the treasure," Rundle said, taking, Liv thought, a malicious pleasure in scaring the boy.

Roseanne stood up. "If he was looking for the treasure, he wasn't the ghost, because the ghost would already know where it was. Only there is no ghost. Come on, Leo, let's get this trash thrown out." She pulled Leo to his feet and hurried him away.

"Girl don't know nothing." Rundle's mouth curved into a smile that Liv wished she hadn't seen. There was nothing friendly about it. "Nothing at all."

"Let me guess, gold stolen from the British ships?" Liv said.

"Or the document. It weren't never found," Rundle said mysteriously. "The blue barrel! Dang kids." He jogged off toward Roseanne and Leo.

"Document?" Liv asked, keeping an eye on Rundle. Roseanne seemed to have things under control, but Liv didn't like the way the gardener treated the volunteers. Someone should ask Pastor Schorr if he was aware of how Rundle was acting.

Ted was looking, too, and he said distractedly, "Some people persist in the belief that there's a chest of gold; others are positive there's a secret document that either truly exonerates Henry and names the real traitor, or proves he really did the dastardly deed they claim he did."

Rundle stood over Leo and Roseanne while they dumped their trash, then, after a few more orders, he walked away.

"Which was warning the British about the attack?" Liv asked as she watched Rundle disappear around the far side of the house. "Are you sure this is a good environment for the community center kids?"

"He's gruff but not usually this mean with the kids. He just doesn't seem to like Leo. Had a little dustup last month when Leo was delivering some groceries. I'm not sure it's a good idea to have the kids here with only Rundle to oversee their work. I think I'll give Phillip Schorr a call when we get back to the office."

"I was just thinking the same thing."

"Anyway, rumors have always circulated about treasures and secret documents." He broke into a grin. "Over the years the truth, or what they thought was the truth, got mixed up with speculation and imagination. Gallantine *was* hanged as a traitor and later exonerated, but it wasn't about gold. Or a battle. It was worse. He informed on a group of patriots planning a proclamation against King George."

"The Declaration of Independence?"

Ted shrugged. "Let's just say it might have turned into the Declaration of Independence if any of them had lived to complete it. But they were slaughtered on their way to meet with other revolutionaries while they were secretly bivouacked with an army patrol."

"Ugh. I think I prefer the parade. Let's do this and get back to the office." Liv took the clipboard that held the map of the reenactment.

She turned so she was facing the river. "So the bleachers will be behind us over there," she said, pointing to a flat piece of lawn between her and the street. "And the ships . . ."

Out on the lake, the wooden depictions of the British ships floated on the water. They weren't actual ships at all but mock-ups attached permanently to docks, from which the fireworks would be discharged.

"This is perfect," Liv said. The trees that lined each side of the property were thick enough to hide the boathouse, the garage, and the neighboring houses, and made the tableau on the water look just like a stage set. "We're lucky Henry Gallantine is so amenable to letting us use his property."

Ted nodded. "We've been holding it here in one form or another for the last ten years. There was never a question of holding it anywhere else."

"I can definitely see why." Liv turned to the right and peered up the façade of the old stone house. It looked more like a gothic castle to Liv, with a turret on one side and a huge chimney on the other. Various sections were stacked like building blocks made of stone, until the last one rose in a peak toward the sky. Dark windows gave it a sinister feel even in the daylight.

"Where does Henry, the ghost, stand to give the signal?" Liv asked.

Ted pointed about a third of the way up the three-story

mansion, where a wide flat roof was surrounded by a stone parapet. "Henry G stands facing the crowd and flashes the signal with a lantern. Well, to be accurate, with a powerful LED lamp that can be shuttered and opened so he can 'one if by land, two if by sea' it in style."

"I think that was Paul Revere."

"Whatever works. Ours is more elaborate; a virtual light show of 'the British are coming.' "

"And this is already rehearsed?"

"For years. Rufus Cobb and Roscoe Jackson have been in charge of the patriots for at least a decade. Rufus is the left flank and Roscoe the right. They have their teams rehearsed and ready to go by the middle of June.

"Daniel Haynes, scion of General Delmont Haynes, who *was* a Revolutionary War hero, no question, leads the attack on horseback, just like he did at the Battle of Ticonderoga."

"Which you neatly appropriated for the Battle of the Bay."

Ted grinned. "If it works . . ." He shrugged. "Actually they should be showing up soon. Tonight's dress rehearsal."

"Are you participating?"

"God no. I'll be sitting in the bleachers with a hot dog and a root beer."

"And which unfortunate souls have to play the British?"

"Well, we don't have any British. We used to when we first started doing the reenactment. But after a few drinks people forgot it was just playacting and the punches started flying. That's when we came up with the idea of the ships."

"Good thinking. Seriously, is it safe? There's no chance of the ghost falling over the parapet?"

"Relax. They all can do this in their sleep. You have to earn your place in this patriot army. And the fireworks are handled by the same company that we've hired for the last five years. You worry too much."

"It's my job. Anyway, I don't worry exactly, I just try to make sure all my bases are covered."

Though Liv had to admit, she'd pretty much let Ted

oversee the reenactment without her while she prepared for the parade and made the final security arrangements for the weekend. They were expecting record crowds, and her new security team would be out in full force.

A.K. Pierce, the head of Bayside Security, ran a tight-but-friendly ship. He'd hired extra personnel to cover the grounds and waterfront for the fireworks and would continue to supplement the police during the rest of the weekend. EMTs and ambulances were in position.

As for the safety of the fireworks, they were profession-ally rigged and set off behind the "British" ships moored out in the lake and couldn't be reached except by boat. Ted assured her that none of the pieces would come near to fall-ing on anyone's head.

Liv had double-checked with the fire department anyway.

The entire event was ready to go.

The only thing, or rather person, who was missing was Chaz Bristow, the editor of the local paper, an avid fisherman who took out fishing parties to supplement his journalistic income.

He'd left town without warning right in the middle of his busiest fishing season. Not to mention the middle of the town's tourist season. So instead of the *Clarion* publishing features and schedules of events, Liv had to print posters to display in the windows of restaurants and stores, and flyers to be handed out by volunteers at information booths at each corner of the village green.

Other than that, Liv didn't miss him, exactly. He was obnoxious and lazy. He had the attitude and looks of a land-locked surfer dude: muscular, blond, really handsome—with a big attitude that needed some serious adjustment.

He could be annoying as all get out, but in spite of his outward laid-back persona, he still had the mind of the inves-tigative reporter he'd once been in Los Angeles. Unfortunately he was very reluctant to get involved in any of the recent wrongdoings in Celebration Bay.

Maybe she did kind of miss him.

"Seen enough?"

"Huh? Oh yeah. No, wait. Are those two men in uniform Rufus and Roscoe?"

"In the flesh."

The two council members strode toward Liv and Ted. They had to be sweltering in the top boots and breeches and the woolen coats of the American patriots. Each was wearing a black hat and had a powder horn slung across his chest. Roscoe also wore a heavy cape that he'd thrown behind one shoulder and held a musket that ended with a serious-looking bayonet. Rufus held a long gun that was almost as tall as he was.

"You two look great," Liv said enthusiastically, though she couldn't stop herself from casting a dubious look at their weapons. "Is that bayonet real?"

"Absolutely," said Rufus, brandishing the musket over his head. "But we're trained to use them safely."

"Good," Liv said, not entirely convinced.

Rufus chewed on his mustache. "It used to be that the first line actually shot."

"With real bullets?" Liv asked, thanking her lucky stars there would be no real shooting that night.

"Not anymore," Ted assured her.

"They didn't use bullets in the Revolutionary War," Roscoe said, "but powder and ball. . . . You see, you keep the powder in this horn, and when you're ready to load, you pour the powder into the . . ."

"You had to ask," Ted said under his breath. "Ah, here comes Daniel Haynes. I wanted Liv to meet him before tomorrow."

Roscoe looked a little disappointed.

"But some other time I would love to learn how to load a musket," Liv said, and turned to wait for Daniel Haynes to reach them.

He looked like a military hero, tall and lean, with longish

dark hair graying at the temples and a neatly trimmed goatee streaked with white. Liv knew he was a local lawyer, though she'd never met him.

His uniform was a cut above the others, with tan breeches and shiny black boots. He wore one of those military hats whose shape always reminded Liv of a taco. He also wore a sword at his side rather than carrying a musket, though he might have one of those, too.

Ted made the introductions. Liv and the "general" shook hands. Daniel Haynes had a deep voice that Liv could imagine mesmerizing a courtroom—or leading an army of patriots. But he seemed distracted. Probably concentrating on getting into the part.

"Have you seen Rundle?" he asked. "He was giving the driver from the stables a hard time about where to park the horse trailer. We park it in the same place every year. And every year he complains. I don't know why Henry keeps him on. Oh, there he is. I must get this cleared up now. So nice to meet you, Ms. Montgomery. Gentlemen." He touched his hat and strode across the lawn toward the gardener.

"And we should be getting back, too," Ted said. "Have a good rehearsal." He took Liv's elbow and steered her toward one of the gates in the wrought-iron fence that fronted the mansion.

Once on the sidewalk, he slowed down. "Sorry, but if we didn't get out of there, Roscoe would have finished his lengthy explanation of musket loading. Trust me, now is not the time."

Liv laughed. "They take this so seriously."

"That they do."

They both looked back at the lawn. Roscoe and Rufus had split up and were walking to their opening positions, but Daniel Haynes and the gardener were standing toe to toe and almost nose to nose.

"Do you think we should go referee?" Liv asked. "After all, I am the coordinator."

Ted grabbed her elbow again. "Absolutely not. This happens every year. Rundle complains about the horse's hooves tearing up the lawn, about the tire tracks the trailer leaves. He rants and raves.

"And Daniel gets his way—every year. Nothing ever changes. Nothing much can go wrong." He grinned. "But the parade tomorrow. Now, that's a nightmare."

Chapter Two

....

Out on the street, food and souvenir vendors were already setting up their vans and trucks. The lighting truck that was responsible for all the special effects until the fireworks took over was cordoned off by a barrier of orange sawhorses.

Liv and Ted walked back toward town down streets with houses decorated for Independence Day. The whole town had been festooned in red, white, and blue since the day after the strawberry festival.

The one-day festival had been a piece of cake—literally—and lots of fun. The day began with the Miss Strawberry pageant, a milder and pinker version of the beauty pageants that were shown on television. Afterward, there was strawberry ice cream, cakes, pies, shortcake, pancakes, Belgian waffles, jams, syrups, and ices. And when you tired of eating, there were strawberry-themed things to buy: pot holders, aprons, hats, and jewelry.

But on the day after the Strawberry Fest, all the stores around the square pulled the pink from their windows and changed over to red, white, and blue. And the town became the epitome of the American Way.

A Stitch in Time displayed freedom quilts, needlepoint flags, and eagle pillows. Bay-Berry Candles was all decked out in vanilla, cherry, and blueberry candles. The Bookworm New and Used Books displayed histories of the revolutionary period for all ages, from recent biographies for adults to classics for children, like *Johnny Tremain* by Esther Forbes and *The Midnight Ride of Paul Revere*.

The tables outside the Apple of My Eye Bakery were covered by red-checked tablecloths topped by a centerpiece of carnations and little American flags.

The square was filled with people. School had been out for several weeks, and families had poured into the area, staying at the local inn or the several bed-and-breakfasts in town. Others made day trips from nearby vacation spots.

The weather was humid but not too hot and, if it weren't for the mosquitoes, life would be perfect. Though Liv really couldn't complain. She spent most of her days and nights inside working.

Ted and Liv waved to locals and smiled at visitors as they walked along the east side of the village green. In front of Town Hall, a construction crew was building the grandstand where the parade would pass, and where the floats would stop long enough to be judged: Best All-Around, Most Patriotic, Most Colorful, Most Inventive.

Everyone won something.

The front door of Town Hall was draped in bunting of stars and stripes. As they climbed the steps, they met Mayor Worley coming down.

Gilbert Worley had been mayor for three terms. He was short, fat, and friendly—especially in an election year—with graying brilliantined hair and a gold tooth that flashed when he smiled, which he did a lot—especially in an election year.

Unfortunately it wasn't an election year, and the mayor was frowning.

"Afternoon, Gilbert," Ted said

"Ted, Liv, glad I caught you." He glanced past them as if he was looking for someone else.

He pursed his lips and stretched his neck, but since he was wearing a plaid shirt unbuttoned at the top, it couldn't be that his collar was too tight. But he was definitely on edge.

"It seems we have more than one ghost this year, and the latest one is causing trouble."

"What? More than the usual pranks?" Ted asked. "We have some fake ghost sightings every year," he told Liv.

"This wasn't a prank. Evidently someone broke into Gallantine House last night."

"Mr. Rundle didn't mention it when we saw him this morning," Liv said.

The mayor shot her an impatient look. "It was the housekeeper who reported it. She has rooms on the first floor. She called Bill Gunnison and he went over there. He didn't find any evidence of a break-in, but Hildy swears things were missing. Some eggs or something."

"Eggs?" Liv asked a bit incredulously. Her neighbors liked a good tale and a bit of exaggeration, but to call the sheriff over eggs?

"Maybe the ghost was hungry," Ted said with a perfectly straight face.

"Hildy thinks it was the kids who were helping clear out the underbrush. But Rundle says he saw the ghost running from the house."

Ted snorted. "You know you can't place any dependence on anything Jacob Rundle says. If he's not drunk, he's just plain ornery. He told us he saw the ghost down by the lake."

"It's a bunch of hooey, but Hildy's on her way over here to complain about the sheriff not taking her seriously. Awful woman."

"And you have urgent business elsewhere?" Ted asked.

"Yes. Oh Lord, here she comes now." The mayor

practically jumped to the sidewalk and took off down the street in the opposite direction.

"I don't think I've ever seen him move so fast," Liv said as she watched the mayor sprint around the corner.

"We should have joined him. And we don't even have the intrepid Westie to warn her off. Tomorrow you bring Whiskey to work." He turned and smiled. "Hildy. What a pleasant surprise."

"Well, I never." Hildy Ingersoll was several inches taller than Liv, at least five nine or ten, built along Valkyrie lines, with gray hair tied back so tightly that Liv was surprised the woman's face moved at all. She was dressed in a gray cotton dress and orthopedic shoes. She held a black purse clutched tightly in the crook of her elbow.

She took a moment to suck in several quick breaths. "Government officials drinking on the job. You should be ashamed of yourselves. I have a good mind to report you to Mayor Worley, but don't think I didn't see him running off down the street."

"He had to see to some urgent business."

Hildy snorted.

"And you heard Ted saying I should bring Whiskey to work," Liv added.

Hildy shook with indignation and turned to Ted. "That's what happens when you start bringing sinners from the big city into town. We'll all be going to hell in a handbasket before you know it." She glared at Liv. "You mark my words."

Ted didn't make a move to explain.

"Whiskey is my Westie terrier," Liv explained. "He's a sweetheart. We, of course, would never drink on the job."

Hildy sputtered, not at all mollified. "Stupid, heathen name to give to a poor, defenseless animal."

Liv had to force herself not to roll her eyes. Sometimes she wished she'd named her dog Snowball instead of Whiskey. But in Manhattan, no one blinked at the name. It was a fine Scottish dog name and a fine Scottish liquor.

"What brings you here?" Ted asked. "I heard about the break-in last night. There's been no more trouble, has there?"

"Nothing but." Hildy pulled her purse closer, as if she thought Liv might snatch it and run. "It's those kids. Have to keep an eye on them every second or they'd rob Mr. G blind. I told him. I said, 'Mr. G, those kids will rob you blind while you're not looking.'

"But did he listen? No, he did not. And now look what's happened."

"What has happened?" Ted asked innocently.

"One of them Fabergé eggs Mr. G thinks are so pretty is gone. Keeps a whole row of them on the parlor mantel. They were all there when I was cleaning the other day. Now one of them's gone." She shook her head. "Mr. G took great store in those eggs. If you ask me, they may cost a lot, but they're just plain gaudy. Them kids stole one of 'em right off the mantel."

Liv and Ted exchanged looks. *Eggs. Of the Fabergé variety.*

"Are you sure it was the kids?" Ted asked. "It doesn't sound like something they would take. Maybe it was the ghost."

For the first time Hildy hesitated. "Why would any ghost want one of them eggs?"

Ted shrugged, looking serious. "I don't know, but Jacob Rundle told us he saw the ghost down by the lake looking for . . . something."

Hildy frowned, chewed on the inside of her cheek as she thought. "Can't believe anything that Jacob Rundle tells you. Half drunk most of the time. Probably got the DTs or something. Got them pink elephants mixed up with the ghost. Don't know why Mr. G lets him stay on.

"It weren't no ghost. I caught two of them kids red-handed in the larder yesterday. Ran off with two of the pies I was saving for the bake sale. They've been stealing stuff for I don't know how long, but Mr. G, he just let's them keep coming. Especially that Leo. The two of them act like a couple of children, all the time playacting. It ain't healthy."

"Can we help you, Hildy?" Ted asked.

"You can't. I came to see the mayor to tell him that Bill Gunnison's next to useless, but he goes running off. And the two of you standing here doing nothing. Not even five o'clock and already there's nobody working."

Liv forced herself not to tell Hildy Ingersoll just how hard they worked. That event coordinating wasn't a nine-to-five, five-day-a-week job, but weekdays, weekends, all hours.

"Would you like to leave him a note?" Ted asked.

"I. Would. Not. I would like our elected officials to do the work our tax dollars pay them to do. And you can tell Gilbert Worley I'll remember that in the next election. And it weren't no ghost," she repeated, only this time she didn't seem too sure of herself. "This is just the beginning, you mark my words." Then with a sharp dip of her chin, she turned and stormed off the way she had come.

"Shades of Mrs. Danvers," Liv said.

Ted chuckled, and they went inside.

The telephone was blinking in the Events Office, and Ted sat down at his desk to listen to the messages. Liv put her bag on the floor and perched on the edge of his desk to listen.

Nothing seemed urgent, although there was a call from Bill that asked Ted to call him at his convenience.

"Tell me more about the ghost-sighting situation."

Ted leaned back in his chair and stretched his hands behind his head. "Let's see. Every year between the Strawberry Fest and the Fourth of July, people start seeing the ghost of Old Henry Gallantine. Some of the sightings are in the eye of the beholder—figments of over-imagination or too much hooch on a Friday night. Some are kids playing pranks. Harmless, and makes the 'real' "—he made air quotes with his fingers—"sightings all the more thrilling." He shrugged.

"The real ghost?"

"The official ghost," Ted amended.

"Oh."

"Then there are others that are unaccounted for."

He reached just the right tone to make goose bumps break out on her arms. Probably the air-conditioning.

"Not pranksters?"

Ted shrugged.

"So, does Jacob really believe in the ghost?" Liv asked a bit incredulously. Her neighbors liked a good tale and a bit of exaggeration. And Ted was the master of drawing out a story.

"Well, I'm guessing he was just trying to scare Leo and the other kids. But there are people who do believe. And there are others who would take advantage of them."

"I take it that the current Henry Gallantine doesn't dress up in a sheet and run into town scaring people."

Ted shook his head. "Cuts out as soon as the signal is given and before the crowd disperses."

"Does every generation of Gallantines name someone Henry?"

"I haven't really looked into it, but my guess is that each had at least one, sometimes more than one. Don't forget he was exonerated, and he was—before and after the scandal— a hero."

"And does the current Henry have any offspring?"

"None that we know of. An old bachelor, though as to offspring . . ." Ted shrugged. "The Gallantines have always been a prolific bunch. Another trait they evidently inherited from the original Henry, who was the welcomed guest of many ladies up and down the thirteen colonies."

"Why am I not surprised?"

"Probably saw it as his patriotic duty," Ted said, fighting to keep a straight face. "Doing his bit to add to a growing country, and he probably convinced the ladies it was their duty, too."

"That's a come-on I haven't heard before." Not that Liv

had been hearing any come-ons lately. She was a dedicated workaholic, even in idyllic Celebration Bay. She did get a little flutter whenever A.K. Pierce walked into her office, but since she'd hired him and she never, with a capital N, mixed business with pleasure, that was out of the question.

Her mind took a stupid turn toward Chaz Bristow before her good sense could stop it. But that would go nowhere. And really, did she have the energy or the patience to deal with the newspaper editor's slovenly, complacent, lazy, unhelpful, snarky, annoying self?

But there was that smile. And that kiss at Christmas.

And the fact that he was missing in action. He'd left town sometime in the spring and hadn't returned. The town had been without a local paper or a fishing guide ever since, and as much as she complained about the snail's pace of getting things scheduled in the newspaper, it was worse not having it at all. She had no idea where he was and when or if he was coming back. If anybody knew where he was and why, they weren't telling . . . her at least.

"So," she said, drawing her mind back from that treacherous subject. "We have the reclusive Mr. G, the angry, avenging Hildy, and the rascally Jacob Rundle. Why on earth would people like that put up with hundreds of strangers on the grounds, plus a good fifty musket-toting reenactors, and someone on the roof wielding a lantern, not to mention all the fireworks?"

Ted gave her his driest look.

"Wait. I know. It's their patriotic duty."

It was six o'clock before they finally closed up for the day. Liv had learned no more about who the "official" ghost was. It was one of the best-kept secrets in Celebration Bay, where normally secrets made the rounds faster than the Indy 500.

Ted didn't seem to be worried about the extra ghost sightings, so Liv let it go.

It was a warm but not uncomfortable evening, and she cut across the park on her way to her home, a delightful little carriage house behind her landladies' big Victorian, several blocks from the center of town. Miss Ida and Miss Edna Zimmerman were retired schoolteachers, and they had lived their entire lives in their childhood home. Rumor had it that both their fiancés had died in the war—which war was rather vague—but Liv guessed the Korean one. Neither had ever married.

They were excellent dog sitters and loved Whiskey to the point of spoiling him. But tonight was their potluck night at the Veteran's Hall, so Liv knew they would have left Whiskey in the carriage house, fed, pampered, and sleeping off a day of fun.

Liv was looking forward to a little sleep herself. Right after dinner. And for once the fridge was semi-stocked. Thanks to the 4-H's July kickoff barbecue, there were leftover spare ribs, potato salad, and rhubarb pie in her fridge, as well as a bottle of crisp, chilled pinot grigio, not from 4-H, but from the local wine store.

As soon as Liv opened the front door, a white whirlwind shot past her, ran a maniacal circle around her feet, and raced back inside.

"Good to see you, too," Liv said, and followed the excited Westie inside.

Whiskey was sitting by his bowl when Liv entered the kitchen. There was fresh water and a cleanly licked food bowl.

"Nice try," Liv said. "I'm going to have to change your name to Roly-Poly if we don't start getting more exercise." It was still early, but Liv had no desire to drag on jogging clothes and spend the remaining daylight pounding the pavement.

She yawned. "You get a reprieve tonight. But Saturday morning—no, Sunday morning, right after church—you and I are going for a run."

Whiskey's ears flipped up to alert. Muzzle down, tail up, and ready for flight.

Liv laughed. "Not tonight. Tonight I put my feet up." She reached into the fridge for the platter of ribs.

Miss Ida was out sweeping the sidewalk the next morning when Liv and Whiskey left for work. She was the slighter of the two sisters, with white hair that she kept pulled back in a bun. She had a penchant for twin sets and floral dresses, and today she was wearing a shirtwaist of tiny blue flowers and a lightweight red sweater.

"Morning, Liv." Miss Ida slipped her hand into the pocket of the sweater, and Whiskey sat at her feet. "Just a little bit of biscuit," she told the attentive Westie and handed him a morsel. "Everyone will try to feed him today. And Dolly has the cutest little flag d-o-g b-i-s-c-u-i-t-s," she told Liv.

Whiskey stood, barked, and gave Liv a reproachful look.

Miss Ida laughed. "I'm afraid he may have learned to spell."

Great, Liv thought, *a singing, spelling dog*. What would be next? "Have a nice day, Miss Ida. I'll see you later."

Whiskey pulled on the leash.

"Heel," Liv commanded.

"Arf." Whiskey started down the street, dragging Liv with him.

"Edna and I are helping with the DAR float this morning," Miss Ida called after her. "We'll pick him up and bring him home with us after l-u-n-c-h. And keep him for the fireworks. All that noise can't be good for his little ears."

"You're not going to the reenactment and fireworks?" Liv asked, walking backward as Whiskey pulled her toward town.

"We never do, too many mosquitoes. And we can see well enough from an upstairs window."

"Thank you-u-u-u," Liv called back as Whiskey picked up speed. "Heel," she commanded again. "Unless you want to go back to obedience school."

Whiskey sneezed, shook his head, and slowed down.

There was already a line out the door to the Apple of My

Eye Bakery. Dolly must have been watching for them, because she ran out with a bag of goodies for Liv and Ted and a rectangular American-flag doggie biscuit. It even had the thirteen stars made of some kind of icing, which Liv knew would be healthy. Dolly's recipes had passed inspection by Sharise over at the Woofery, who now sold Dolly's Doggie Treats from her grooming business.

Next door, BeBe Ford, proprietor and barista of the Buttercup Coffee Exchange, was doing a brisk business. All lush curves and dry wit, BeBe was also Liv's best bud in Celebration Bay.

"Crazy weekend," she said as she steamed the milk for Liv's coffee.

While she waited, Liv looked around at the small area where a coffee bar lined one wall and a few small tables crowded every inch of non-pedestrian space.

"You and Dolly should combine forces and get a larger place."

"We've talked about it a hundred times. Can't find one that suits our needs for a price we can afford. And then outfitting new surroundings—ugh." BeBe slid a cardboard tray with Liv's latte and Ted's tea across the counter. "No time to talk. Maybe tomorrow. No, I can't. Dinner next week?"

"Sounds like a plan," Liv said.

Ted was waiting for Liv and Whiskey at the door to the office. He was wearing a bright-blue buttoned shirt and a red striped vest.

"How's my favorite da-a-awg today?" Ted crooned and leaned over to scratch Whiskey's ears.

"Aroo-roo-roo."

"Well, I'm so glad you feel that way. But if we're going to sing at the parade tomorrow . . ." Ted sighed dramatically and gave Liv a look reminiscent of the one Whiskey had shot her while she was conversing with Miss Ida. "We're woefully under-rehearsed. Yankee Doodle went to town . . ."

"Aar roo roo roo aar roo roo-o-o-o-o."

Liv groaned, hurried into her office, and closed the door. So far Ted had taught him to sing "Jingle Bells," the "Hallelujah Chorus," and "Danny Boy" for St. Patrick's Day, all of which sounded very much the same. "Yankee Doodle" promised no surprises.

But it entertained the both of them. And there were some people in town, namely her landladies and Dolly Hunnicutt, who thought it was a clever trick.

Liv spent most of the day at her desk making last-minute phone calls and double-checking everyone's schedules. For the first few hours, she jumped every time a firecracker went off, but gradually became inured to the sound.

Miss Ida and Miss Edna picked Whiskey up at four, and Ted and Liv walked to the Gallantine House early to triple-check that everything was in order, the fireworks were set up, the troops were ready, the boats were in position out on the water. But when Liv suggested they double-check with Henry Gallantine about manning the lantern that night, Ted dug in his heels.

"Already done. You worry too much."

"It's—"

"Your job, I know. But everything is fine. Spray yourself with bug spray and let's go get some lemonade."

Liv held her breath and sprayed. There were few times when she missed the city, but mosquito season was definitely becoming one of them.

The crowds were already milling around the street vendors, loading up on food and drink. At six o'clock, security opened several designated entrances in the gates, and people flooded through only to be stopped by volunteers who searched their bags and took their tickets.

As soon as they were inside the gates, veterans rushed to get the prime seats on the bleachers. Within the hour, most of the seats were taken, and the standing-room area was shoulder to shoulder.

Liv and Ted took their seats on the bleachers one row below

the mayor, Jeremiah Atkins—local banker and one of the town trustees—and Janine Townsend, the ex–event coordinator, who still managed to put herself wherever the action was.

It was a perfect summer night with a sliver of moon just appearing as the afternoon turned to dusk. As it grew dark, glow-in-the-dark necklaces and bracelets competed with the fireflies and turned children into shadowy aliens.

Only the mansion was spotlighted from below, which cast eerie shadows against the stone and ramparts, making the old mansion look like a movie set. Liv was sure she could see Henry Gallantine's hand in the presentation.

The ships looked like black silhouettes against the water.

The crowd became quiet. Children strained forward to see what would happen next. Anticipation rippled through Liv.

A voice worthy of reciting the Declaration of Independence began the story of the Battle of the Bay: "It was on a summer night when General Haynes received word that the British had begun moving ships toward the fort of Ticonderoga, but they were never to arrive. For from the roof of his house on the lake, Henry Gallantine signaled the British approach and called the patriots of our great state to arms. Here is the story of those brave men who preserved the freedom of all New York."

It was thrilling, if mainly hyperbole and a good deal of imagination.

Just as the sun completely disappeared behind the crowd, someone cried, "There. It's the ghost of Henry Gallantine. Up on the parapet."

All eyes turned to the roof of the mansion.

A figure hovered behind the stone parapet, perfectly framed in an eerie light that made him look otherworldly. Liv was duly impressed. And she let herself be pulled into the action as the figure lifted the lantern. It blinked once, twice, and again. Then the light went out, and the lantern and figure disappeared.

From the shadows of the trees, the patriots crept stealthily onto the lawn. The lights rose just enough to see their uniforms, swords, rifles, and deadly bayonet-tipped muskets. First the left flank, then the right, until fifty men met in the middle of the lawn, waiting for their leader.

"You're positive none of those rifles and muskets work?" Liv asked.

"Authentic, but not loaded. We used to fire them but it was a pain in the butt. Sometimes literally," Ted whispered. "Another reason we added the British ships,"

Out on the lake light rose on several "British" ships.

And as the American army joined as one and turned toward the lake, a rider and horse galloped from behind the mansion. Daniel Haynes reined in before his troops and brandished his sword as the stallion rose on its hind legs.

There were exclamations of delight and awe from the bleachers. Liv had to admit it was pretty spectacular, and the fireworks hadn't even begun.

With the general leading the way, the patriots rushed to the lakeshore, where the general rode out of view—to dismount at the horse trailer, Liv supposed. The others dispersed, climbed into boats and started to row.

All the lights went out. Even those of the vendors across the street. Only the ships were backlit from some unseen source, and the silent black boats fanning out around them were silhouetted by the moon.

As they rowed closer to the ships, the final light blinked out, leaving total darkness except for the starlit sky as the patriot boats disappeared into the night.

Where, Liv knew, they would be tied up at neighboring docks until the next morning. The men would return to the Elks' hall and hand in their uniforms. They'd change back into street clothes to enjoy the rest of the fireworks with everyone else. But for now it was magical.

"Good timing," Liv whispered to Ted.

"Got it down to a science," Ted said as the first spray of brilliant red fireworks lit the sky.

The crowd *aah*ed. A baby started crying.

Liv leaned toward Ted. "Now, that is very effective."

But Ted wasn't watching the fireworks. He was looking back at the roof, where the figure with the lantern had reappeared. The light was flashing. In short and long bursts.

"Is that part of the show?" Liv asked.

Ted shook his head.

"What is it?" Liv demanded, suddenly alarmed.

"It's Morse code for SOS." He was already climbing down the bleachers.

Chapter Three

....

Ted jumped down from the bleachers and reached back
to give Liv a hand, but she was already on the ground and
running toward the house.

"Liv, wait," Ted called, jogging after her.

She slowed long enough for him to catch up.

"Do you have a plan?" he asked, only slightly out of
breath.

She shook her head.

"Then follow me." He led her around the side of the
house to the front door, where two security people were
posted to prevent tourists from bothering the inhabitants.

They stopped Liv as she ran toward them. "Sorry. The
house is off-limits to visitors. If you're looking for a bath—"

"I'm the event coordinator," Liv said, reaching for her
ID card. She had to yell over the exploding fireworks. The
sky was lit up in reds, greens, yellows, blues. "There's a
problem with the production."

The guard looked at the card, looked at her.

"Please hurry," Liv said, then caught a glimpse of a very

large man striding down the street. He passed beneath the light of the street lamp, and Liv recognized the shaved head and wide shoulders of A.K. Pierce, head of Bayside Security, whom Liv had hired as additional event security. "Mr. Pierce. A.K.! Over here!"

A.K. looked up, zeroed in on her, and strode through the wrought-iron gates to meet her.

"Ms. Montgomery? Is there a problem?"

"There might be. Ted saw an SOS signal coming from the parapet where the ghost signals the patriots to attack."

"Isn't that a part of the show?"

"The first signal, but the second SOS signal didn't start until after the fireworks began," she explained, then looked to Ted for confirmation.

"That's right, someone is up there flashing an SOS. I think we should see what the situation is."

"Absolutely." A.K. strode past them and up the front steps and pounded on the heavy wooden door. When it didn't open immediately, he pounded again. "Security," he boomed.

He waited a few seconds while he looked around the outside of the house, possibly considering the efficacy of breaking one of the windows. He raised his hand to pound again when the door opened several inches and Hildy Ingersoll peered out.

"This house . . . is . . . off-limits," she huffed out.

Liv was reaching for her ID but Pierce already had his open.

Hildy looked at it. "What's this?"

"Are you the lady of the house?"

"The housekeeper," Ted said. "Hildy. It's Ted Driscoll. There's trouble up on the roof."

"What kind of trouble, to get me running to the door with all that banging?" She sucked in a deep breath. "Those kids up to their tricks? I told Mr. G not to let them in the house. Nothing but trouble. We're not responsible, I told him. But he don't listen. Got a soft spot for them rascals. The more fool he." She had to stop to suck in air. "But you can believe those bleeding-heart do-gooders will make trouble if one of us so much as sneezes at them. I say spare the rod—"

"Are there children in the house now?" Ted asked.

"Well, no, not now. But Mr. G—is something wrong with Mr. G?"

"Excuse us." A.K. moved her aside and went through the door.

While she stared in surprise, Ted and Liv slipped in after him.

"You can't just . . ." the housekeeper began.

"How do you access the roof?"

"Well, I—"

A look from A.K. and she clamped down on the words. "Upstairs. There's pull-down stairs on the third floor."

A.K. was already bounding up the wide staircase.

"You can't go—" The housekeeper hiked up her skirts as if she meant to run after him.

Ted mumbled, "Sorry, Hildy, an emergency." He ran past her to the stairs, Liv following.

Liv took the wide staircase two steps at a time and quickly passed Ted, but when she reached the second floor, she could hear A.K. running overhead. She sprinted down the hall and hauled up the next flight to the third floor.

She found A.K. pulling a folding stair down from the ceiling. He immediately began climbing toward a rectangular opening in the ceiling. As soon as he'd disappeared through the opening, Liv climbed after him. Ted stopped to catch his breath, then followed her.

The stairs led right to the roof and Liv reached the top just as another spray of fireworks lit the night.

A.K. had stopped a mere two feet away and was shining a flashlight around the periphery of the roof. The roof was flat; the stone parapet that surrounded it was about hip-high.

As Liv reached him, A.K. abruptly held out his arm, preventing her from moving forward.

She heard Ted climbing up through the opening, huffing slightly. He needed to get more exercise. Maybe she'd suggest he and Whiskey take up jogging instead of singing.

"See anything?" Ted asked, coming up to her.

"Nothing yet."

The powerful beam from A.K.'s utility flashlight panned across the roof surface in meticulous order. No wild searching for this marine. He slowed as his light picked out dividing walls; illuminated dark corners only to plunge them into deeper darkness when the light moved on to the rounded walls of the turret, the square corners of the asymmetrical house; then ran along the individual stones of the parapet.

And out in the night the fireworks continued to light the sky. They only made the roof seem darker.

Liv was just beginning to think it was a false alarm when the light stopped, moved back, and came to rest on something lying on the floor.

A man dressed in the long brown coat of the Minutemen lay on his side. On the ground next to him, the lantern lay on its side, its light extinguished.

A.K. stepped forward and shined the flashlight beam directly on the man's face, spotlighting the longish, lank hair covering his cheek.

"Stay here," A.K. said, and bent over to peer at the fallen figure, checked for a pulse.

"Should I call nine-one-one?" Liv asked.

A.K. held up a hand for her to wait.

"Ted." A.K. motioned him forward. Liv went, too.

A.K. thrust his flashlight into Ted's hand and turned the man over.

The flashlight jerked in Ted's hand. Liv recoiled. A.K. sucked in his breath.

When the light once again shone on the man, it also showed the gaping hole in his stomach and the Rorschach of blood that covered his uniform.

Liv covered her mouth.

"If you're going to be sick, move away," A.K. said.

She shook her head.

"Do either of you know who this is?" A.K. asked.

Ted had to clear his throat before he could answer. "It's Henry Gallantine's gardener. Jacob Rundle."

"Shouldn't we call the EMTs?" Liv asked. "Maybe they can—"

A.K. shook his head. "The crime-scene boys. But there's no hurry. He must have bled out in a matter of seconds."

Liv swayed back and Ted put a sustaining arm around her shoulders.

The three of them stayed that way, Liv and Ted standing together and A.K. crouched down over the body, while the sky lit up with white stars. Then with a *pop pop pop*, the stars exploded and rained down in a waterfall of red.

*Ooh*s and *aah*s wafted up from the crowd below and became silent. And that's when they heard someone moaning. And close by.

A.K. was on his feet faster than a man his size should be able to move. He took the flashlight from Ted and searched the darkness at the far end of the roof.

"Oh Lord," said Ted.

In the far corner, pressed against the parapet, was a crouching figure. When the light shone on him, he scuttled even closer to the wall and brandished a rifle at them. Its bayonet glinted in the lantern light. The blood that covered it turned to black.

For a moment none of them moved, then Ted asked uncertainly, "Leo?"

Leo was shaking so violently that he flickered like an old movie. And Liv was having a hard time reconciling the boy with the "gentle soul" with the strapping young man clutching the musket and bayonet.

Ted took a step toward the boy. "It's okay, Leo. Put the rifle down."

"Stay back," A.K. ordered under his breath.

"It's all right," Ted told him. "It's one of the boys from the community center. He's harmless."

"He might be harmless, but he's armed and may be dangerous. We're not taking any chances."

Ted ignored him and took a step closer. "Leo, put down the rifle. Everything's going to be okay."

Leo shook his head in spasmodic jerks. "He's gonna get me."

Liv was amazed at Ted's calm. She didn't think she could move if her life depended on it. Which, now that she considered it, might just be the case.

Leo let out a wail, something like an animal cry, as Ted approached.

When he was several feet away, Ted crouched down, vulnerable to any harm Leo might have in mind. But Liv was afraid to call him back and risk startling the obviously traumatized teenager.

A.K. stood still but was poised to move. Liv could feel the energy vibrating off him in waves. It was almost as frightening as facing a possible killer, and in a weird way, exhilarating.

"Where did you get that rifle, son?" Ted's voice was quiet, soothing.

Leo twitched. "Found it. Over there." His head jerked toward the dead man. "Heard something. I know he was coming to get me."

"Who?"

"The ghost."

"Leo, the ghost can't hurt you."

"Yeah, he can. He hurt Mr. Rundle. He's mad. He said so."

"The ghost?" Ted had somehow managed to inch closer.

"No-o-o-o. Mr. Rundle. He said the ghost was mad and it was my fault and he was gonna get me."

"We won't let him get you. Why don't you let me hold that for you?" Ted reached out his hand for the rifle, but Leo flinched away and clutched it tighter to his chest.

"Tell me about the ghost."

Leo shuddered. "You know him. He's Old Gallantine, who hid the treasure."

"You saw him up here on the roof tonight?"

Leo bobbled a nod.

"Did you recognize him?"

"He was the ghost."

"Can you tell me what he—what his face looked like?"

Leo moaned. "Didn't have no face."

"You couldn't see it in the dark?"

"No. Ghosts don't have faces. Just all shadowy."

"What did he do when you saw him?"

"Disappeared."

"Disappeared?"

Leo nodded spasmodically. "He hurt Mr. Rundle. Now he's gonna come after me. Don't let him get me."

"We won't. He's not going to come after you. We'll protect you, but you need to give me the rifle." Ted reached for the musket.

"No-o-o."

His cry was drowned out by rapid-fire explosions. It must be the finale, Liv thought, because one display followed another, and the blasts continued until the whole night sky was filled with color.

Leo dropped the musket and covered his head with his arms. Ted snatched it from the floor and held it out for A.K., who was lightning swift to take it and move it out of range.

Ted sat down by the cowering boy and put both arms around him. Liv couldn't hear what he was saying to the boy, but she saw his lips moving, and he rocked Leo back and forth until the last explosion died away and the color fell from the sky.

And then there was silence. A calm descended and seconds passed before the sound of people talking and gathering up their belongings replaced their exclamations of delight. But this time they sounded far away as they moved

on to their next stop or returned home, while three people
and a frightened boy were separated from the rest of the
world by a stone wall and a murdered man.

"There," Ted said. "It's all over. The fireworks are finished and the ghost is gone."

Leo peered out between his arms.

Ted patted his shoulder. "See? No ghost?"

"He won't come back?" Leo spoke so quietly, Liv could
barely hear him, and she found herself moving closer.

A.K. stopped her. "Just stay back until we have him in
custody."

"Custody? Surely you don't think—"

"Liv—Ms. Montgomery. Just do as I say."

"Can you tell me how the ghost disappeared?" Ted
continued.

Leo looked around. Lifted a finger and pointed to the
parapet. "Jumped up right there on the wall, then . . ." His
hands jerked up and his fingers splayed, an action that made
Liv jump back and had A.K. reaching for his side.

"Presto. Like that."

Liv let out her breath.

Ted looked over. "I think you'd better call the sheriff."

"Already have," A.K. told him. "I have a squad of my
men surrounding the house. Though it's my guess they won't
find anyone."

When had he done that? Liv hadn't seen or heard him
make a call.

"You think whoever killed Mr. Rundle already got
away?" Liv asked.

"I think we're looking at him."

Chapter Four

....

"You can't think Leo killed him."

"When you find two people on the roof, one is dead, and the other one is holding the murder weapon . . ." A.K. didn't bother to finish his sentence. It was all too evident. And it *was* a pretty damning situation.

"So now what do we do?"

"Wait for Bill Gunnison to come take custody of the suspect."

Ted, who had been consoling Leo, looked up at that. His mouth tightened, but he didn't bother to argue. The writing was pretty much on the wall.

"Perhaps we could take him downstairs to wait? Maybe Hildy can be coerced into giving him something to drink."

A.K. reached for his hip and a pair of cuffs.

"Oh, A.K. Is that necessary?" Liv asked.

"He acts like a child, I get why, but he's a powerfully built young man. That wound was caused by someone who was either very strong or running on a lot of hate and adrenaline—or both."

"Or fear?"

"You mean self-defense?"

"It's possible, isn't it?"

A.K. lifted a shoulder, not exactly in agreement but not dismissing the idea altogether.

A.K. opened his phone and began texting.

"Well?" Ted said, sounding for the first time slightly impatient.

"I have a couple of men coming up to transport him downstairs."

Liv flinched. It sounded so impersonal.

While they waited, no one spoke. Liv tried to just stare into space or at her feet and not think about the gruesome scene that was right behind her. Trying not to focus on Leo or the dead man but just looking. It was one of those moments that she just fell into naturally, not thinking anything in particular, just looking. Letting her mind focus on the area itself. It was a technique she used to spot a poor traffic pattern, an overcrowded table setting, clashing colors, drooping décor.

It came naturally to her tonight. She took in the position of the body and Leo, the place where Leo said the ghost had disappeared. The angle of the wall that jutted out halfway across the floor. The tower door looking like a black rectangle.

Like a set waiting to be dressed, like a ballroom after the dancers were gone, like a murder scene with the victim lying in situ.

She shivered. It wasn't cold. And she jumped when she saw a head appear through the opening to the stairs. A man, followed by a second, climbed onto the roof. They were dressed in jeans and T-shirts. One had long hair, the other a standard barber cut. They looked like any other tourists, except they'd climbed onto the roof without a sound.

"Todd, Kemp, escort this young man down to wait for

Sheriff Gunnison. Mr. Driscoll and Ms. Montgomery will accompany you. Wait there for me."

One of the men stepped foreward. "The housekeeper is none too happy about us being here."

"Use your charm," A.K. said.

"Sir."

Kemp and Todd moved simultaneously toward Leo as precisely as a marching band. *Or a military parade*, thought Liv. Were they all marines? The thought was comforting and also a little unnerving.

Leo saw them coming and scrambled back, so close to the wall that Liv was afraid if he stood suddenly, he would fall over backward and plunge to his death. Or even worse, he might jump just to get away.

The men stopped simultaneously.

Ted took Leo's arm. "These men have come to keep you safe." He glanced at Liv.

And she saw the misery on his face. The men had come to hold him until the police arrived.

They parted as Ted led Leo toward the stair opening.

Liv marveled that they were going to let him go down ahead of them. Weren't they afraid he might try to run? If she were in Leo's place, she would be inclined to get as far away as she could.

But she understood when Leo froze and stubbornly refused to go any farther.

Then she heard a voice below. "Come along son, everything will be fine."

Ted urged him forward, and they both climbed back into the house.

"Like a frightened animal," A.K. said, almost to himself.

Liv cut him a sideways look.

A.K. nodded. A dismissal. "Go downstairs. Kemp, see that the lady gets down safely and send the sheriff and the CSI team up when they get here."

* * *

"I don't know what Mr. G will say when he finds out that people have been traipsing through his house all night," Hildy said as she clanked glasses on the table in front of Liv, Ted, and Leo.

A.K.'s men had refused refreshments. They stood around the periphery of the room, four of them, at attention, which was strange looking considering their summer casual wear.

"And just what *is* going on up on the roof? You been causing trouble, Leo?"

"No ma'am. I don't think so." He cast a worried frown at Ted.

Ted patted his shoulder.

"Where's Mr. G?" Hildy demanded.

"Mr. Henry's gone."

"I know that. The fireworks is over." The housekeeper threw her head back and looked at the ceiling. "Lord save us from this ignoramus."

One of the security men visibly tensed. "Ma'am, if you could keep those opinions to yourself."

Hildy Ingersoll snorted. "I'll just go find out for myself. And if you've done anything—"

"Ma'am."

"I'm going." And, mumbling to herself, she left the room. One of A.K.'s men followed her out.

Leo watched them go, then turned his attention back to the security guards. His eyes kept darting from one to another and to the windows. One of them moved a step closer to the window, and Leo seemed to relax a little. It occurred to Liv that Leo wasn't thinking about getting away. It was as if he thought the ghost might outwit his protectors and swoop in through the window to snatch him away.

He didn't seem to have any idea that he was being detained, not protected.

Time crept by with no one speaking. They heard Bill

Gunnison and the crime-scene people arrive, but when Ted attempted to go out into the hall, the guard casually stepped in front of the door.

Ted sat down. "I think I should call Silas Lark." He punched in the number on his cell.

Liv nodded. It certainly looked like Leo might be needing a lawyer, and Silas was the best lawyer in town. He also did pro bono work.

"I want to go home," Leo mumbled, and shrank down in his chair.

"We all do," Liv said. "Hopefully it won't be much longer."

But the minutes ticked by. Leo put his head down on his arms and seemed to fall asleep.

At last they heard a commotion in the hall.

Leo's head came up and his eyes widened.

"It's just some people coming down the stairs," Ted told him. He was beginning to look a little stressed himself.

Footsteps clattered down the stairs, followed by metal clicking as the EMTs unlatched the wheels of a gurney.

Bill walked measuredly into the room. His sciatica was definitely acting up.

"Hello, Leo. What are you doing here?"

"I wanna go home."

"And we'll try to get you there as soon as we can. Can you tell me what happened when you were up on the roof?"

"The ghost did something bad to Mr. Rundle."

A piercing screech erupted from the hall, and they all turned to see Hildy Ingersoll standing in the doorway and clutching the frame for balance.

"Hildy, didn't I tell you to wait for me in your sitting room?"

"Who's that they're taking away on the stretcher? Is that Mr. G they're carrying away with his head all covered up? Oh, Lord, save us!"

Leo moaned.

Hildy stormed into the room and lunged toward Leo. "What did you do, you hooligan? You've killed him. He was nice to you and now you've gone and killed him. Devil's spawn!"

"Hildy! Stop it!" Ted was on his feet and barring her way. "It isn't Henry Gallantine."

Hildy blinked. "Then who was it?"

"It's Jacob Rundle," Bill said.

"What was he doing up there? He knows better than that. Mr. G don't like him coming in the house. Dirty and half drunk more times than not."

"Well he was up there tonight."

Hildy tried to look around him to where the EMTs were rolling the gurney toward the front door. "What happened to him? If I told him once I told him a hundred times, drink would lead him to a bad end." She punctuated her sentence with a sharp nod. "And what was that boy doing up there?" She lifted her chin toward Leo. "Where is Mr. G?"

Leo's eyes rounded. "He's gone."

Bill took her arm. "I will want a statement from you, Hildy."

"I'll give you a statement," Hildy said. "We haven't had a moment's peace since Mr. G let that Phillip Schorr talk him into letting those delinquents from the community center help out around here.

"And bringing him meals, like I didn't cook for him and leave things in the freezer."

Beside her, Ted smothered a snort.

"And coming to play games with him." Another snort. "Games, as if he weren't a grown man, passed sixty a good time ago. I told him they were up to no good. Stealing things every time I turned my back. And now one of them has gone and killed off the gardener, though he weren't no great shakes himself. Heathens. All of them."

"Thank you, Hildy," Bill said. "If you could just hold

your thoughts until your interview, I would appreciate it." He took her elbow to escort her from the room.

"You let go of me, Bill Gunnison. Won't have nobody manhandling me, even if you are the sheriff. I know where I'm not wanted." She paused to glare at Leo. "I know Jacob was mean to you, boy, and that weren't right. But there was no need to go and murder him. And if you've hurt Mr. G . . . well, I hope you get everything that's coming to you."

She huffed out of the room. One of A.K.'s men slipped silently after her, no doubt to keep her where Bill wanted her.

Leo looked at Bill, then at Ted, then Liv, and back to the sheriff. He didn't seem to understand that Hildy had just accused him of killing Jacob Rundle.

"Hildy's just upset," Bill said. Which was an understatement.

Liv couldn't help but be impressed with the Bayside Security team. They'd worked several events for her since last winter, but never before had she seen them in action.

Normally she wasn't even aware of who they were. They were like chameleons blending into the crowds seamlessly and effectively. She knew there were also women working for the company. She just hadn't ID'd any of them, and they certainly weren't here tonight.

"I didn't hurt Mr. Henry." Leo said. "He's gone. He always goes away in July. He said he would teach me to play chess when he got back."

"When did you see him last?"

"Huh? Um . . ." He was silent for a few seconds, then his eyes got a mischievous look. "Wednesday. He said he was gonna get old Rundle good."

Even Bill flinched at that statement.

"Then he said we'd play when he got back."

Liv wondered if they were finding any evidence on the roof. A.K. hadn't made an appearance downstairs. Was he still with the crime-scene team? Could a civilian do that?

Though the more she got to know the man, the more she thought he might have more ties with law enforcement than she imagined.

Bill didn't seem to be in a hurry. Maybe he was waiting for A.K. to finish up whatever he was doing and take his men away.

The only one besides Leo who seemed anxious to get out of there was Liv herself.

She felt bad for the dead man and was concerned for Leo, but she was neglecting her duties. The main event was over, but she should be touching base with Fred Hunnicutt to make sure people got safely out of the grounds to their cars and homes or to one of the many restaurants and cafés open for the occasion.

And do it without letting a possible leak about the murder set off a widespread panic.

She had complete confidence in Fred, who was the coordinator of vehicular and pedestrian traffic, to take care of things in her absence. And there *were* extra law enforcement officers and A.K.'s staff of security guards.

But Liv wondered how many of them had been reassigned to the crime scene. She'd paid for an extra two details for the fireworks, an event that drew the biggest crowd of all the events she'd organized for Celebration Bay so far. That was twelve extra staff, but six of them were standing in the kitchen looking like refugees from a tour bus, which cut her down to one extra detail.

Was that enough to insure the safety of the hundreds of visitors? Especially if there was a murderer at large? She considered asking Bill if she could leave in order to find out, but one look at his face stopped her.

Bill pulled out a chair facing Leo and eased himself into it.

"You know I'm your friend, Leo," Bill said.

The boy nodded. "The police are our friends. You can always go to them and they'll help you."

Liv's gut clenched. It sounded like a quote from a school safety lesson. She cut a glance toward Ted. She was pretty sure Leo shouldn't be talking to the sheriff without having his rights read. Though from what she'd experienced, she wasn't sure the young man would understand what the Miranda warning meant.

Leo looked pleadingly at Bill. "But I wanna go home."

"I know you do. But could you help me and answer some questions first?"

Leo nodded.

Liv slowly tilted her head for Ted to meet her at the other side of the room. They both eased out of their chairs.

"Shouldn't he have read him his rights?" Liv whispered.

Ted looked toward the other end of the table. "So far he's only taking a statement. He doesn't want to befuddle the boy with all the hoopla. He'll get closer to the truth if Leo feels comfortable."

"And he feels comfortable with all these people listening?"

"He trusts Bill. But yes. If it starts getting incriminatory, Bill will stop him."

"Are you sure?"

"Liv, Bill would never do anything to entrap Leo. Or any of us."

"Do you think he killed Rundle?"

"I don't know what to think. I don't think he would, but maybe if he were frightened and he thought Rundle was the ghost . . . I just don't know."

A.K. Pierce appeared in the doorway about as silently and surprisingly as the ghost of Henry Gallantine himself. He nodded slightly to Bill and lifted his chin, and his men filed silently out of the room. It sent goose bumps up Liv's arms.

She'd never look at a tourist in the same way again. Any of them could be a well-trained agent.

They were replaced by three officers in uniform, not nearly as quiet and much more obvious.

"Now," Bill said, turning his attention back to Leo, "why were you up on the roof tonight, Leo?"

"Needed to see Old Henry's ghost."

"And you thought you would see the ghost on the roof?"

"Oh yeah. Everybody knows it's the ghost that gives the signal to start the fighting. Just like he did before they hung him."

"How did you get up on the roof, Leo? Did Hildy let you in?"

Leo had been looking at Bill, but now his eyes drifted to the door. He hunched over closer to the sheriff, and said in a lowered voice, "Came in the secret way, so Hildy wouldn't catch me and chase me out."

"Not the way we came up the stairs?" Bill asked.

Leo shook his head. "The secret way."

"You can show me that way later?"

"Yeah, I can. Old Hildy won't find us that way."

Liv frowned at Ted. Once again Leo sounded like he was quoting someone. One of his friends?

"Okay then, when you got to the roof, what did you see?"

Leo thought back. "Somebody lying on the ground. It was Mr. Rundle. So I went over to see why he was lying down. I don't know why he was up there. Mr. Henry, he doesn't like him. He came in the house once and Mr. Henry yelled at him. Hildy knows she's not supposed to let him in." Leo licked his lips. "Don't know how he got up on the roof. He don't know the secret way."

Leo stopped and took two deep breaths.

"And then what happened?"

Leo shuddered. "He was mad."

"Rundle?"

"The ghost. He jumped out of nowhere and ran right past where I was. And I got awful scared and tried to hide."

"Are you sure he was a ghost, Leo?" Bill asked. "And not Mr. Henry?"

Leo frowned, thinking. "No. It was the ghost."

"How do you know he was the ghost?"

"Cause he had a cape like a general. Old Rundle was dressed like a soldier."

Liv exchanged a look with Ted. "Did Rundle participate in the reenactment?"

"Never." Ted raised his eyebrows.

"So what was he doing in a uniform on the roof?"

"A good question," Ted said, and turned his attention back to Bill.

"Then what happened?"

"He ran right past me growling, like this." Leo made growling noises. "Then he jumped on the wall and raised up his arms like this." Leo raised his arms like a bear on his hind legs. "And then he disappeared." Leo flicked his fingers in the air. "Presto!"

It was the same thing he'd said on the roof.

"That's some story, Leo." Bill said.

"It's the truth, Sheriff. The real truth. Honest." Leo licked his lips. "Didn't even wait long enough for me to ask him."

"Ask who what?"

Leo just stared at him.

"Did you want to ask Mr. Rundle something?"

"No. Old Henry's ghost." Leo's face scrunched in frustration. "Just wanted to talk to him."

"You needed to talk to the ghost?"

Leo nodded. "Yes sir."

"Why?"

"Wanted him to tell me."

Bill waited, but Leo wasn't more forthcoming.

Bill let out a slow, controlled breath. "What did you want the ghost to tell you?"

"Where the treasure was."

"Leo, there isn't really any treasure. It's just a story that people made up a long time ago."

"It's true. Mr. Henry told me. We found lots of treasure but not the real treasure. So I thought if I asked the ghost.

Well, I thought if the ghost knew we needed the money, he'd tell me where he hid it."

"You need the money, Leo?"

"Yes sir."

"What do you need the money for?"

Ted started to say something.

Bill held up a peremptory hand.

"For the community center."

"The community center?"

"Yes sir. A man came to talk to Pastor the other day. Said we had to give him money right away or he was gonna take the center away. That isn't fair. We need it."

"You're right, Leo. The center is very important."

Leo nodded. "But I wish I hadn't done it."

Everyone snapped to attention.

"Hadn't done what?"

Ted stood up. "Bill, I don't think he should answer any more questions without a lawyer present."

Bill stood, too, but more slowly. "I believe you're right. Leo, you just sit here for a minute. How would you like a ride down to the police station?"

"I want to go home."

"And you will go home, just as soon as we finish up some things at the station."

"Can we turn on the siren?"

Bill hesitated. "Sure we can. You'll like that, won't you?"

Leo nodded, looking less scared than he had all night.

"You know Officer Meese, don't you? You just go on out to my cruiser with him, and I'll be out in a minute. Okay?"

"Okay."

Meese waited for Leo to amble over to him, then he smiled and took him away.

Bill came over to Ted and Liv.

"I think it would be a good idea to call Silas Lark and have him meet us. Then I'd appreciate it if you two would come out to the station and give your statements there."

"Of course," Ted said. "What do you think?"

"I think this isn't looking good at all."

"You don't really think Leo killed Rundle?"

"No. But I think he saw who did. And if the murderer saw him . . ."

"What?" asked Liv.

"He might come back for Leo."

Chapter Five

....

Neither Ted nor Liv felt like talking as they made their way back to Town Hall to get Ted's SUV. Since Celebration Bay didn't have its own police department, Ted drove the nearly ten miles to the Sheriff's Office.

Liv had a million questions bouncing around her brain, but she knew better than to discuss things before she gave a statement. Memory was easily befuddled by discussion.

It sort of freaked her out that she knew information like "don't discuss a case"; "don't compare notes of a crime scene"; "don't make conjectures before giving your statement." The kind of knowledge she should only know from television and not from experience. She certainly hadn't needed to use that knowledge on the mean streets of Manhattan.

But since moving to Celebration Bay nearly a year ago, she'd been involved in several murder investigations. Not because she was from Manhattan, which Roseanne Waterbury thought gave her an eye for crime. Not because she was nosy, according to Chaz Bristow, the missing *Clarion* editor.

But because she was the town's event coordinator, which put her in contact with vast numbers of people, kept her knowledgeable about the details of various sites, and made her the first person anyone called when they had a problem, including, it seemed, murder.

She'd never been called on to help with an investigation in Manhattan. She'd never even come close to murder or even accidental death. Once she'd seen a taxi hit a bag lady who had stepped off the curb before the light changed, but the driver had stopped—causing a huge traffic jam—and helped her across the street, where she continued on her way.

Celebration Bay was a small, quaint town with good people and holidays galore. It was also the scene of small-town secrets and smothered anger and was so tightly knit and taciturn that any wrongdoing could fester until it finally exploded either in a yelling match, a fight at the pub, or something more violent.

But why the gardener? And why had he been portraying a historical figure in full view of several hundred people when he wasn't even supposed to be there at all?

Liv thought back to when he'd first appeared, an eerie white aura surrounding him. It was a great effect. His uniform, in her mind's eye, shone in a ghostly way, which she guessed was the whole point.

Hundreds of people watched Rundle give the signal, but Liv couldn't remember seeing his face. Then he backed away from the wall and away from view. And into the killer's bayonet?

Not unless the killer was also one of the reenactors, dressed in military garb. The man certainly couldn't have walked into his own bayonet. And besides, if he was supposed to be the ghost, why did he have a bayonet at all? And what were both of them doing on the roof when it should have been Henry Gallantine?

"Liv, we're here."

"What? Oh."

The Sheriff's Office was a utilitarian building built on a section of rolling hill, with a well-lit parking lot large enough to accommodate at least forty vehicles. There were only a handful of cars in the lot, and Ted found a spot right in front of the main entrance.

They met Reverend Schorr on his way inside. Phillip Schorr was pastor of the First Presbyterian Church where Liv had attended services with her landladies. He was also the director of the town's community center. He was young for a pastor, Liv thought. Mid-thirties, a dynamic speaker, and a kind man. And his slightly longish hair and his boyish charm helped fill the pews each Sunday.

Tonight he looked a bit incongruous with his clerical collar sticking out from the opening of a bright-red polo shirt.

"I got here as soon as I heard," he told them. "Leo wouldn't hurt a soul. There's been a terrible mistake."

Liv was glad he'd come. Maybe he could explain why Leo wanted to ask the ghost for money to give to the community center. He would be a respected advocate. And right now it looked like Leo could use all the allies they could muster.

The three of them walked inside and stopped at the sign-in desk. The desk sergeant sent them straight through to Bill's office.

Liv was surprised to see Leo sitting at a rectangular table drinking a soda and helping himself to a box of cookies.

Silas Lark was also there. He came over to meet the three as they entered. He was a small man with thinning dark hair, mild mannered, but he took no prisoners according to Miss Edna. Liv had seen him in action. She was glad he appeared to be representing Leo—if the young man needed representing, which she ardently hoped he wouldn't.

Liv leaned over to whisper to Ted. "Where are his parents?"

Ted frowned. "Tell you later."

Pastor Schorr went straight over to the table and said with

a smile, "I hear you've been having some adventures tonight, Leo."

Leo shrugged, looking contrite. "I wanted to talk to the ghost."

Schorr placed a comforting hand on Leo's shoulder. "Now, you know, son, that there's only one ghost and that's the Holy Ghost and he loves all his children."

Leo nodded, but he frowned, as if he weren't sure. Liv didn't know what was different about Leo. He was slow in the way he moved, the way he talked, the way he thought, though he went to high school with the other local teenagers.

"You know you're safe with God?"

Leo nodded.

Liv thought that was all well and good, but if the person who had murdered Rundle and had attacked Leo thought Leo may have recognized him, the boy would probably need a little more get-down-and-get-dirty earthly protection.

Which made her think of Chaz Bristow, something that was happening more often the longer he stayed away from town. He'd taken Leo and some of the other kids out fishing more than once. Any other man would call it mentoring. Chaz said it was a pain in the butt, but it was the only way they would stop pestering him.

"So, you don't have to worry about any other ghosts."

Leo shook his head.

Liv didn't think it would be so easy. Leo had feared for his life up there on the roof.

"Is Leo eighteen?" she asked Ted.

Ted nodded, tight-lipped. So if it came to it, he would be tried as an adult. She looked over at the boy happily separating the two sides of the cookies and licking out the cream filling before eating the outsides.

She didn't for a minute think he'd killed Jacob Rundle. But she'd only met him a few times and those times were when Whiskey had been with her. Boy and dog had bonded over the "Hallelujah Chorus" last December. Now they were fast friends. Of course, Whiskey was Mr. Congeniality.

On the other hand, he knew a bad guy when he smelled him, and he liked Leo. Could dogs testify in court?

Bill came in a few seconds later. "Sorry, I hope I didn't keep you waiting too long, but I stayed to ask Hildy a few questions."

Leo looked up and actually smiled at the sheriff; there was a chocolate ring around his mouth from the cookies, and in spite of his size he looked so young that Liv longed to protect him, which was strange, since she didn't have a maternal bone in her body—not yet anyway.

Ted pulled Bill aside before he got two steps into the room. "Are you charging him?"

"Not at this point. I don't think he's a flight risk, and all the evidence is circumstantial so far. We'll know more after the tests come back from the state lab."

Which could take months, Liv thought. She glanced at Ted and knew he was thinking the same thing. Plenty of time to find the real killer and just hope to heaven it didn't turn out to be Leo.

They each gave their version of what had happened that night and then were sent home. Leo was released into the custody of Reverend Schorr, though how adept the young bachelor would be at caring for the teenager, "gentle soul" or not, was anybody's guess.

Silas Lark and Ted had a short conversation on the sidewalk after they left the station. Liv gave them their privacy because she knew Ted would tell her what was said, and she didn't want to cramp the lawyer's style.

After almost a year, she was still considered an outsider. Not in the day-to-day happenings, but when things got dicey and the town drew together. She didn't feel too bad; BeBe had lived in Celebration Bay for twelve years and she was still considered a newbie.

"What do you make of Leo's story?" Liv asked as she and Ted were driving back to town.

"Well, if I didn't know Leo—and really, I haven't had much interaction with him—I would say it's pretty far-fetched." He slowed down at a crossroad and looked both ways before proceeding.

"But I've never heard of him being in any kind of trouble. He's liked by the other kids, except for the bullies of course. He spends a lot of time at the community center. I think he lives with a single mother and several siblings."

"You think? Don't you *know*?" she asked half-teasingly. Ted was Gossip Central, he generally knew everything about everybody, and it seemed to Liv that he didn't even have to try. The weird part was that nobody knew much about him.

He wasn't secretive; he just didn't talk about his past or his personal life. And where that would usually run up red flags for Liv, it didn't with Ted. He was a man unto himself. A gentleman—intelligent, dependable—and he loved her dog.

"Okay," Liv said, bringing her mind back to Leo's dilemma. "He really does believe in ghosts?"

"Seems so."

"And he really thinks there is a treasure."

"Yes. You saw his face when Rundle was talking about it out in the yard."

She had. "Do you believe in the treasure?"

Ted cut her a quick look but kept his eyes on the road. It was dark and late and country roads were notorious for accidents, especially on holidays, when the drinks flowed to excess.

"I don't discount the possibility."

"Really," said Liv, intrigued.

"Though I tend to think that if something is still hidden after all these years—over two hundred of them—it would be a document of some kind. And if someone actually found it, it would probably disintegrate the moment they picked it up."

"Hmm," Liv said. "The other thing—" Her sentence was stopped by a jaw-cracking yawn. It was after midnight; they'd both been working nonstop and had to get up early the next day for the parade. "When the housekeeper saw the gurney, she thought it was Henry Gallantine. I thought you said he left town every July to visit family."

"I did."

"Let me rephrase that. Does Henry Gallantine leave town every July?"

Ted shrugged.

"He doesn't."

"Let me put it this way. He does. But not until after the Fourth and the reenactment. He likes to keep up the mystery of the ghost appearing on the roof. So he makes a big show of leaving town, then comes back for a final appearance before he really leaves for the summer. It's part of his mystique: It's a big secret, only everyone is in on it, but they pretend not to know. It's more fun that way. A true eccentric."

"Along with a lot of other people in this town. So that's why Hildy was so upset? She knew it should have been Henry Gallantine on the roof." *And covered up on the gurney.*

"Hmm."

"I wonder if the murderer thought he was killing Henry?"

"I have no idea."

"And if Henry Gallantine was supposed to be there and wasn't, where is he?"

Ted smothered a yawn. "Oh Lord, I couldn't even follow that question, much less try to answer it."

"Ted, don't be obtuse. Do you think whoever killed Rundle was after him or Gallantine?"

"I don't know. I'm going to drop you off at home. There's no need to go back to the office tonight."

They passed Town Hall, passed the square where chairs lined the parade route. And turned onto Liv's street.

"Do you think he's dead, too?"

Ted slowed down to make the turn into her driveway, drove all the way to the end, and stopped in front of her carriage house.

"I haven't the foggiest. Good night, Liv."

Interrogation closed. She wouldn't be learning any more from Ted tonight. It was standard operating procedure, making her work for information. It heightened the drama and Ted's entertainment. Though tonight he didn't seem to be enjoying the game.

"Good night," she said. It didn't matter. She'd find out. Eventually. She always did.

Liv's alarm went off way too early the next morning. For a few minutes she just lay blinking into the darkened bedroom. But she got up and was halfway to the bathroom before she remembered why she'd stayed up so late last night. Leo . . . She didn't even know Leo's last name.

She showered and went back to her bedroom, where a sleepy Westie opened one eye, then closed it again. He thought it was way too early to wake up on a Saturday morning.

"It's parade day," she said as brightly as she could manage.

He blinked, then lowered his muzzle to his paws and settled back down onto his plaid doggie bed.

"People will be dropping food all day."

Whiskey sneezed.

"And your friend Leo is in big trouble."

His ears flew up, he wriggled up to all fours and barked.

"Thought you'd want to know. Though I don't see how any of us can help. Nasty stuff is going on out there." Hopefully the parade would go off without a hitch.

Liv looked in her closet. It was going to be a scorcher. Somehow a flowered sundress didn't strike her as appropriate parade wear, but she'd just about exhausted her red, white, and blue options.

And it was really hard to care about clothes when a man

had been murdered and a young teenager was the most obvious suspect.

But she couldn't stand staring into her closet all morning.
She had a responsibility, a job to do—a red, white, and blue
job to do.

She pushed back some hangers and began rummaging
through the contents of her closet. She'd had to invest in a
whole new wardrobe since moving to Celebration Bay.

She hadn't realized when she'd interviewed for the job that
theme was the almighty arbiter of fashion. Even on nonspe-
cific holidays, anyone with a store or a function dressed to
the hilt. Liv had made it through fall okay, thanks to one
late-night Internet shopping spree right before she left Manhattan. She'd been buying haphazardly and at the last minute
ever since.

She pulled out a pink T-shirt. She'd meant to recycle some
pink and red from the strawberry festival. Unfortunately the
T-shirt, as well as other garments, were hopelessly stained,
as the berries had been sweet, juicy, and detergent-proof.

She pulled on a pair of jeans. Not exactly the blue of the
flag, but they would have to do. The only other blue she had
were dark-wash jean shorts, and they were way too short for
the public, according to her landladies.

She selected a white T-shirt, ran a scarf through the belt
loops, and carefully twisted the Hermès pattern to accent
the red. Hopefully the purple swirls would look like blue.

But one glance in the mirror made her cringe. Not only did
she look like she'd seen a body and spent most of the night at
the police station, she seriously needed a wardrobe upgrade.

Next month. August would be fairly easy. She would
organize her coming year and purchase accordingly while
she had the chance. She never had time for shopping once
the holiday season began.

She brushed her hair back into a ponytail and pulled it
through the opening of the blue cap she'd bought on the
street the day before. Hopefully she would look official

enough to be authoritative if the need arose and patriotic enough to pass local opinion.

Sensing adventure—and breakfast—ahead, Whiskey rolled out of bed, shook vigorously, and trotted down the hall to the back door.

She let him out and put out a bowl of food, which he scarfed down immediately when he came back inside.

"And now your favorite part," she told him. She leaned down to tie on a stars-and-stripes kerchief that she'd bought at the Woofery for the occasion. Sharise, the groomer, tried to talk her into a top hat with red and white stripes, but Liv had put her foot down.

After years of Liv buying cute little doggie outfits and having Whiskey refuse to wear them, he'd suddenly become a Westie fashionista. He and Ted even had matching bow ties at Christmas.

Liv shuddered to think what Ted would be wearing today.

She clipped on Whiskey's leash and they headed out. It was still early, but already Liv could tell it was going to be hot and humid again.

Whiskey trotted ahead of her down the driveway, ready to show off his bandanna and get a tiny treat. He was much more enthusiastic than his barely-put-together mistress.

But neither Miss Edna nor Miss Ida was out yet. Probably still picking out their outfits for the parade. And then she remembered . . . they were *in* the parade.

Liv felt a rush of pride and excitement. She'd only been here a little less than a year—so she'd be considered an outsider for the next fifteen years at least. She might never be asked to ride on a float in the parade or host the Winter Ball. But she was home.

They walked the two blocks to the square, where the sun was just coming up over the eastern mountains and cast a shimmer of gold over the lake. Already vendors were setting up in the green. Food and souvenirs, charities selling raffle tickets for prizes that would be announced later that day.

BeBe and Dolly both had tables out on the sidewalk that crisscrossed the park. Miriam Krause and her quilting club would be selling patriotic quilts and donating the proceeds to rehabilitate wounded soldiers. There were voting-registration tables and free blood-pressure check stations. Petitions to sign, though Ted and Liv had carefully scrutinized each group that registered to set up a booth.

This was a day to celebrate and appreciate freedom, not to engage in political debate of any kind. There was plenty of grumbling and threats to sue the town when certain extremist groups were turned away, but not even the mayor backed down. Evidently there had been some pretty nasty encounters in the years before, and he didn't want a return of that, and Liv wholeheartedly agreed. No politics on the Fourth of July.

Security would be doubled for the parade. Between the county police and Bayside Security, Bill Gunnison had a full force of officers and patrolmen.

Liv had been told that the parade drew mainly local families and tourists who were traveling with small children. But Liv knew quite well that, while the reenactment could be more carefully controlled by limiting the entrances, the parade-goers would be free to roam the town.

She'd been the event planner to the rich and the sometimes infamous, but except for a few angry words or a drunken brawl, she'd been confident of the safety of the attendees. But these open venues and free-flowing events were out of her comfort zone; she was adapting, but she still checked and triple-checked the schedule before each event.

Liv walked along the sidewalk that surrounded the park. Lawn chairs had been set out for days, chained to parking meters or tied together, to save places for the parade. The judging stand in front of Town Hall was finished and was decorated with bunting and American flags.

Apple of My Eye was busy but not crowded yet. Whiskey

was a big hit in his festive kerchief. And Dolly had a special star-shaped doggie treat for him.

Dolly herself looked like Betsy Ross, pleasantly plump with a frilly white mobcap over her honey-colored hair. A white kerchief collar covered the shoulders of a red figured dress. Even her normal apron was white and starched so that it barely moved.

Behind her, the pink cupcake wall clock supported two American flags, one current and one of the thirteen colonies. The display case was filled with red, white, and blue cupcakes, cookies, blueberry muffins, raspberry turnovers, even striped Rice Krispies snacks.

Liv ordered a raisin scone. Dolly bagged the scone but, instead of handing it to Liv across the counter, she motioned to her part-time helper to take over. She accompanied Liv to the sidewalk.

"Is it true?" she asked, looking around to make sure no one was listening. "That poor Leo Morgan found the body of Jacob Rundle last night?"

Liv nodded; there was no point in denying it. Everyone would know soon enough, and she didn't want to jeopardize anyone's trust in her by lying and acting innocent.

"How did you and Ted figure out that something was wrong?"

"Well . . . Ted noticed something off about the signal and went to see if something was wrong. I just followed him."

"Well, let us know if there's anything Fred or I can do, though I'm sure you and Chaz will get to the bottom of it."

"Chaz isn't here, Dolly."

"Oh, are you sure? Fred said he thought he'd seen his SUV in the Quickie Mart parking lot."

"I don't know," Liv said. "I'd better get going."

Dolly hurried back to the bakery, and Liv went next door to the Buttercup Coffee Exchange. The sign for today's special advertised the YankeeSnickerDoodle blend.

"How do you come up with these names?" Liv asked BeBe.

"It's a knack," BeBe told her. "And too sweet for you. You won't like it. But, the One if by Land is a double shot of espresso with a dollop of whipped cream and cinnamon. It's pretty good."

"I'll have—"

"I know, a double-shot latte, plain." BeBe made her latte, then placed a tall cardboard cup on the counter. "Ted came in earlier for his tea." BeBe sighed. "He wouldn't try the Boston Tea Party brew, either."

Liv took her coffee. "Hey, I tried the Jingle Bell Jamaican last December."

"Once. That's okay. You have other good qualities."

"Thanks," Liv said. "Well, I'd better get going. A line is forming behind me."

She nodded to several women she sort of recognized and continued to the door, where she stopped with her hand on the knob.

"They say Bill Gunnison has taken that Morgan boy into custody. Always thought there was something wrong with him. Now we know," one of the women said as Liv passed.

"I wonder how they caught him so fast?"

"They must have gotten a tip."

The gossip was starting already. And this bunch had it all wrong.

"Well, I don't believe it. He's a little slow, but he's always seemed so nice. Oh, good morning, BeBe, did you hear . . . ?"

Liv let herself out and hurried down the sidewalk. They'd had a tip all right. An SOS. But if Rundle had bled out immediately like A.K. said, who gave the signal of alarm?

Chapter Six

....

Liv was a little unnerved from that whole encounter. She sure hoped people didn't assume Leo was guilty just because he was a little different. Though people tended to do just that. What did that one woman say? *He always seemed so nice.*

Of course, that's what they always said about psychopaths that went on killing sprees. *Not funny, Liv.* Leo was just a kid in the wrong place when something bad had happened. She was sure Bill had let him go by now.

But what really worried her was that she hadn't thought to ask Ted who he thought had signaled the SOS.

She stepped up the pace, hoping to catch Ted before he left the office for parade duty.

Some kids saw Whiskey and came over to pat him. Then others joined them. Whiskey preened and licked hands and made himself adorable. Liv finally managed to pull him away, but this was just the beginning.

While they were standing there, Quincy Hinks came out of the Bookworm. "Just heard about Rundle. Heart attack?"

Liv shrugged and held up her hands, pulled Whiskey

away from the kids, and kept walking, right past Bay-Berry Candles. Now if she could just—

But everyone she passed wanted to stop and chat. Ask questions about what had happened the night before. Most didn't know exactly what had gone on other than there had been a lot of cop cars around the Gallantine estate and that someone thought they'd seen the coroner's van.

Liv just nodded, shrugged, and kept walking.

"Yoo-hoo, Liv?" Miriam Krause, the owner of A Stitch in Time fabric-and-quilting store, stuck her head out the front door and motioned Liv over. "I was talking to Mr. Valenski at the newsstand earlier this morning, and he said that Hildy Ingersoll came in for Henry's newspaper, and she told him that Leo Morgan killed Jacob Rundle last night."

Liv did not want to be drawn into any gossip this morning and had meant to keep walking. But this stopped her. "She went in for Mr. Gallantine's newspaper? But I thought he had left for the summer."

Miriam flipped her hand. "Should have. He usually has the car packed and waiting. As soon as he plays the ghost in the reenactment, he drives out of town."

So where was he? And why was Hildy getting his paper if he wasn't here? Did Hildy know where he was?

"What else did Mr. Valenski—"

Unfortunately, the same Westie who would have sat and played with the children just a few minutes ago suddenly realized they were near the office, where he would be given his star biscuit, and he pulled at the leash.

"Heel," Liv said. Whiskey barked and pulled harder. "Sorry. Too much excitement."

"Don't you worry about it. He's cute as can be. I tell you, I don't believe it for a minute."

It took a beat before Liv realized she was back to talking about the murder and not Whiskey.

"Poor boy, he never did anybody any harm, and you tell Bill Gunnison not to be too quick to judge."

"Will do," Liv called back as Whiskey took off down the sidewalk. "Sorry, Miriam, gotta run."

Liv and Whiskey practically ran the rest of the way to Town Hall. Liv didn't even reprimand him. She needed to see Ted before he left for the parade.

Ted was just coming out the door as they reached the Events Office.

"Who's my favorite dawg?" Ted crooned.

"Aroo-roo-roo."

Ted laughed. "Yankee doodle . . ."

"Arroo-roo-roo."

"Ted, come inside, now."

Song forgotten, Ted followed her back inside. "What's up?"

She told him about the women at the Buttercup.

"Bunch of old—well, never mind, there's always a few."

"So, have you heard from Bill this morning?"

"Yes, and don't worry. Leo is a witness, not a suspect."

Liv let out a huge pent-up sigh. "Bill won't charge him?"

"No. Not unless he gets some real evidence." He eased Liv's latte out of the tray, flipped the tab of the cup top back. "Drink. We've got a parade to attend."

"In a minute," Liv said. "Who signaled the SOS?"

Ted frowned. "I assume Rundle must have."

"A.K. said he bled out almost immediately. So he couldn't have."

"Maybe he . . . I don't know, Liv. Let Bill figure it out. Now, I've got to get over to the parade start."

"Okay, but listen to this."

Ted tilted his head and looked at her. "Yes?" he said patiently.

"Miriam Krause was at the newsstand this morning and Mr. Valenski said Hildy picked up Henry Gallantine's newspaper this morning. Why would she do that?"

Ted's eyes widened slightly. "A creature of habit, maybe."

"Or she knows where Henry is."

"Or she knows where Henry is. I'll call Bill on my way over. Unless you want to."

"Not me."

Ted grinned. "Want me to be the one who gets in trouble?"

"Hey, I didn't ask any questions. I was just walking to work like I do every day, minding my own business . . ."

"Uh-huh. Now, you sit down at your desk and drink your coffee and then go get a good seat for the parade."

"I was thinking of maybe watching from my office window."

Ted raised an eyebrow. "This is not the Macy's Thanksgiving Day Parade. It's more fun down in the thick of it."

"I wasn't worried so much about the fun, as I thought it would give me a good bird's-eye view."

"So you can see any snafus as they occur? And what on earth would you be able to do from up here?"

"Call you?"

"I'm turning off my cell. See you on the sidelines." He slipped out the door before she could answer.

She gave Whiskey his biscuit and went to her office to look out the window. She could see Ted striding down the street.

"He wouldn't really turn off his phone, would he?"

"Arf," said Whiskey and curled up on his pillow where he proceeded to demolish the doggie star.

Liv found a place for herself near the grandstand. The crowd was three deep in some places, children sitting on the curb in front of the lawn chairs, people standing behind.

The parade was everything Liv had expected from a small-town celebration. It was led by Mayor Worley, smiling and waving from the front of a vintage Cadillac convertible, his brilliantined hair catching the light and shining from sea to sea. He was followed by the reenactment army, looking a little bleary-eyed from their battle and, Liv suspected, an after-reenactment party at McCready's Pub the night before.

She was surprised to see slings and bandages and even one guy on crutches. Daniel Haynes led the cadre on horseback, and Liv couldn't blame the soldiers for keeping a good distance behind the horse. Haynes didn't look extremely happy to be there, but at least he didn't have to march. Those uniforms had to be sweltering in the sun.

Liv just hoped they were staying hydrated.

"So, what do you think so far?" Ted asked, slipping in behind her.

"It's great. The army has even bandaged itself up like they have been in a real battle."

Ted snorted a laugh. "Those are real and mostly self-inflicted. It's the same every year. Scrapes and cuts and whatnot. I was just talking to Rufus and Roscoe at the starting location. Winston Carew tripped over a root and knocked his tooth out. He spent most of the battle at the dentist's office. Clarence Moffat broke his collarbone jumping from a rock. One of the new guys had five stitches where he walked into a Do Not Enter sign in the parking lot. A few miscellaneous cuts and bruises. Surely the original patriots were more coordinated than these guys." He chuckled. "Even Daniel Haynes sprained his ankle when his foot caught in his stirrup as he tried to dismount. Almost missed the whole thing taking a call of nature right before the signal sounded." He laughed. "And a good time was had by all. You gotta love them."

"I don't suppose they get workmen's comp."

"No. But they do have to sign a waiver form so that the Reenactment Committee is not held responsible for acts of stupidity. All right, I've got to make sure the floats are fanning off at the end and not blocking traffic in front of the post office. See you later."

His last words were drowned out as the high school marching band stopped in front of the grandstand. They were followed by several antique cars, a fire engine, and a police bagpipe-and-drum corps. There was a group of young girls twirling batons and wearing sequined outfits and another group of tap dancers from a nearby dance school.

Two trucks of veterans came next, one filled with young men and women returned home from the current fighting around the globe, and another where five wizened old men, survivors of World War II, sat in one corner, holding on for dear life. Liv thought they should have gotten a smaller, more comfortable vehicle. They looked very lonely up there by themselves. But they were cheered just as enthusiastically as everything and everyone else.

Floats were sponsored by local businesses, churches, service organizations, and schools. And in between came clowns, Boy and Girl Scouts carrying banners, parents pulling their children or pets in wagons decorated with crepe paper, convertibles carrying dignitaries.

Kids from the community center pushed shopping carts along the parade route for people to fill with canned foodstuffs for the food pantry. Liv saw Roseanne Waterbury, but Leo wasn't there, and she thought how much he would have liked to walk in the parade.

An Uncle Sam walking on stilts bowed and doffed his top hat to the crowd. Celebration Bay was nothing if not patriotic, and on July Fourth they outdid themselves.

Every fire engine in the area must have been in attendance, honking their horns to the delight of the children. Liv shuddered to think what would happen if there were a fire somewhere. Would they just pull out of the parade and rush to put it out?

Ida and Edna, riding on the DAR float, spotted Liv and waved. The flatbed was crowded with people who could trace their ancestors back to the War for Independence. All standing or sitting in front of a giant depiction of the original thirteen states made from crepe-paper flowers. The float stopped in front of the grandstand to be adjudicated by a panel of judges before moving on.

Next came clowns stuffed into an old VW bug, which

stopped every few yards for the clowns to jump out and perform a Chinese fire drill.

The Garden Club's "Where Democracy Found Fertile Ground" float followed the clowns and also stopped at the grandstand. Liv thought it looked like Dexter Kent's nursery had been transferred to the flatbed. The members sat on bales of hay in their patriotic outfits.

Liv enjoyed it immensely. The only thing she missed was Chaz Bristow making snarky comments.

She couldn't imagine where he was or what he was doing, but she could be sure it involved sleeping and fishing . . . and really, couldn't he just do that here?

Someone nudged her.

"Forget something?" she asked, turning around. But it wasn't Ted.

Roseanne Waterbury, who must have finished the march, looked serious and worried.

"Can I talk to you?" she asked.

"Sure," Liv said, wondering what on earth she could need to talk about. "Would you like to come to the office?"

Roseanne nodded.

"Fine. When would you like to come?"

"Now. Please, it's important."

"Of course."

They squeezed through the crowd that had bottlenecked around the grandstand and went inside. Whiskey, who had been left inside for the festivities, met them at the door. He saw Roseanne and began dancing at her feet. She crouched down to pet him.

"Would you like a bottle of water?" Liv asked. "I'm afraid it's all we have."

"No . . . thank you." Roseanne bit her lip. She'd matured during the last school year. When Liv first met her, she'd been a tall, skinny girl with cinnamon-colored hair that she usually wore in a long braid down her back. Today her hair was pulled back into a high, messy bun. She was wearing jean shorts and a tight-knit white camisole with blue stars sprinkled across the front. She'd developed a few curves in the last few months.

"Come on in and sit down."

Whiskey led the way into Liv's office, and when Roseanne sat down, Whiskey sat down beside her chair.

As soon as Liv pulled up a chair, Roseanne blurted out, "Everybody's saying Leo killed Mr. Rundle."

Taken aback, it took Liv a second to recover. "Everyone?"

"Well, no. But a bunch of kids were saying it this morning when we were waiting for the parade to begin."

And if kids are saying it, that means their parents are, too, thought Liv.

"And one of the center kids took a punch at one of them and there was a big fight. It isn't fair. Leo didn't even get to be in the parade today because Bill Gunnison thought there might be trouble. And there was."

"How did you find this out, that Bill said there might be trouble?"

"We were supposed to pick Leo up to go to the parade this morning. But when Dad got in the truck he said Leo wasn't going. And when I asked why, he told me that Mr. Gunnison called to say Mr. Rundle had been killed and they'd taken Leo in for questioning."

Roseanne's eyes were dark and intense, and Liv had an uncomfortable feeling she knew where this was going.

"It's just for questioning," Liv assured her. "As a witness."

Roseanne shook her head. "You have to help him."

"I'm sure Bill is investigating thoroughly."

"I know, but you helped my dad when he was accused. He might still be in jail if not for you."

Liv shook her head.

"And everybody knows you're the one who solved that murder at Christmas."

"Rosie, stop right there. I nearly got myself killed at Christmas because I was clueless. And your dad would never have been charged. And Leo won't be either." *If he's innocent,* she wanted to add, but she didn't. She also started to say that the sheriff was more concerned about Leo's safety, but thought better of it. She didn't want to give any false hope.

"Please, just come. I told him you'd bring Whiskey. He's good for when you're feeling down, aren't you, boy?" She reached down to scratch Whiskey's head. "He's at Pastor Schorr's and I told him I'd bring you both. Maybe you could talk to him."

"Wait, why is he at Pastor Schorr's? I thought you said he couldn't come to the parade."

"He couldn't. That's why you have to come. I called his cell just to cheer him up, and he said someone threw a rock through the window of his house. His mother said she couldn't keep him there. It was too dangerous for the younger children. She kicked him out. Can you believe that? He didn't know what to do. So he went to the center but it was closed, so he went to the rectory. Pastor Schorr took him in. He's there now. Please."

"Does Bill know?"

"I don't know. Leo's really scared. Please say you'll help him."

Roseanne looked like she was about to cry. And Liv remembered the fall night when Roseanne showed up at her door having driven her father's truck into town, though she was only fifteen, just to talk to Liv.

"Okay. I'll come with you just to talk to him and let Whiskey work his magic."

"Thank you. Whiskey's good when you're feeling scared."

And isn't that the truth, Liv thought. *Or lonely, or sad, or depressed.*

It was only two blocks to the Presbyterian parsonage. The parade was just wrapping up, and Liv hurried them along the sidewalk before they had to fight the crowds going back to their cars, to restaurants, or to one of the park vendors.

As soon as they'd left the square, they slowed down. They passed the cemetery, showing its share of American flags on the graves, turned the corner at the First Presbyterian Church, and climbed the steps to the parsonage next door.

It was a nice stone "cottage," large enough to accommodate growing families. Of course, Pastor Schorr was a bachelor, but he wouldn't be for long if the ladies of Celebration Bay had their way.

He opened the door looking serious but welcoming. "Thanks for coming. He's in here." He gestured them into what must be his study, a smallish, cozy room filled with books and papers, a couch and wing chair, a desk, a table with a stack of books in one corner, a globe on a stand—and Leo Morgan sitting on the corner of the couch.

"Look who's come for a visit, Leo."

Whiskey ran right up to him, and Leo slid off the couch to sit on the floor and scratch his ears. Whiskey licked his face and climbed into Leo's lap. Leo hugged him so tight, Liv was afraid Whiskey might wriggle free.

"I really don't know what I can do," Liv said to the reverend in a low voice.

"This is just what he needs right now," Pastor Schorr said, gesturing to boy and dog.

"He's the best comfort dog ever," she agreed. Actually, she thought he was the best dog ever. Period.

Roseanne went to sit on the floor beside Leo and reached over to ruffle Whiskey's fur. "Leo, Ms. Montgomery has come to talk to you."

Leo looked up. "They threw a rock." He rested his cheek on Whiskey's back.

"I'm so sorry," Liv said.

Reverent Schorr caught her eye. "Let's step outside for a moment."

They went across the hall into a living room that was also small and filled with comfortable furniture. "I have to confess," the pastor said, once they were seated, "when Roseanne said she wanted to bring you here, I wasn't in favor of it. The less said the better. Leo is a good boy, but he's special, he lives life slow, his IQ isn't the greatest, but he's . . ."

"A gentle soul," Liv said. "That's what you said back in December."

He smiled, a little sadly. "Sometimes 'the world is too much with us.'"

Liv recognized the quote, but didn't understand why the pastor was quoting it now.

"Sorry. I'm a little out of my element. Squabbles and crises of faith I know how to handle. I can give comfort and guidance. I can even replace Velma Morgan's window." He sighed heavily. "I trust in Bill Gunnison to get to the bottom of this. But what am I to do with Leo?"

Liv shifted in her seat. "Is that a rhetorical question?"

He laughed sadly. "Unfortunately, yes. He's eighteen . . ."

"You don't think he really killed Mr. Rundle?"

"No, of course not. I'm more worried how he'll fare with the town's opinions. And I'm even more worried that someone might try to hurt him."

"An angry citizen?"

"Or the killer."

Just what Bill had said. "He said he'd seen the ghost; surely if the killer thought he'd recognized him, he would have killed him, too, but he didn't."

"I said that Leo is slow, but he gets there eventually. It might take him a while. I'm afraid he might see someone in town and suddenly he'll recognize him as the 'ghost' he saw on the roof. He might even blurt out something that would name the man as the murderer. Can you imagine?"

Liv tried not to. There was a killer out there, and maybe no one was safe.

"But I'm not sure what to do with him. Oh, he can stay here. But he can't stay inside all the time, and I'm not sure he'll feel comfortable being left alone when I have to go out. And I don't know if he can withstand the outside world blaming him."

"Surely they won't," Liv said, knowing that of course some people could and would and already did.

"I don't know how much he really understands about why people act the way they do. He's been the brunt of some bullying in school. Just a few kids and they didn't get far."

"He fights back?"

"Oh heavens, no. The kids from the center and from his church group keep an eye on him. Form sort of a buffer around him. But they can't do that outside of school. And they certainly shouldn't in a situation like this that could be potentially dangerous."

He shook his head. "I don't know where Leo got this notion of helping the center by asking the ghost for the treasure."

"I'm afraid it was Jacob Rundle, himself. Though I believe he was trying to frighten him."

"Why would he do that?"

"Why does anyone feel like they have the right to be hurtful?" Liv asked.

"A question the sages have been trying to answer since the beginning of time. And then there are people like Leo." He smiled. "What a selfless act, to want money for the center, when he could have wanted it for himself, or his mother; when you think of all the young people who rob and steal just for the fun of it—oh dear, listen to me.

"I can't help but get a little"—he smiled sheepishly; he was charming—"righteously angry at the injustice of it all."

"Pastor Schorr . . ."

"Why don't we cut out the formalities? Call me Phillip. 'Pastor Schorr' can get to be a mouthful after too many repetitions."

"Phillip. Is the center in trouble? Leo said that night that you had been talking with a man who said he was going to take the center away."

"Ernie Bolton. He owns the building. Owns several pieces of property over on the next block. We've been paying him two hundred dollars a month for an old storefront. Now he says the taxes are too high and he's going to raze the whole lot and sell it off as one big parcel."

"Where will you move to?"

"That's the problem. We can meet other places, but I want the kids to have a place that's all theirs. That they don't have to share." He laughed deprecatingly. "I know this doesn't sound very charitable of me. But some place that isn't associated with social services, or school, or even religion; we have kids at the center from different ethnic backgrounds and religions."

"I think I understand. A place to call home."

He looked up, sudden interest lighting his face. "Exactly. I don't think we could find another place that's large enough and that we could afford. We've been surviving on bake sales and car washes for years."

He slapped his knees and stood up. "Speaking of which. Let's see what those two young people are doing. Knowing Leo, he's ready for lunch."

While Phillip got out the makings of sandwiches, Liv washed lettuce. From the sink she could just make out the back of the *Clarion* office on the next block.

"Does Chaz Bristow mentor the kids from the center?"

Schorr laughed. "Better not let him hear you say that. It's one of the better-kept secrets in Celebration Bay, and he swears he does it just to get them to leave him alone. I hope he doesn't let that all get lost in the shuffle."

"What do you mean?" she asked, looking at him over her shoulder.

"Well, it will be good to have the paper up and running again. But I hope Chaz doesn't let this story grow too big. It might take a long time for the center to recover. Some of the kids have been in a bit of trouble. Not so much anymore." He smiled that boyish grin. "There are always temptations out there. And if Leo . . . but he didn't, and Chaz won't turn it into something sensational. He's pretty loyal."

"Chaz?"

The pastor nodded and handed her a tomato. "The first out of the garden," he said.

"Do you know when he's planning to come back?"

"Chaz? Oh, he's back, I saw a light at the paper on my way home from the fireworks last night."

Chapter Seven

....

They all sat around the kitchen table eating lettuce, tomato, and turkey sandwiches.

Leo ate enthusiastically, as if he hadn't just witnessed a murder and been cast out of his home.

Roseanne sat next to Leo, her sandwich barely picked at. She'd been giving Liv pointed looks since she'd sat down. Actually the pastor had given her a few himself.

Liv put down her sandwich. "Leo, would you like to tell us about last night on the roof?"

He shook his head and kept eating.

"Leo," Roseanne urged, "you can tell Liv, I mean Ms. Montgomery. She wants to help you."

He shook his head.

"Leo. Why?"

"Sheriff said not to talk to anybody, not even you, Rosie."

"But Liv is . . ." Roseanne began.

"The sheriff is exactly right," Liv said. She couldn't really help Leo if she didn't know what he'd seen, but she didn't want to be able to coerce it out of him. Because if she could, so could someone else.

Leo nodded seriously. Knit his brow. "I can't go home."

Liv glanced at the pastor.

"Well, I would like you to stay here with me for a few days. Like a vacation."

"Never been on a vacation."

"Chaz takes you fishing," Schorr said. "That's like a mini-vacation."

"Yeah."

"Would you like to stay here on a vacation?"

"Don't have a toothbrush or clean clothes."

"We'll go pick them up at your house."

Leo shook his head. "Mama said don't come back. She's afraid the ghost will come looking for me and hurt one of the young'uns."

The other three protested together.

Finally, Pastor Schorr won out. "Leo, what did I tell you about ghosts?"

Leo thought about it. "There's only one ghost, and he's a good ghost."

Schorr scratched his head. "Right . . . and besides . . . Old Gallantine's ghost only comes out for the Fourth of July. What's today's date?"

"The fifth of July," Leo said proudly. "He won't come out no more?"

Schorr hesitated, and Liv knew he must at least be wrestling with what he should say—if not with his conscience—because at last, he said, "No, he won't come out anymore."

Liv and Whiskey left after lunch, but Liv promised to bring Whiskey back for a visit. She needed to touch base with Ted about the parade, plus she was sure that by now he would have the inside scoop on the investigation, since he and the sheriff had been friends for decades.

But first she took a detour to the *Clarion* office. The office had once been a charming clapboard bungalow with a front porch and a peaked roof. It had been painted white at one time but now had faded to gray. It had been terribly neglected inside and out. The rooms were square and still had the original details but were crammed with old printing equipment and new computers, not to mention mountains of paper.

She suspected Chaz lived upstairs, though she'd never ventured that far into the house.

It certainly looked deserted, though it was hard to tell. There were no papers piling up on the porch, though, being the editor of the local newspaper, he didn't have to have it delivered. And the mail went through a slot in the door.

Still it looked forlorn, lifeless.

Recognizing it as a place filled with wonderful things to snuffle and roll in, Whiskey started up the steps. Liv followed him and knocked on the front door. She didn't expect an answer, but she knocked again anyway. Since there was no Gone Fishing sign hanging on the door—Chaz's usual signal that he was out or not interested in having visitors—she turned the knob. The door was locked, and she began to wonder if Pastor Schorr had been mistaken.

If Chaz was home, the door would be unlocked.

Quelling a sense of disappointment that she attributed to not finding someone who could help Leo out of this mess, she walked back to the Events Office.

"How'd you like the parade?" Ted asked once he and Whiskey had gone through another of their "singing" rituals.

"I thought it was great," Liv said distractedly.

"You don't sound like you thought it was great." He followed her into her office.

"I just got back from the rectory."

"Details, please."

"Roseanne Waterbury found me toward the end of the parade. Someone threw a rock through Leo Morgan's window, and his mother threw him out. He's at Pastor Schorr's. I went with Roseanne to let him play with Whiskey."

"How could you say no to a request like that? So, what are you upset about?"

"Other than a man being murdered during the reenactment? A young man was a witness. A couple of the women in Buttercup this morning were blaming him because Leo is different. And now someone is threatening the family."

"A pretty nasty situation and bound to get worse," Ted said. "We have our share of hotheads. Prejudiced bigots and stupid to boot."

Ted wasn't usually so adamant, but this murder seemed to have struck a nerve with everyone. Why this time? Celebration Bay thrived on gossip and opinions. Most of it was out of habit, sometimes just to be ornery, and occasionally tempers did flare. But this felt like an attack on the community.

"Why would someone kill the gardener?" Liv asked.

"First, we need to know what he was doing up on the roof."

"Instead of Henry Gallantine? The real Henry Gallantine."

Ted shrugged.

"Even Hildy was upset. She thought it was Gallantine on the roof. So why wasn't he there last night? And where is he?"

"Not a clue."

"Are you sure you don't know? You always get the news first."

"Not this time. If anybody knows, they're not talking."

"Leo said the ghost wore a uniform like Rundle's. Do you think it was someone in the reenactment?"

"Not necessarily. Anybody with access to a uniform could make those visitations. That's close to a hundred participants plus all the dressers, cleaners, and anyone who could walk in and borrow a uniform, not to mention anyone who has a uniform at home."

"People have patriot uniforms at home?"

"We're a patriotic group."

"And to think I couldn't find a backup Santa suit last Christmas."

"Well, I for one think Revolutionary Santa would be right up there with Golfer Santa, Surfer Santa . . ."

"Ugh, don't remind me."

"Oh, I don't know. Every town should have one tacky Christmas shop."

"Not this town," Liv said.

Ted laughed.

"So you don't know where Gallantine is?"

"No. And that is worrisome. He doesn't seem to be in town, that anyone is aware of. Bill called his sister in Buffalo. He usually visits her, but she said he'd called to say he wasn't coming this year. He didn't say why.

"Bill even tried the nephew. Lives over in Connecticut somewhere. Left a voice message to call him, but as far as I know he hasn't returned his call. Not that Henry would visit him."

"Why not?"

"Don't get along. The nephew has a bit of a gambling problem. Tried to get Henry to help him out on more than one occasion. Had some pretty unsavory characters after him. Henry helped him a couple of times but then put his foot down when it became clear he wasn't going to get help with his addiction."

"And Hildy doesn't know?"

"Evidently not. She told Bill that she thought he was on the roof and that he would leave afterward like he did every year."

"Well, that doesn't get us anywhere."

"Us?"

"The royal 'us,' meaning Bill, the town, everyone."

"Uh-huh."

"Has he found out anything?"

"Nothing that he can share anyway."

"So can you give me some background?"

"Is this a need-to-know question or just curiosity?"

"This is a forewarned-is-forearmed question."

"Very appropriate adage for the season."

"Ted," Liv said sharply.

Whiskey barked.

"Two against one." Ted shrugged. "Okay, here it is. Henry may be retired from the movies, and he is a bit of a recluse, but he still has a flare for the dramatic.

"And since his was one of the founding families of Celebration Bay, he sees it as his duty to carry on the good part of the Gallantine myth."

"He went from fame to seclusion?"

"Not all at once. But he grew up, and as often happens with child stars, he didn't make the transition to adult actor. He tried to make a couple of comebacks, but nothing panned out. He came back to stay, oh, maybe thirty years ago. And now he's a local legend. And terribly eccentric."

"From Hollywood to Celebration Bay. Wow. Which reminds me. Did you know Chaz is back?"

"I heard he was."

"And you didn't say anything?"

"Should I have?"

"Have you seen him?"

Ted shook his head.

"Aren't you curious as to where he's been?"

"Not really. Are you?"

"No, but I thought he might want to know about Leo. They seem to be acquainted. He might want to—I was about to say help, but Chaz never wants to help."

"I'm sure he has his reasons. Let's go mingle with the crowds in the park."

Whiskey immediately stood up, looking alert, and Ted hadn't even mentioned either of his two favorite words, "food" or "eat."

"Come on, Liv. I haven't had lunch, and it will give us a chance to test the climate."

Liv knew he wasn't talking about the weather.

*   *   *

The green was filled with people enjoying the afternoon. A sidewalk sale was busy along the walkway in front of the stores. Restaurants were open and picnic blankets were spread over the grass. Fragrant smoke rose from the Firemen's Auxiliary ribs-and-burgers stand. Lemonade and iced tea, sno-cones and ice cream were sold from stands or handcarts throughout the park. And if anyone wanted something a little stronger, McCready's was open for business.

Ted stopped at the first Italian sausage stand, and they walked through the park, Ted munching and sipping a root beer while Liv nodded to people and listened for gossip. But everyone seemed more intent on relaxing and having a good time than worrying about murder.

The quilting group had assembled their frame on the lawn and were giving a demonstration on how to make star-pattern squares.

A group of children ran past them, their faces decorated with painted flags and stars. Each held red, white, and blue pinwheels, compliments of the Veterans of Foreign Wars.

Ted finished his sausage and root beer, and they stopped at a gelato cart, where he was looking over the flavors when Liv saw A.K. Pierce headed their way. He was strolling with a nice-looking woman in slacks and a skimpy T-shirt.

"Hmm," Liv said. "Is he off duty or is that one of his operatives?"

Ted burst out laughing. "Operatives? Well, I guess that is what they're called. Sounds very cloak and dagger."

"Cloak and dagger," Liv repeated, as something flitted into her mind before floating away again.

"Having a nice time?" Ted asked as A.K. and friend slowed down as they reached them. Liv didn't miss the twinkle in his eye.

"This is Adrienne," A.K. said. He introduced her to Liv

and Ted but was already moving away. "I'll see you Monday morning with the report from the weekend," A.K. told Liv.

Liv smiled. "Ten o'clock."

He nodded to Ted, then he and Adrienne strolled off down the walk arm in arm.

"Hmm," Ted said. "What do you make of those two?"

"Coworkers," Liv said, shoving away the little irritation she felt at seeing the two agents so chummy.

The rest of the day went along with no unusual problems coming to Liv's ears. She didn't see Bill at all.

"Probably investigating," Ted said as they closed up the office. "See you Monday."

"Call me if you find out anything?"

"Sure will. Now try to enjoy your day off."

Her day off began with church services at the First Presbyterian Church. She didn't go every Sunday, since Sunday sometimes was her only day off. But even though she was tired, she wanted to be there today. To see if Leo attended. And how people treated him.

Pastor Schorr looked a little tired as he read the scripture. And that was sure to elicit concern from more than a few ladies, who would then rush home and make him food, and he and Leo would eat well for the whole week.

Liv wondered if he'd had a rough night. Had he and Leo had any problems? She couldn't do anything, and maybe she was just curious like everyone else, but she did care about Leo. And she didn't want him to come to any harm.

So she sat with Miss Ida and Miss Edna, who had eschewed red, white, and blue for their usual Sunday attire. The whole congregation had thrown off their patriotic clothes and everything looked back to normal.

If only that were the case.

"Let he who is without sin among you cast the first stone . . ." the pastor intoned in a voice that always caught

Liv by surprise. But not nearly as much as his subject matter did today. Pastor Schorr was a turn-the-other-cheek kind of guy, but he sounded a little hellfire and brimstone today.

And it didn't let up through the reading of scripture or his sermon, and culminated in the final hymn, when they sang, "Within your shelter, loving God . . . no evil shall come near." As they sang the final "amen," Liv was still wondering if he'd chosen that hymn as solace or as a threat.

It only got worse at coffee hour. News of the murder was out. And people could barely get to the fellowship room before they began speculating about who had done it and why. Most folks were stymied to think of why the gardener would be on the roof, and couldn't begin to guess why someone had followed him there to kill him.

Some had convinced themselves it had been an accident.

"Everyone knows that Jacob Rundle drank too much. He probably fell on his own musket."

That's when Rufus Cobb and Roscoe Jackson joined forces.

"He wasn't supposed to be up there at all," said Rufus, and chewed on his mustache like he did when he was upset.

"He's never even rehearsed giving the signal," Roscoe added.

"Are you sure he even gave the signal? I heard they didn't find anybody up there but Leo Morgan, scared out of his wits."

Liv hadn't even thought about that. They'd all just assumed that Jacob had given the signal, because there had been no one else. Just the way they hadn't thought about who had given the second signal, the SOS.

"Maybe Henry Gallantine gave the signal, stabbed Rundle, and got the heck out."

"If it had been Henry, Leo would have recognized him."

"Where is he, then?"

"Hiding out in that big mansion of his."

"Don't be ridiculous. That's the first thing the police did, search the house."

"What do you think, Liv? You were up there." Roscoe Jackson's question turned all eyes toward Liv.

"I don't know any more than what you've heard. We were sent downstairs to wait, so I don't even know what the police did or didn't do."

"Somebody oughta tell us what's going on."

"I'll tell you what's going on."

"Well, not to speak ill of the dead, but . . ."

Pastor Schorr came into the room, and the conversation suddenly changed to small talk.

Liv slipped out the door and made her getaway.

Once outside, she stood indecisive on the sidewalk. She probably should have skipped church and taken Whiskey to visit with Leo while Pastor Schorr reminded everyone to be a good neighbor and not jump to conclusions. Which they had been for as long as it took them to get to the fellowship room. Then all bets were off. But she couldn't blame them. Everyone was affected when something like this happened, and they couldn't get back to normal until the crisis was over.

But should she wait for Miss Ida and Miss Edna in the parking lot or walk home to get Whiskey?

She did neither, but turned in the opposite direction. If the sisters couldn't find her, they would figure she had walked home and wouldn't be worried. But she didn't go home. She'd done a lot of thinking last night. Both Ted and the pastor said that Chaz had returned home. But he obviously wasn't broadcasting the fact. And why was that?

Of all the times to revert back to his totally lazy, bonehead self, now was not it. Leo needed him. And he probably didn't even know about what was going on or care if he did.

Really, the man was beyond annoying; he was downright callous. She marched right past the rectory and crossed the street. She wasn't really dressed for a confrontation, since she was wearing heels and a summery dress.

But she'd held her own with some pretty out-there clients while wearing higher heels and shorter skirts than she was wearing now.

Mr. I-Won't-Get-Involved Newspaper Editor was about to get a taste of event planner on a tear.

Chapter Eight

....

Liv wasn't surprised to find the *Clarion* office locked and dark. Undaunted, she tried the front windows. Of course, she would never climb in without calling out first. But they, too, were locked.

She tested each reachable window as she circled the house to the back door, which of course was locked. But knowing Chaz, she was pretty certain that if he bothered to lock the door . . . She rose up on her toes, reached up to feel the top of the bracket that held the porch light, and—*voila!* There was the spare key.

She inserted the key in the lock and turned it; the door opened, and Liv had her first qualm.

"Chaz? Chaz, are you here?"

She got just what she expected. Nothing, not even the rustle of someone turning over in his sleep. She stood there deliberating. She needed to talk to him. And besides, he might be sick, he might have fallen, though a thirtysomething-year-old man could probably still reach for his cell phone. Or he could be the victim of a robbery and lying bleeding to death.

She stepped all the way into the house. Was that a creak she heard?

"Chaz!"

Maybe he really was sleeping; maybe he was sleeping with someone; maybe that's why no one had seen him. He was having a torrid . . .

"Chaz are you decent?" Still no answer. "Okay, that does it. I'm coming in."

She stepped through the door into what she thought was the kitchen, groped for a light switch. It was a kitchen. A very messy, dirty, disgusting kitchen, though when she looked farther than the pizza boxes, dirty plates, and rows of beer and milk bottles, she could see that it once had been very nice.

Wooden cabinets, a wooden table in the middle of the room piled with cast-off newspapers. Not the *Clarion*, she realized as she looked closer. The *Los Angeles Times*. And recent editions. Was he feeling homesick? Why didn't he go for a visit? No one was stopping him.

Or maybe that's where he'd been. She picked up one of the folded newspapers. Coverage of a trial of some banker accused of killing his wife. She shivered. Who would want to live in a place like that?

Of course, who was she to judge? She'd spent most of her life in New York City, where things like that happened. So far she didn't miss too much about it, except maybe Bloomies, SoHo, the Met, Central Park. . . .

But she'd been here for a matter of months, and Manhattan was only a few hours away. Chaz had been here for several years, and LA was not in commuting distance. Was he finally missing his former profession of investigative reporting?

She tossed the paper back on the table. Well, if he wanted a murder to investigate, she just happened to have one on hand. She opened a cabinet under the sink, found a box of trash bags, and began methodically dumping food and take-out cartons into it.

"What the hell are you doing?"

Liv squeaked and whirled around. A man was standing in the doorway. Tall, thin, scruffy beard, beady eyes, and dirty hair that fell into his eyes. He was wearing a grungy white T-shirt with the evidence of the pizza she'd just thrown away dribbled down the front.

She opened her mouth to ask, "Who are you and what are you doing here?" when she recognized him.

"Chaz?"

"Who else did you expect?" he said in a gravelly voice.

"You're back," she said. Which was self-evident, a fact that Chaz should gleefully point out. Only he didn't.

He stepped farther into the room. In the overhead light he looked even worse than before.

"Good heavens, what happened to you?"

"What? You broke in here just to ask stupid questions?" He moved slowly into the room, looked around. "Since you're here, do you see a can of coffee somewhere?"

"Are you sick?"

He shrugged.

"Is that yes or no? Should I call an ambulance?"

He snorted.

"Where have you been? You look . . ."

He smiled, but it was a tired parody of his usual leer. "Beat to shit? Thanks for sharing."

"Well, you do look a little tired."

"Long day."

It looked like it had been a long seven weeks . . . if she had been counting. Which she hadn't been. Not exactly. Not all the time.

"It's only noon. Have you been working on a story?" She said it mainly to get a spark of the old snarky Chaz. She'd even be happy at this point to learn he'd been staying out late to research the spawning habits of lake trout. Anything but this . . . she groped for a word: Dejection? Defeat? Apathy? Whatever it was, she didn't like it.

"Ah," Chaz said, and lifted a coffee can from beneath the pile of papers, sending most of them to the floor.

"Why don't you go take a shower and pull yourself together while I make the coffee?" She snatched the can from his hand and looked around the mess for the coffeemaker.

And was sorry when she found it. The carafe was half full, and there was green stuff floating on top. She gingerly put it in the sink and turned on the hot water.

"Actually I hadn't intended on pulling myself together."

"Go," she said over her shoulder. "Before I use all the hot water trying to get this coffeepot disinfected."

"Did you walk all the way over here in those shoes just to nag me?"

"No, I wore these shoes to go to church—"

Chaz made a sound that might be a derisive laugh. Or maybe a cough. "If you haven't noticed, you missed the church and came to . . ." He seemed to lose his train of thought and looked vaguely around the room. "Here."

"Are you on drugs?"

"I wish."

"Chaz, what's wrong?"

"God, I'll go take a shower just to shut you up." He wandered out of the kitchen.

Liv stared after him. Okay, he was lazy and uninterested in current affairs. He was sarcastic and smarmy, but there had always been an underlying humor to it . . . until today.

She didn't like the Chaz she saw today. The humor was gone, the obnoxiousness was gone; he just looked angry and depressed.

She scrubbed the coffeepot and started the coffee, then began to gather up the newspapers that littered the floor and table. Picked up the section with the article about the banker on trial for murder. Grabbed for another section and found a follow-up article with the headline "Banker Freed on Murder Charges."

Another section. Another article about the same trial.

She put the papers on the counter and began to read. She heard the shower come on above her head. She hadn't read two paragraphs before she forgot about the reason she had come. Forgot everything but what she was reading.

She recognized the guy's name. She'd seen it when she'd first met Chaz and had Googled him to find out what his story really was. A hotshot investigative reporter, respected by his peers, whose last story—that she could find anyway—was about the kidnapping of a banker's wife. Liv bet dollars to donuts this was the same man.

He'd been accused of planning the whole kidnapping and ransom, and killing his wife while playing the inconsolable husband. Knowing Chaz, he'd followed the case to the very end, maybe had been responsible for uncovering the banker's plot. Is that where he'd been? At the trial? As a witness? Or to make sure justice was done?

The guy had been acquitted. Chaz must have thought the man was guilty or he would be elated and celebrating instead of holed up like a hermit.

The water turned off above her, and she hurried to wash the least disgusting mug.

When Chaz came back a few minutes later, clean and shaved, he looked more like his old self. Which gave Liv a little thrill of pleasure . . . to see him looking better.

She handed him his coffee.

He took it with a scowl. "You're like a midge, you know that?"

"Those little bugs that sting the heck out of you?"

"Yep, those bugs."

"Just because I couldn't stand the mess in your kitchen?" she said, glad to see him beginning to get back some of his old attitude.

"Because I know you want something and it isn't my hot self. So why did you come?"

"Actually, are you aware there was a murder Friday night?"

Chaz bobbled his mug and coffee splashed on his hand. "Ow," he said, quickly putting the mug down and flinging coffee off his fingers.

"I guess that's a no."

He raised one sardonic eyebrow, and she felt the stirrings of hope.

"Well, let me tell you about it."

"Do I have a choice?"

"No, because I think even you will be interested in this case."

Another snort. "I doubt it." He picked up his coffee.

"At the reenactment Friday night everything went perfectly, the ghost signaled from the roof, General Haynes galloped across the lawn, the patriots swept down the lawn, got in their boats, and the fireworks started."

"Fascinating."

"Then the lantern started flashing from the roof again."

She saw a brief flicker of interest and hurried on. "Ted recognized it as being Morse code for SOS."

"Henry does love his little bit of drama."

"We went to investigate."

"Of course you did."

Liv gritted her teeth.

"Jacob Rundle had been stabbed with a bayonet."

"Jacob Rundle doesn't give the signal."

"Well he did Friday, and someone killed him."

"Where was Henry?"

At last, a show of interest, small though it was.

"He wasn't there. Just Rundle in a patriot uniform."

Chaz shrugged. "Bill will handle it."

"I'm sure he will, but there was a witness."

Chaz let out a long sigh. "Okay, I'll take the bait. Who?"

"Leo Morgan."

She had his attention. He went absolutely still. "What was he doing on the roof?" He tried to ask the question casually, but Liv could see the wheels already turning. She had him.

"He wanted to ask the ghost of Henry Gallantine where the treasure was hidden."

"Oh my God. What would make him do something like that? Never mind. That was a rhetorical question."

"Well, I'll give you a non-rhetorical answer. He wanted to find the treasure and give it to Pastor Schorr for the community center. We found him cowering on the roof, holding the musket that killed Rundle."

"He was shot with an old musket? No one heard? It would have to have happened before the fireworks began, though it would have made more sense to wait and have the noise camouflaged. Just another one of the explosions."

Thank you, thank you. At least he was asking questions. "He wasn't shot, he was bayoneted."

"Ugh." Chaz went to the coffeepot and poured himself another cup.

"Bill questioned Leo and sent him home. But someone threw a rock through the window of his house and his mother kicked him out. He's staying with Phillip Schorr for the time being. We're all concerned for his safety. Both from the killer and from some of the hotheads who were quick to accuse him of the murder because he's a little different."

"Leo wouldn't hurt anybody." Chaz ran a hand over his face. "Bill will take care of it."

"He's investigating the murder, of course, but I'm more concerned about Leo."

"Bill will put a security detail on him."

"He doesn't have that kind of manpower."

"Then have your big marine from Bayside Security do it."

"Chaz, Leo needs your help. He trusts you. Are you going to throw him to the wolves?"

"Don't be overdramatic."

"I'm not. Bill may have to put Leo into protective custody until the murder's solved."

"What? No way. Leo would be totally confused and frightened. It's a terrible idea."

"I thought so, too, but Pastor Schorr doesn't think he can keep him safe at the rectory, since he'd be left alone while Phillip goes about his church duties."

"So it's Phillip now? You do get around."

"Chaz, for crying out loud. Do you want Leo behind bars, even if it's only for his own safety?"

"Bill can't do that," said Chaz. "Did Leo recognize the killer?"

"He said it was the ghost. That he had a cape and no face."

"Probably covered in a nylon stocking, oldest disguise in the book. No leads?"

"How would I know? I didn't even know *you* were back."

Chaz put his mug on the table. "Is Leo there now? I'll go talk to him."

At last, Liv thought, and followed him toward the door.

He turned on her, stopping her mid-step. "Where are you going?"

"With you."

"I thought you were here to clean my house."

"Then think again."

He leered at her, that smarmy smile, the humorous eyes. She never thought she'd say it, but she was relieved and happy that the old Chaz was finally making a comeback.

They left through the back door, and Liv noticed that Chaz didn't bother to lock it. It wasn't a safe thing to do, but it was definitely a Chaz thing to do. Things were suddenly looking up.

No one answered the bell at the rectory.

"I doubt if Pastor Schorr is back from the service yet," Liv said.

Chaz rang again. "He's probably been told not to open the door to anyone."

"Then we'll have to wait."

They sat on the front steps.

"People might get the wrong idea, us waiting here for the preacher," Chaz said. He gave her knees an appraising look.

Liv didn't bother to answer, just pulled her skirt down.

It was only a few minutes before they saw the pastor striding home, his black cassock whipping behind him.

He lifted a hand when he saw Chaz and Liv sitting on his front steps.

"Greeting or benediction?" Chaz said under his breath.

Liv cut him a quelling look and stood.

"I thought you might be here," the pastor said without preamble. "Chaz, good to see you. I saw your lights the other night and figured you must be home. Leo will be glad to see you, too."

He unlocked the front door and ushered them in. Leo was sitting on the couch in front of the television, watching a cartoon that appeared to be *Davey and Goliath*.

Phillip Schorr smiled apologetically. "I figured since he couldn't be at Sunday school this morning, he could study his Bible. Though I suppose it's rather inappropriate, considering my sermon today."

"Throwing the first stone," Liv told Chaz.

Leo looked up from the television and saw Chaz. "The ghost killed Mr. Rundle."

"So I heard. How've you been, man?"

Leo jumped up. "Okay."

Chaz stuck out his hand, and he and Leo went through an elaborate handshake. "Learned in the Watts district of Los Angeles," Chaz explained. "And good for what ails you."

He took Leo over to the couch. "So the ghost killed old Jacob Rundle, huh?"

Leo nodded.

"Wow, I would've been really scared if I'd seen Old Henry Gallantine's ghost."

"I was," Leo said, his eyes growing rounder. "I tried to hide where it was shadows so he wouldn't see me."

"Smart move. See him but not let him see you."

Leo nodded again.

"Huh," Chaz said. "I sure wish I could've seen him. What does Old Henry look like anyway?"

"Like the ghost."

"Ah, so sort of like Mr. Henry?"

Liv watched as Chaz maneuvered his way through the most astute questioning she'd seen yet. A combination of back-country hillbilly and *Boyz n the Hood* that elicited more information than several prior questionings had. Leo seemed to completely forget that he'd been told not to discuss the events.

The man was good, she had to admit.

After a while, Chaz slapped Leo's knee. "You've got the makings of a good reporter, you know that, Leo?"

"I do?"

"Yep. You do. Now I'm going to go have a look at where that ghost was myself."

Chaz started to get up, but Leo grabbed at his sleeve. "He's mad. Don't let him get you."

"Not to worry. If he tries to bother me, I'll kick him in the shins."

Leo laughed. "Ghosts don't have shins, Chaz."

"Oh yeah." And, extricating himself from Leo's grasp, he said good-bye to Pastor Schorr and headed to the door.

Liv waved good-bye and followed him out.

He stopped on the steps. "Where do you think you're going?"

"With you."

He gave her the once-over. "In those shoes?"

"Yes, so no more of your sarcasm or I'll kick you in the shins."

He shook his head. "You'd better stop listening to those violent sermons. Throwing stones. Kicking shins. Yeah."

He started off down the street, cocky as he ever was. He didn't think she could keep up. But Liv hadn't been an event planner in Manhattan for nothing. Once you learned to navigate potholes, delivery hatches, steam grates, and unrecognizable garbage in four-inch heels, running after Chaz in your Sunday shoes was a walk in the park.

"You know, Hildy will never let you in," Liv said when she caught up to him. "Even you at your most charming."

"Aw," he said in a saccharine singsong. "Don't need her to."

"How are you—?" Liv stopped, then had to run to catch up with him. "You know the secret way."

This time it was Chaz who stopped, surprised. "Do you?"

"There really is a secret way? Leo said he came up the secret way. I wasn't sure if it was really secret or just an outside stairway or fire escape."

Chaz smiled his slow, lazy smile. "Oh no, it's much better than that."

Chapter Nine

....

They didn't go in the front gate but walked past the house and turned into someone's driveway a half block later.

"Who lives here?" asked Liv. "We're not going to get shot for trespassing, are we?"

"Hope not," Chaz said, and kept walking.

Several yards later, and without warning, Chaz ducked into the shrubbery lining the drive and disappeared from view.

Liv's first thought was that he was trying to lose her, and that just wasn't going to happen. She thrashed her way after him.

He was waiting for her in a small clearing that backed up to the outside of an ivy-covered stone wall that must be the same one that surrounded the Gallantine property. Though here the wall was much higher than in front, several feet over her head.

She had no doubt that Chaz could scale the bricks, but she had qualms about herself. She could probably climb it, but it wouldn't be pretty and it definitely wouldn't be modest, which was sure to set off Chaz's sleaziest comments. "Does this wall go all the way down to the water?"

"Yep, but we're not going that way." Chaz motioned her to follow him and, hoping that the vine covering the ground wasn't poison ivy, she plowed ahead.

They came to a rusted gate mostly covered with ivy. She would have walked right past it, except that Chaz had stopped and, once she'd looked, she could see where the vines had recently been stripped away. Leo must have come this way. And maybe the murderer.

Chaz pushed the vines aside and pressed down on a rusty lever. It didn't move.

"Used to be a key."

Oh great, they were going to have to walk all the way to the water and back. She glanced down at her shoes in a final farewell; they wouldn't survive the trek.

Chaz stepped back and looked up, began testing the strength of the vines.

"Don't even think it." She started down the wall to the water.

"Hey, where are you going?"

"To go around."

"Liv, Liv, Liv." He pushed the ivy aside and pressed the latch; the gate creaked open. "You are so easy."

"You wish." She followed him inside.

They entered onto a narrow strip of lawn behind the old mansion. The back of the house was even more uneven than the side close to the bleachers. Additions that appeared as mere afterthoughts were linked and stacked haphazardly together like so many building blocks, making the turret seem like it was the only thing holding them up.

The grass was brown and trampled down. A few yards away a thick stand of trees separated the property from its neighbors and blocked any sun from filtering through to the ground. It made the air chilly and the atmosphere spooky.

Several yards from the house proper was a square stone outbuilding. Chaz headed for it, jogging on tiptoe, knees lifted high, like a cartoon detective. He threw himself up against the stone wall and motioned Liv to hurry.

She hurried. He might think this was funny, but she didn't relish being caught trespassing on a crime scene.

They crept along the back of the building. Chaz peered around the corner; Liv peered around Chaz. To their left was the kitchen. The outbuilding must have been the old icehouse. Liv could see Hildy standing at the window. Doing the dishes?

Liv grabbed Chaz's arm and pointed toward the window. Chaz thumbed his nose at the housekeeper. She didn't look up.

"Nearsighted," Chaz said in a stage whisper. Liv was sure he'd done it just to amp up the excitement. Hildy turned from the window and moved out of sight.

"Now." Chaz motioned for Liv to follow him, and she did. As closely as possible without stepping on him. Until he stopped at the base of the stone turret, and then she did plow into him.

He turned and gave her a look. "Lucy."

"Sorry, Ricky."

Chaz shook his head and pulled at the heavy wooden door that was barely five feet high.

It didn't open. He went through the looking-for-a-key routine.

"If this is another of your tricks . . ."

"Nope. This one is always locked. But I . . ." He began to inspect the stonework around the wooden doorframe. "Ah." He wiggled a piece of stone until it fell into his hand, and along with it a key.

He set it in the lock and pulled the heavy door outward. Put the key and piece of mortar back, then felt inside.

"No light." He pulled the door all the way open. And stepped back.

"What are you doing?" Liv whispered.

"Giving the creepy-crawly things time to get out." He

looked down at her shoes and shook his head. Smiled. "Ready?"

Liv was not ready at all. "Are you sure they're all gone?"

"I think so. If I hear you scream, I'll know I was wrong."

"Chaz."

"Come on. Don't tell me you're afraid of a few spiders?"

"I was thinking of something larger."

He stopped to look at her. "Like a psychopath? Do you really think I would let you go somewhere you could get hurt?"

Liv shook her head. For all his annoying ways, she trusted him. She grabbed the back of his shirt and followed him into the darkness.

She couldn't see a thing, but she felt the damp and smelled the dead, cold air. Suddenly a dim light appeared in the black. Chaz was using his cell phone as a flashlight, not that it gave off much light.

Slowly a door to the left came into view, but Chaz ignored it and continued forward, Liv holding on to him. About ten shuffling steps later, he stopped again. The light went out.

"Watch your step."

She felt him grow taller. Her toe hit something hard. A step. They were going to climb to the roof.

Her shoes weren't made for this, but she was afraid to take them off when she couldn't see where she was stepping. And she refused to let him go on without her.

They felt their way upward, Liv holding on to Chaz's shirt with one hand and feeling the rough stone wall with the other as they climbed the curving staircase. It was an airless corridor, the darkness only relieved by an occasional small rectangular window.

And it seemed to go on forever. Surely they weren't going to the top of the house. The roof where they'd found Rundle had only been about halfway up.

A few minutes later, Chaz slowed. As Liv took another

step, she realized he hadn't moved upward but had shuffled over to make room for her.

They were standing on a small platform, she guessed. It was dusty and claustrophobic. And much too small a space to be sharing with Chaz. They were standing so close, she could feel his body heat.

On cue, he said, "This is cozy."

"And we are where?" Liv heard a squeak, resisted the urge to flee or climb up Chaz's back, and then realized it was the squeak of a door opening, not a creature.

She blinked against the sudden light.

Chaz stuck his head out, looked around, and opened the door more fully. Motioned Liv out. She came with alacrity. They were on the roof. It was sunny, and it took a few seconds for her eyes to adjust.

The first thing that came into focus was Chaz's face.

"Okay, give me the blow by blow."

Liv looked around until she found the trapdoor where they'd entered the night of the murder, which was now covered over. She walked over to it. Stood there getting her bearings, setting up the scene from the night of the murder. Moved several paces to the center of the roof. Turned in a slow circle.

It looked different in the daylight. Made the events of the night seem remote. But she could see it all. The position of the body lying along the wall closest to the bleachers, curled on its side until A.K. turned it to its back. She turned slightly to the right, Leo cowering in the corner, and farther along the parapet to the place where Leo said the ghost had disappeared.

It was all there like a snapshot. She turned to explain it to Chaz, but he was leaning against the turret wall, arms crossed, head tilted, watching her.

"What?"

"Nothing." He pulled away from the wall. "Just trying to

decide if you were actually looking for clues or arranging the banquet tables."

She gave him her iciest look. "Mock all you want, but in my profession it pays to notice details."

"So tell me about them."

"We came up from the stair." She paused to give him a saucy smile. "A.K. had a *real* flashlight. He found Rundle lying not far from the place where he'd given the signal." She pointed to the place. "Or at least from where somebody gave the signal. We just assumed it was Rundle because the lantern was lying on its side at his feet.

"A.K. went over to see what was wrong." She closed her eyes, reconstructing the scene. "Rundle was lying on his side, dressed in one of the patriot uniforms. A.K. turned him over. There was a gash in his stomach. A lot of blood. A.K. said it looked like a bayonet wound, but there was no musket."

Chaz walked over and squatted down by the place she'd pointed out.

"A.K. said he'd probably bled out in a few seconds." She hesitated. "So he couldn't have given the SOS signal, could he? Unless he'd done it before he was attacked. But that doesn't make sense. Anyway, A.K. said to call Bill but to wait on calling the EMTs. He said it was too late for Rundle, and he didn't want them messing up any evidence."

Chaz looked back at her. "How many times are you planning on saying 'A.K. said'?"

"Sorry, but he did."

"Huh." He went back to studying the floor.

"I'm sure Bill already searched the area."

He stood up, gave her a sour look. "Are you just going to bitch at me after you interrupted my comfortable sloth and dragged me over here?"

She was about to point out that she'd only asked him to go talk to Leo, not to play amateur sleuth. But she didn't. She was glad of his help. And he wasn't exactly an amateur.

He looked over the parapet onto the lawn. "And no one saw any sign of a skirmish from below?"

"Not that I've heard."

"Okay, then what happened?"

"The fireworks started in earnest, and when there was a pause, we heard moaning and found Leo pressed into the corner over there." She winced. "Chaz, he looked so frightened. He was clutching the musket. Even from across the floor I could see the bayonet. It was black in the dark, but I knew even then it was covered with blood."

Chaz walked over to the corner, turned sharply back to her. "What did he do?"

"Nothing. Just moaned that the ghost was going to get him, too. Ted tried to take the musket, but he was just too frightened. He said he'd tried to hide, but the ghost rushed at him and then . . . disappeared. Then the fireworks finale started. It was really loud and continuous and it frightened him even more. He dropped the musket and covered his head with his arms. Ted grabbed the musket and handed it to A.K., then sat beside Leo on the floor until Bill came." She ran her tongue over dry lips. "It was awful."

Chaz didn't seem moved by her story, but Liv was feeling sad and sick all over again. It was such an outlandish story, no wonder A.K. hadn't believed it. Could Leo have gotten confused and killed Rundle thinking he was protecting himself? But would he lie about it? He seemed guileless to Liv. She didn't really know him, but Phillip Schorr did and he believed him.

"So he was in the corner? And the ghost disappeared about here?" Chaz walked over to the place where the killer had disappeared. He looked down, leaned over the parapet.

"Would you not get so close?" Liv warned. "You're making me nervous."

"Would you miss me when I was gone?"

"Maybe. Is it worth the test?"

He grinned, a real Chaz grin. Then he switched back into reporter mode.

"So where was Leo when all this happened? Not in the corner?"

"I got the impression he'd just come out of the tower."

Chaz raised an eyebrow. "Impression?"

She ignored him. "Which would put him somewhere around . . ." Liv walked over to where they had entered the roof. "Here."

Chaz joined her. "Go on."

"If the ghost had just killed Rundle, he would have been coming from over there. And would have run past Leo to there." She pointed toward the space where Leo had pointed.

Chaz walked it step-by-step. "Whoever it was must have killed Rundle and then was trapped when Leo came up. He came from over here?" He walked back to where Rundle's body had been found.

"That's about where Leo said."

"And he came at Leo like this?" He made a beeline toward her, slowed down as he reached her. "Then what?"

"Leo said the ghost jumped on the parapet, lifted his arms, and disappeared."

"Like this?" Chaz ran across the roof.

Before Liv realized what he was doing, he'd jumped to the parapet, turned around, and threw out his arms. The movement knocked him off balance. He stumbled backward, arms windmilling to regain his footing.

There was an awful moment when everything hung in a tenuous balance. And then, as if he had just given up, Chaz dropped his arms and plunged from the roof.

Chapter Ten

....

"Chaz!" For a second, Liv couldn't get her feet to move. "Chaz!" The second scream released her and she rushed to the edge of the parapet, adrenaline, compounded by fear, coursing through her.

She barely felt the rough stones scraping her hands as she dragged herself across the stone wall and peered over.

Only to let out a wordless scream as she came almost face-to-face with a grinning Chaz Bristow. Her breath whooshed out. "What?" was all she could get out.

"Aw. I didn't know you cared."

"I don't, you jerk. You scared me to death. That was an awful thing to do." And to her dismay she felt her eyes fill with tears. Only to be displaced by red-hot anger as she realized he was standing on a ledge not five feet below her.

"It would have served you right if that damn ledge had given way and you'd plunged a hundred feet to your death. And I would be left up here staring down at your mangled body."

"And you'd have to go down those creepy stairs all by

yourself." He lifted an eyebrow. "Or, heartbroken, you could have thrown yourself after me."

"Don't count on it. How did you know that was there?"

"Used to climb up here when I was a kid. It was our secret clubhouse."

Liv looked down at him and tried to imagine him as a kid. Probably one of those smart-aleck boys who was always in trouble.

"Don't you want to know what we did up here?"

"No," she said, peering down at the stone ledge. Now that her heart rate was returning to normal, she saw that, even though it was probably four feet wide, wide enough to catch anyone's fall—she swallowed hard—it would still have been very easy to overshoot and lose one's balance and . . . It was a sheer drop below.

Pushing the possible consequences from her imagination, her rational mind began to understand that the murderer must have known about the ledge, maybe even practiced the drop in case his normal means of escape proved unusable, which it must have done when Leo came to the roof.

"And how do you plan to get back up?"

"Well," Chaz said, as he bent over and appeared to be scrutinizing the wall, "I could keep going the way I started."

Liv leaned farther over and looked past him.

"Careful."

It wasn't a sheer drop to the ground, as she'd thought. There was another ledge another few yards below, and another one below that, offset just enough that a person could jump from one to the other. Still, it was a pretty difficult exit route. It would take time, and one misstep could leave a person dead or seriously injured.

"I think you'd better climb back up."

"Nah, I'll just do this." He disappeared again.

"Chaz." This time Liv was more annoyed than frightened. She waited until Chaz's head appeared from out of the stone wall, and he grinned up at her like the Cheshire cat.

"Let me guess. There's an open window."

"Yep," he said. "I'll meet you back on the street."

"The heck you will. I'm not going down that way by myself." She pulled off her shoes and held them down for him to take.

"This I gotta see."

"No, you don't. You're going to come back out here and help me down. And don't back off the ledge by mistake."

He hesitated. "Liv, really, it's too dangerous. I'll go down and let you in the house."

"And risk running into Hildy? I don't think so."

"I'd rather you take on Hildy than drop from the roof like a bale of hay."

"I'll remember you said that."

He grumbled but crawled back out the window and onto the ledge.

"And no smarmy comments," she said as she tried not to think about what she was doing and how far it was to the ground. She just kept reminding herself that it couldn't be worse than breaking an ankle and having to hop down that awful staircase, across the yard, and through the underbrush on one foot.

No. She'd take her chances with Chaz.

"And pay attention to what you're doing." She hiked her skirt up.

"Yes ma'am." But his smile faded as she threw her leg over the stone wall.

And she didn't complain when his hand grabbed her butt and lowered her to the second ledge or held on to her a little longer than necessary when she was on her feet again.

Neither of them spoke until they'd both climbed through the window and were standing safely on the inside.

Chaz closed the window and turned to her. "What a view." Then he grew serious again. "I shouldn't have let you do that."

Liv, who was pulling her dress down to where it belonged,

frowned, confused. "You couldn't have stopped me. Now, where the hell are we?"

"One of the storerooms. And scene of many teenage trysts." He waggled his eyebrows.

Ignoring him, she looked around. It was a real junk room. Cast-off furniture, stacks of old magazines. Trunks and cardboard boxes, filled with God knew what. And all of it dusty. "Do you think the killer escaped this way?"

They were both talking just above a whisper, though Liv doubted if anyone could hear them, even if they were standing in the next room.

"Possibly. If Leo's version can be believed."

"You have doubt?"

"Always. About everything. Leo thought he saw the ghost. Maybe it was the killer, maybe it was his expectations of seeing the ghost . . ." He trailed off as he began looking around. "Don't move and don't touch anything."

Normally she wouldn't, but she hardly had space to turn around. Which meant the killer would have been cramped, too. Even to make a getaway, especially if he had to hide for any length of time. She couldn't even see the door from where she stood.

She looked around. Boxes and crates rose to the ceiling. Everything was covered with unrelieved dust. And then she saw something. Maybe it was nothing, but . . .

"Chaz," she whispered. "Look at this."

He squeezed in next to her. She pointed at a cardboard box that stood about knee-high. "Something disturbed this dust."

It was an uneven disturbance in the dust surface. As if someone had quickly and ineffectively passed a dust cloth over it. Which Liv recognized because she was pretty ineffective with a dust cloth herself.

"A dust cloth or. . . . Leo said he wore a cape. Do you think—?"

"No."

"Why not? The hem of the cape might be just this height, depending on the length of the cape and the height of the killer, and the ratio of the two."

"But he would really have to be a ghost."

"Why?"

"Look." Chaz pointed to the floor. "Dust, dust, and nothing but dust. Not even the ham-footed evidence of a bungled police investigation."

"Surely Bill had his men search."

Chaz cut her off. "Nope."

"In other words, all this has proved nothing," Liv said, disappointed.

"At least it might cut down on the possible escape routes. Because, unless this guy could fly, he didn't come through here."

"Are there other windows?"

"Lots of them—and ledges and roofs."

"Great. We're right back where we started. No suspects."

He patted her on the back. "You give up too easy."

"But why not just go back the way he came? No, never mind. Leo. Leo cut off his escape. Except Leo was so petrified. He probably could have run right past him and down the stairs. But he didn't, so it still means he was someone who knew about the ledge."

"Well, don't look at me."

"Don't be absurd," she sighed. "But who? How many people knew about the ledge."

"Everybody who grew up around here knows about the ledge." He waggled his eyebrows. "Jumping off the roof was a rite of passage, and it really impressed the girls."

Liv huffed out a breath, sat down on a dusty trunk, and began brushing off the bottom of her feet before putting her shoes on. "Who would go to all this trouble to kill Jacob Rundle? Surely there are more convenient places to kill a gardener."

"Maybe they weren't after Jacob."

"You think they were after Henry Gallantine?"

"Or maybe Henry was after Rundle."

"On the roof?" She swung her shoe by the strap. "Unless he killed him because he was on the roof."

Chaz choked out a laugh.

"No, really. Hildy said Henry told Rundle that if he caught him in the house again, he'd fire him."

"That's interesting." Chaz scratched his head and sat down beside her. Watched her slide her foot into her shoe.

"What?"

"Nice ankles. Maybe they killed Henry, too."

"So where is the body?"

Slowly, Chaz looked down into the space between them.

Liv jumped to her feet. "You think he's in the trunk?"

Chaz shrugged. "Let's see."

Liv stepped back, forcing herself not to close her eyes.

Chaz leaned over the trunk, squatted down, and tested the lock. "It's not locked."

"Maybe you should wait and call Bill."

He opened the top. His breath caught.

"What? What is it?"

Chaz gave her a long hard look. "If I tell you, I'll have to . . ."

"Kill me?"

"No." He held up his hand. Crooked his little finger. "Pinky swear."

"Aargh. Let me see." She leaned over and came face-to-face with what looked like a crate full of old velvet curtains.

"Not just curtains," Chaz said, when Liv told him so. "Stage curtains. Back from when Henry decided to try his hand at directing and opened a little theater in town. Alas, we're not a very cultured lot."

"We're wasting time."

"But who would you rather waste time with?"

He just wouldn't let up. But for once, her relief at having

him back on the job, and as smarmy as ever, trumped her annoyance. It made her think maybe he would get involved. For Leo's sake.

"I'd rather someone caught the murderer."

"I thought that's what we were doing."

"It's useless. There are too many possibilities and all of them absurd. Jacob Rundle killed Gallantine so he could take his place on the roof. Or Gallantine found out Rundle was impersonating him and killed Rundle. But could that old man actually jump up to the parapet, much less jump backward off the parapet and land without breaking every bone in his body? Scale the walls to the ground or climb in the window and teleport over this junk and let himself out the door?"

"Henry's not that old. And he's pretty good about keeping himself in shape. These actor types."

"Or it's someone we haven't discovered yet," Liv suggested. "With their own priorities, their own motives, and their own means of escape." She did a quick three-sixty turn in the narrow space.

Chaz shook his head. "It's amazing you get anything accomplished, ever."

"Why?"

"The way your mind flits all over the place."

She sank into one hip. "Among intelligent people, it's known as multitasking."

"Huh."

"So, what do we do now?"

Chaz looked around. Surveyed everything once more. Liv thought she could see him memorizing the room. Or maybe she was just hoping that he really did have an idea.

"I say we have lunch."

Great. She should have known better than to think he would show a continued interest in the case. Even for Leo.

"You have lunch. I'm going to do something to help Leo."

"Don't forget your shoes."

Liv snatched her shoes from the floor. Now her feet were all dusty again.

Chaz crossed his arms and frowned at her. "You know, you dragged me out of my slough of despond, where I was very happy, badgered me into talking to Leo, and now you're yammering on about I don't know what. I need sustenance. Now, be quiet."

He walked past her and turned the knob to the door.

"Chaz, no," Liv whispered urgently. "What if someone catches us?"

He grinned. "I'll throw you in front of me and hope for the best."

He opened the door and stepped out into a hallway, Liv on his heels.

"Stop right there."

Liv recognized the voice, but it wasn't until Chaz froze and she peered around him that she saw what had caused his sudden reaction. Hildy Ingersoll was standing not five feet away, frown on her face, feet apart, and pointing what looked like a double-barrel shotgun right at them.

"Hands up." She shoved the shotgun in the air.

Liv lifted her hands.

"Now, Hildy . . ." Chaz began.

"I said hands up."

Chaz slowly raised his hands. "You've been watching too much television, Hildy. You know I'm always welcome here."

"Not when Mr. Henry ain't home."

"Where is he?"

"I'm the one asking the questions."

"Definitely too much television," Chaz said out of the side of his mouth.

"Chaz," Liv whispered. "Stop it." She was beginning to shake. Would Hildy actually shoot them? Liv supposed she would be within her rights, especially in Celebration Bay, where more people than not owned guns.

"What were you two doing in there? How did you get up here? And none of your tricks, Charlie Bristow."

Chaz winced. And if Liv hadn't been frozen in terror, she would have enjoyed his discomfort.

"I already called the sheriff. People traipsing in and out at all hours with no respect, no respect at all, and on the Lord's day. He shall smite those who . . ."

"Aw, Hildy," Chaz said in his best good-old-boy drawl. "You know we always liked playing up here."

"I know what you boys were doing up here. Smoking and drinking and having your way with the girls." She turned her beady eyes on Liv. "No good white trash, that's what I say." Looked Liv up and down. "And you. You oughta be ashamed of yourself. And you representing the community like you do. Shame on you and your filthy city ways."

Liv started to protest that they weren't up to any . . . what? Smoking, drinking, or having their way with each other? She couldn't think of a term that wouldn't set off the righteous Hildy on a new tirade. On the other hand, neither could she tell the housekeeper that they were looking for a murderer.

And Chaz was no help. He just grinned at Hildy like he'd been caught out. And he hadn't. At least not with Liv.

"Hildy, it's not what you think," Liv began.

"It's worse," Chaz said. "Now, come on down and let us out the front door before the sheriff gets here."

Hildy jerked the shotgun toward the staircase leading downstairs.

Chaz shrugged and gestured to Liv. "After you."

The look Hildy gave him sent a chill up Liv's spine, but she started down the hall to the stairway. Liv moved as close to Chaz as she could without looking like the chicken she was.

Just as they reached the first floor, the doorbell rang, a hollow gong that only added to the gothic atmosphere. Hildy shuffled across the foyer and, shifting the shotgun into one arm, she opened the front door.

Liv had never been so glad to see Bill Gunnison in her life.

He, on the other hand, didn't seem to be glad to see her or Chaz at all.

"Trespassers," Hildy said, taking up the shotgun again and holding it cradled in her arms like a baby.

Bill's mouth tightened. "So I see. I'll take them off your hands now, Hildy. Thanks for calling me."

He motioned Liv and Chaz toward the door.

"Now, you just wait a minute, Bill Gunnison. Aren't you gonna frisk them? They broke in the window upstairs and were messing around in one of the rooms. No telling what they took."

Bill nodded. "Well, Hildy, they look like pretty desperate characters. I'm going to take them down to the station where I have backup waiting, and if they have anything they ought not to have, I'll make sure you get it back."

"I want to press charges."

"Aw, Hildy," Chaz began.

Bill shot him a look.

"I'll take care of it," Bill said, and practically pushed Chaz and Liv out the door.

Hildy watched until Bill opened the back door of the cruiser and Chaz and Liv crawled in. And even though Liv was pretty sure it was for Hildy's benefit, she thought that Bill pushed Chaz's head down with a little too much enthusiasm as he guided him into the cruiser.

Bill got in the front and drove away.

Chaz started humming under his breath. "Seems Like Old Times."

Liv nudged him with her foot.

"Bill," she began.

"Don't," Bill warned. "I don't want to hear what the heck you two were doing in there. You're lucky Hildy didn't fill you both with buckshot."

Liv's stomach flip-flopped. "She'd really shoot us?"

Bill ignored her but turned to Chaz. "What were you thinking?"

Chaz shrugged. "Liv made me do it."

"I did not."

"Be quiet, both of you."

"Are you going to arrest us?" Liv asked.

"Not if I can help it." Bill pulled to a stop in front of the *Clarion* office. Turned around so he could see them both, though it was a little hard to talk comfortably separated by the bulletproof glass.

"So, what did you find out?"

Chaz scratched his head, leaving his hair standing up in spikes. "That somebody could jump off the parapet and land on the ledge below without hurting themselves. Which we knew."

"Somebody who was athletic."

Chaz shrugged. "So we can guess Hildy didn't kill Rundle."

"And Leo was sitting on the roof when Ted and I arrived," Liv said, not sure what point she was trying to make.

Chaz cut his eyes to her, warning her to shut up, she guessed. But she didn't think Leo had killed him. If Leo had come up the "secret" way and killed Rundle, he could have easily escaped the same way, instead of sitting whimpering on the floor.

"See anything else?"

"It's more like what we didn't see," Chaz said.

"Which is what?" Bill asked.

Liv wondered, too.

"Well, the biggest question is, where is Henry Gallantine?"

Bill glared through the bulletproof glass that separated them. "I wish people would stop asking me that. I've contacted his sister, where he usually spends summers.

"She said he would normally be there by now. But he called last week to say something had come up and he wasn't coming. She said she'd call us if she hears from him. Okay? That's not classified. Or have you already made your own inquiries?"

Liv shook her head.

"Not me," Chaz said.

"Uh-huh. We've also tried to get in touch with the nephew, but he's not returning our calls."

Ted had already relayed this information. Surely they had found something new by now.

"Henry would never go there," Chaz said. "The last time Frank was here—Frank's the nephew—" he told Liv, "Henry told him to get out and stay out, that he'd paid his last gambling debt. Or do you already know that from *your* inquiries?"

"Chaz," Liv warned quietly. "Stop it."

"We've checked the hospitals, have an APB out on his car."

"His car is missing?"

"He had his car serviced over at Jerry's, just like he does every year, got it back on the third, just like always. No one's seen it since."

"And that's it?" Chaz asked, a slight edge to his question.

Bill kept his pointing forward. "Hildy says she hasn't seen him since Thursday night." He glanced at Liv. "Which is no surprise. He doesn't see anybody on the fourth. He likes to prepare for the role and leaves as soon as it's completed."

He sniffed. "Used to be an actor. Enjoys a bit of drama, even though he's been retired for years."

"So if he isn't here, and he isn't there . . ." Liv began.

"He isn't anywhere, that darn elusive Pimpernel." Chaz grinned at her, though Liv thought it looked more like a grimace.

"Very funny."

"I think you should search the house."

That was enough to make Bill turn around.

"I thought you and Liv had already done that."

Liv was beginning to wonder what was going on between

the two of them. There was definitely a subtext that she was missing.

"We did search it, the night of the murder," Bill said. "And A.K.'s men surrounded the house until the end of their shift in case anyone tried to escape."

"Huh. A.K.'s men," Chaz said. "Why not the police?"

"Because it was the Fourth of July all over the county, not just in Celebration Bay. Other towns needed support, plus there were several accidents, DUIs. Darn fools."

"So A.K.'s men searched the house for the killer?" Chaz asked at his driest.

"Yes, and I know what you're going to say. There are so many hiding places in that old monstrosity, we could be playing cat and mouse with a killer for days. I do have someone watching the house twenty-four/seven, but I'd appreciate if you two would keep quiet about it."

"I wasn't really thinking about the killer," Chaz said. "I was thinking about Henry."

"Heck," Bill said, "I wouldn't put it past him. Sometimes I think he's lost his grip on reality. Doesn't know the difference between what's real and what's the movies."

"Maybe Hildy is holding him captive." Chaz raised an eyebrow at Liv.

She shot him a look that said, *Don't test Bill's patience.*

Bill snorted. "Why would she do a fool thing like that? Or is this you being sarcastic?"

"Me, sarcastic?"

"Yes," Bill and Liv said together.

Chaz shrugged. "It just occurs to me that lately Hildy has grown more prejudiced, angrier, and possibly a little greedy."

"Hmm. I don't know what Henry pays her, but she's been with him for twenty years."

"And why he's kept her on is a mystery," Chaz said. "She can't cook, her housekeeping skills leave a lot to be desired, she's got a face like an anvil, and she's not even nice."

Liv couldn't tell if he was being serious or just obstructive. His tone was almost conversational, his features perfectly relaxed, as if he had no ulterior motive. But she had seen him in action enough times to know that he had a façade for every occasion.

He usually showed no interest in investigating anything, not even where to hold the next tractor pull, but sometimes he couldn't help himself. He'd once said investigative reporting was like an addiction. One he obviously wanted to kick, but couldn't quite give up for good.

For which Liv was glad. But what toll was it taking? And what was this sudden antagonism between him and Bill? Was it mere exasperation on Bill's part? Liv could sympathize.

"Right now, we're looking at Henry Gallantine as a person of interest."

"A suspect, you mean."

"A person of interest," Bill repeated, pulling the cruiser back onto the road. "Liv, I'll drop you off first."

"Oh," she glanced at Chaz. "We're not going to jail?"

"You're not. What I do with Chaz remains to be seen."

"Bill, you're not serious, are you?"

"Yes."

"Then I guess I'll take that ride."

No one spoke on the ride to Liv's house. Chaz rested his head back on the seat and closed his eyes. Bill kept his eyes forward. Liv felt very isolated with the glass separating them.

When they reached the Zimmerman sisters' old Victorian, Bill pulled the cruiser to the curb. "I'll let you off at the end of the drive, if you don't mind. Don't want Ida and Edna getting all upset."

Liv smiled. "You mean you don't want them to get all excited and start asking you questions."

"That's exactly what I mean." He clicked the locks on the back doors, and Liv got out.

"Good night, Irene," came from the "sleeping" editor in the backseat.

Liv got out, and the door locked again.

Bill rolled down his window a few inches.

"Liv, there's a murderer loose, and I don't want any more civilian casualties. Now, get inside before someone sees you."

"Should I worry about my reputation?" she asked Bill, only half joking.

"No. Everyone will just think you're helping with the investigation."

Liv cringed. Was it resignation she heard in Bill's voice? Or disgust? "Bill, I—"

"Can't help yourself. I know."

"It wasn't Chaz's fault. I kind of badgered him into doing it."

"Aw" came from the backseat. Liv hadn't thought that the intercom was still on.

"You," Bill said, turning around and pointing a finger at Chaz, "just shut up."

Liv stepped back. Definitely a subtext going on between the two of them.

Bill nodded to her, rolled the window up, and drove away.

Liv barely had taken a step before Miss Edna appeared on the front porch. She'd changed from her church wear into knit pants and a striped T-shirt that Liv had seen on the pages of a catalogue the last time she'd visited the sisters.

Edna waved. "Liv, Whiskey's here with us. We didn't know how long you'd be gone. And Ida has just made tea."

Chapter Eleven

....

Caught, thought Liv. Bill had the good sense not to stop too long. Liv should have had him let her off at the corner.

Liar, liar, pants on fire. She had a million questions about Henry Gallantine, Leo Morgan, Hildy Ingersoll, and the dead gardener, and the sisters were a storehouse of information both past and present.

They had lived in Celebration Bay their entire lives and had taught most of the residents under fifty years of age. Liv was sure they would have information on the background of all the players.

Liv veered around to the front walk and climbed the steps to the porch.

The first things Miss Edna saw were the shoes in Liv's hand.

"A long story," Liv said.

"One that I'm sure will go better with tea and Ida's red, white, and blue cake. Come on inside." She held the door for Liv and followed her into the foyer. "Ida!" she called. "Liv is joining us for tea."

At the sound of her name, Liv heard the click of doggie paws on the hardwood floor of the hall. A few seconds later, Whiskey bounded into the room as if he hadn't seen her in weeks instead of a few hours.

Liv knelt down to say hello, and Whiskey took the opportunity to sniff her shoes.

"Just shoes, I'm afraid, no hidden treats."

"Arf," Whiskey barked, and sat back on his haunches. Then lowered his head to his paws. His pitiful pose.

Liv stood up.

"I'm afraid I'd have to give him an A-plus in English Comprehension," Edna said fondly.

"Too bad the only word he doesn't understand is 'no.'" Whiskey whined.

"Okay, maybe he understands but chooses not to listen." Liv sighed. Singing, spelling, and English Comprehension . . . and he was back to wearing his red, white, and blue kerchief, which one of the sisters must have found and put on him when they picked him up from the carriage house.

Whiskey was thriving in his new home. And Liv was, too, sort of. She'd be really thriving if she had a social life outside of tea with her landladies and her weekly dinners with BeBe.

Ida appeared from the kitchen with a tray of tea and cake. Every time Liv came to tea, which was fairly often, they always used the china teapot and plates. At first Liv thought it had been because they had a guest, but she was beginning to think they served themselves from the best china even when they were alone.

Liv felt a rush of affection for the two spinster schoolteachers, her landladies and friends. And they loved her dog. She had a great life. It would be perfect if she had someone to share it with. Someone who was more than a friend or a landlady or a coworker. Someone who was a . . . boyfriend?

"We didn't know where you had gone this morning," Miss Ida said as she poured Liv a cup of fragrant tea.

"I'm so sorry," Liv said. "But I was on a mission of sorts."

"We heard Chaz was home," Edna said as she took her own cup from Ida.

"We've been wondering why he hasn't shown his face since he got back," Ida said, and lifted a piece of layer cake with white icing covered in blueberries and a filling of strawberry compote. She handed the plate to Liv. "Did he say when he's getting the paper back up and running?"

Liv bit back a smile. Her landladies kept their fingers on the pulse of Celebration Bay. Nearly as astute as Ted when it came to gossip. They'd actually been very helpful more than once when Liv had been up against seemingly insurmountable problems. And they hadn't been averse to helping in a couple of murder investigations. In fact, they had been very enthusiastic participants.

The two of them drank tea and cut cake as if they had no other thoughts in their heads, but Liv knew they were waiting for all the news and they would be just as enthusiastic about telling her all they knew in return.

Bill had said that everything he'd told them this afternoon wasn't classified, so Liv had no compunction about sharing the information with her landladies and asking their advice. And if she knew the sisters, they'd already found out about her and Ted finding the body of Jacob Rundle. It was probably all over town by now.

"Well," she said after she'd taken a sip of tea, "when I heard the way people were talking at the fellowship hour, I started worrying about Leo. He wasn't at church, so I guessed that Reverend Schorr had decided to keep him at home. He's staying at the rectory."

"We heard," Ida said. "I've never understood how some people can be so mean, throwing rocks through that poor woman's window. Bill didn't arrest Leo. And the idea of that boy killing that old man. It's absurd." She *tsk*ed.

"Since when do facts have anything to do with the way people act?" Edna asked. She'd been a middle school teacher

and had a more realistic view of the world than her elemen-
tary school–teacher sister.

"I just hope some of them took the pastor's reading this
morning to heart," Miss Ida said. "Starting with Leo's
mother. To think she kicked him out of her house."

"So do I," Edna agreed, "but for my part, I don't think
removing Leo from that environment is the worst thing that
could happen to him."

"Is it a bad environment?" Liv asked.

Edna snorted. "If you call living with an irresponsible
woman with too many children, none of them with the same
father, and who are mostly taken care of by one another . . ."

"It was just awful," Ida said. "She wasn't even sending
them to school until the truant officer and social services
put their collective feet down. Told her to send them and
give them a decent place to live or they were taking them
away. She straightened up for a few months."

"Afraid of losing her welfare checks," Edna added. "That
didn't last, but by then poor Dina, the oldest girl, turned eighteen and left school to take over doing the cooking and
cleaning."

"That's terrible," Liv said.

"An all-too-common story around here, I'm afraid. I
know she'd like to get out of there, but she can't leave the
little ones. To her credit."

"So I guess it's a good thing that she kicked Leo out,"
Liv said. "Maybe he'll have a chance to do something with
his life."

The sisters nodded and murmured their agreement.

"But where will he live?"

"He can't stay with Pastor Schorr. He's got too much on
his plate already." Edna took a bite of cake.

"Maybe get him into one of those residencies," Ida said,
shaking her head. "It seems a shame, but what else is there
to do?"

"But you didn't go to see Leo, did you?" Edna asked,

bringing them right back to the subject Liv had hoped they'd forgotten. Silly her. The sisters never forgot anything.

"No. Yesterday, Pastor Schorr said he'd seen a light on at the *Clarion* office, so today I went over to see if Chaz was back." Liv didn't miss the look that passed between her landladies. She hurried on.

"I thought Leo might be afraid, staying alone at the rectory, and I knew that he and Chaz are friends. I didn't know if Chaz had heard about what happened, and once he did he might want to spend time with him. Like one of those big brother programs. I know he does things with the community center kids. Even though he acts like he doesn't care about anything, he does. Or he wouldn't do it."

"He was always a sweet boy," Ida said.

"He was hell on wheels from the time he got his first tricycle," Edna said. "But so interesting. Lord, always getting into trouble." She frowned. "Not real trouble, just pranks, and so curious about everything. I could have used a hundred students like him."

"A hundred students like Chaz and you'd been sent off for the cure, Edna."

Edna made a face at her sister, ran her finger over her plate, and licked the last of the cake icing off it.

That earned her a frown from Ida. "If you want more cake, Edna, you just need to ask."

"I don't want more. I wanted to lick icing off my finger. The privilege of retirement. So was he home?"

"Yes, but . . ." Liv wondered how much she should divulge about the status of the local editor.

"But what?"

"When I got there, he didn't look very good. Actually he looked awful." Liv paused. He'd probably kill her if she blabbed about his slovenly state to the sisters. Or about the way he and Bill had been acting. And what part her butting in might have played in it. But she needed some advice.

"Well, the house was dark and locked. So I let myself in. The kitchen was a mess."

"Just like a man," Ida said.

"But worse. He hadn't shaved or bathed in I don't know how long. It was like he just didn't care."

Edna nodded. "Took the outcome of that murder trial hard. I was afraid of that."

"You knew about the case?"

"Sure we did. We've been following it on the Internet. And when we heard the outcome on the news last week, we thought he might be upset."

"Probably feels like it's his fault," Ida agreed.

"His fault?" Liv said. "From what I read, the evidence he turned up during his investigation was pivotal in bringing it to trial at all."

Edna put her plate down. "But it wasn't enough to convict the man."

"And you think he feels responsible?" Liv was having a hard time reconciling the lethargic, laid-back Chaz with this paragon of morality and responsibility.

"Of course he must be taking it hard," Ida said. "His father was so proud of him. We all were."

Liv let that sink in before she said, "He was very successful, from what I understand."

"Yes, he was."

"So successful that he gave it up to run his father's local newspaper?" Liv asked.

"Now, Liv," Edna said. "His family needed him. He's also loyal, no matter what some people might think. He came back to his roots."

Ida sighed. "Now, if he'd just settle down with a nice—"

"What do you know about Henry Gallantine?" Liv asked before Ida could finish her sentence.

"Another one who left and came back."

"Leo isn't the only one with a crazy mother," Edna added.

"Henry's mother, Maddie, erred on the opposite side. Smothered that boy with her doting and ambition."

"Poor Henry," Ida said. "She took him to New York to audition for a part in a movie they were making. He was a handsome boy and very photogenic. Next thing everyone knows, she'd packed up the baby and Henry and took them both to live in Hollywood."

"Left her husband behind. No one heard from her again," Edna said.

"Just what we read in the papers. We saw a couple of movies Henry was in. He was a good little actor. Then he had a television series for a while."

"What about the sister? Did she become an actor, too?"

"Not that we ever heard of," Edna said. "I know she came back to visit a few times, but then she just sort of dropped out of sight until she came to keep house for the current Henry. But that was a long time ago."

"So why did Henry leave Hollywood to return home?" Liv asked.

"Sad, really," Ida said.

"The same thing that happens to most child stars happened to Henry," Edna said.

"He grew up and couldn't get parts?" Liv guessed.

The sisters nodded together.

"Stuck it out for a while, picking up small parts in bad movies. Finally I guess he just gave up and came back to live like a hermit in that old mansion, just like his father before him," Edna said. "But I remember the day he came back to town, driving a big old Lincoln, he looked like a young Robert Redford. The whole town lined the streets, waving and applauding. But he just drove straight through town to that big old house without even looking out the window to see."

"I imagine he was embarrassed," Ida said.

Edna nodded. "Sad. At first he tried to get involved in things, but the spirit was just gone out of him. That's when his sister moved in with him to keep house, but talk about your hell on wheels. That boy of hers was incorrigible and spoiled to boot. Henry couldn't stand him."

"Well, he was a horrible child," Ida agreed. "And you know I love children. But this boy stole and lied and made mischief every chance he got. Henry finally had to send them packing."

"Grew up to be a horrible adult from what we hear," Edna said.

Ida *tsk*ed. "A pity. And after all Henry had done for them. Henry was like that. Always kind to the kids, gave to various charitable causes, tried to start up a theater group for a while, but couldn't keep enough people interested."

"And," Edna said, "turned out just like his father. Henry's father never got over his wife and son leaving. And seems like the same thing's happened to this Henry."

"He never married?"

The sisters both shook their heads and sighed.

"Such a shame, such a dashing young man. Ida, is there more tea in that pot?"

Ida poured Edna another cup. "Liv?"

"No, thanks." Henry certainly didn't sound like a man who would commit murder. Unless, as Bill had suggested, he'd gone round the bend. "Just out of curiosity, what happened to Henry's mother and father?"

"Maddie did lose her mind—so sad—ended up in an asylum in Los Angeles," Ida said.

"And Henry." Edna stopped to shake her head. "The housekeeper found him dead one night out by the hedge. They declared it a heart attack, but some people think he threw himself off the roof out of loneliness."

"Which he brought on himself," Ida said with a hint of exasperation, which she seldom showed. "He had good neighbors, and before Maddie and the children left, he had good friends. He could have turned to them, but he chose to lock himself up and pine away."

Unlike either of the sisters when they'd lost their fiancés to war. They had gotten on with their lives, become teachers, taught a whole generation of Celebration Bay men and women. Productive, nurturing, and well loved.

And what about Chaz? Was that what he was doing? Cutting himself off from the world? She wasn't really worried. She'd managed to badger him into helping Leo today. Whether he would continue to do so was another story.

Hopefully Bill would catch the killer before it was put to the test.

Ida leaned over and patted Liv's knee. "You don't worry about a thing. Just stick to your lesson plan like we showed you, and we're sure you and Chaz will get to the bottom of this in no time."

My lesson plan, Liv thought as she and Whiskey walked up the drive to her house. How had it come to this, that a person whose forte was organizing parties and corporate events somehow kept getting involved in murder investigations?

It wasn't just because she was nosy. "I'm not nosy, am I?"

"Arf," Whiskey said, and took off for his nightly inspection of the shrubbery.

"I take that as a no."

When Whiskey reappeared, Liv went inside, but not to bed.

Her laptop was calling. She kicked off her shoes and sat down at her desk.

After a few minutes, Whiskey gave up standing in the doorway to her bedroom waiting for her to come to bed, yawned, padded over to the desk, and flopped down across her bare feet.

"Have I told you lately you're the best dog in the whole world?"

Whiskey made one of those long whining yawns. Shook his muzzle and promptly fell asleep.

Liv clicked on the template she'd made for her last

adventure into things that she shouldn't look into. She'd saved it in a folder labeled LPFM. Lesson Plan for Murder.

She sat staring at the empty columns. She hadn't expected to have to use it after the incident of the Harvest by the Bay Festival, when the sisters had first suggested she approach her questioning as they would a lesson plan.

But she must have had some intuition that she might need it again, since she'd saved it as a template. And here she was again, though Liv was appalled at having to admit that she might consider investigating on her own.

Well, she rationalized, she was just living up to expectations. And besides, even though she insisted she wasn't a control freak and always delegated duties, in truth, deep down inside, she was a control freak. Was it her fault that she wanted to be the best, do the best, hire the best, have the best outcomes?

Which brought her back to the first excuse—reason—for her meddling: looking into things. She had a festival at stake. She began to type.

"Jacob Rundle murdered on the roof as he participated in the reenactment. Gardener. Case of mistaken identity?" Question mark.

The Motive column she left blank. Though in the Comments column she entered: "Why would someone want to kill a gardener?" And another big question mark. *For mistakenly mowing over the daylilies? For overwatering the cactus, for hitting a water main when digging out the—* She didn't write any of that down. It sounded too ridiculous.

She stopped. Thought.

Leo had said he and Henry had found some treasure, but not the "real" treasure. What if the gardener had been digging and accidentally uncovered the "treasure." Would he have turned it over to Henry, or would he have opened it first? If it were gold would he just have taken it with no one the wiser? But if it were a document, as Ted suggested, and if he'd found something incriminating about Henry's ancestor, would he generously hand it over and promise to never tell, or destroy it, nobly keeping his employer from disgrace?

Nah, not the Jacob Rundle she'd seen in action. If it were gold, Rundle would have kept it. And if it were a document, he would have offered to give it back—for a price.

She entered two words in the Motive column to the right of Rundle's name. "Theft, Blackmail??" Put two question marks beside it. Already she was picking holes in that theory. If she were going to blackmail someone, she wouldn't have dressed up as a patriot to meet her victim on the roof in the middle of a pageant with an audience of close to a thousand people sitting below.

She would have just gone into the house, taken Henry aside, and asked for a reward or blackmailed him with what she'd found.

And why on earth would Henry agree to meet him on the roof, when Hildy and Leo had said he didn't like Rundle in the house. Maybe because the roof wasn't the house?

Only, instead of getting money from Henry, Henry killed him?

And that would certainly take care of the question of how the killer had escaped. He'd just gone back inside. Did Hildy know? That would make her an accomplice, even if it were after the fact.

And how had he eluded the police? Ted, Liv, and A.K. had gotten there within a few minutes . . . unless Rundle was dead before the first signal was given. It was possible that Henry had been on the roof to give the signal and had given it.

Then Leo interrupted him, and he had to do something drastic. Like jump over the parapet and climb back into the house. But the dust hadn't been disturbed on the floor; Chaz had said he would have to have flown.

But there was the folding-stair entrance. Maybe he hadn't just disappeared, but made a big show of it, and while Leo

covered his head in fear—which Liv had seen him do—
Henry just climbed back down the stairs.

But why hadn't Leo recognized him?

Or had he and just not made the connection yet? He'd
been dressed like the ghost . . . because he was playing the
ghost, like he did every year. He'd probably planned to get
away before the body was discovered.

She leaned back and looked at her screen. So far the only
motive she had was connected to the treasure or the pur-
ported treasure. But she had a lot of unanswered questions.
Like why do it now with so many people around and when
he was supposed to be at his sister's, where his alibi could
be checked?

It didn't make sense.

And if Henry didn't kill Rundle, someone else had . . .

Henry Gallantine should have been portraying the ghost
on the roof that night. But as far as they knew, he hadn't
given the signal but left Jacob Rundle to do it. And he'd
never made it to his sister's. His car was missing and so
was he.

Maybe he was dead, too.

She added this to her lesson plan and looked over her
columns. So far she had three people—Henry, Jacob, Leo.
Two motives—gold, document. Questions—nearly twenty.
Answers—goose egg. She yawned. She was getting too tired
to think straight. But her mind was turning too fast to go to
sleep.

She went to IMDb, the Internet Movie Database, and
typed in "Henry Gallantine." Spent a few minutes reading
about his movies, looking at photos and video clips. There
were a couple of him at award functions several years back.

He'd been a cute kid and not a bad actor if the short clips
she watched were any indication. He was still a good-
looking man, not terribly tall, maybe five ten, but fit.

Formal, charming, and distinguished looking. Was he in
good enough shape to leap to a parapet and jump to the ledge

beneath, climb through the window or jump through the opening to the folding stairs, and make his escape before the police arrived?

Was he hidden inside the massive old house, and then, once the coast was clear, would walk out to wherever his car was parked and drive away . . . to where? Had he already escaped?

Liv searched the Internet for a stream of his old movies. Most weren't available, but there was a version of *Treasure Island*.

Perfect. A period piece about a treasure. A fitting end to the weekend.

She stretched, dislodging her sleeping dog. Disgruntled, he got to his feet and padded off to his own bed. Liv curled up on the couch and started the movie.

It only took a few minutes for Liv to be hooked. Henry Gallantine was one likable kid on screen. An enticing teen-idol type. And his Jim Hawkins was a perfect foil to Long John Silver.

And she wasn't at all surprised when Henry, being chased around the ship, climbed nimbly up the mast only to swing across the bow on the rigging to land on the other side of the deck.

When Liv woke up the next morning, the first thing she thought of was that she wouldn't have to wear red, white, or blue to work. The second thing she thought was, *Has Bill caught the murderer yet?* And the third, *Did Henry Gallantine do his own stunts?*

She hurried through her morning routine, anxious to get to the office and hear the latest, but when it came time to leash Whiskey, he refused to budge.

"What?"

He padded into the living room and put his feet up on the desk chair. And Liv saw what he was waiting for. His stars-and-stripes bandanna lay where she'd taken it off him the night before.

"You are such a fashion hog." She tied it on him and they started off to work. She was halfway there when she began to feel that post-event letdown funk. It always happened, like walking to a cliff edge—or a parapet—and falling over, the image of Chaz disappearing over the side of the wall still vivid in her mind. Her stomach did a sympathetic flip.

In Manhattan she just tried to keep going, maybe had a morning of exhaustion followed by some retail therapy and it was off to the next project.

Now she was about to have several weeks where she wasn't really needed. Which was a good thing.

She could work on her recap of the year, find the things that hadn't run as smoothly as they should have, bookmark things that were working fine, come up with plans for improvement. Start on her projections for next year. Look for new holidays and events to add to the roster.

She could get back to running consistently. She really needed the exercise—fit body, fit mind.

Maybe even take a few days totally off. Feet up, book open, air-conditioner turned up to near freezing; television on mute while she drank iced tea in her pajamas.

She could take up crocheting, or quilting. There were so many things to do in Celebration Bay if she only had the time.

But she wouldn't have time. Especially if people kept getting murdered. Hopefully the murders they'd experienced were just an aberration and not a trend.

She picked up pastries and coffee, but both places were busy with customers and Dolly and BeBe didn't have time to talk. Which was just as well. They'd only want to talk about the murder, and Liv really just wanted it to be over.

She climbed the steps to Town Hall. Whiskey sat at the closed door of the Events Office while Liv dropped the leash, anticipating his mad scramble to Ted and their daily songfest. She opened the door. Whiskey jumped in. There was no Ted.

Whiskey went to the desk. Sniffed around Ted's chair. Looked back at Liv.

"Beats me," she told him. "Maybe he's taking a late morning." That would be a first. But they had been running at full throttle for seven months. They both could use some downtime.

Liv put the bakery bag and cups on Ted's desk and went back to shut the door. But before she reached it, Whiskey shot out into the hallway.

"Whiskey, come back here." She hurried after him. But instead of turning to the right toward the door to outside, Whiskey turned left and was caroming down the hall. "Where are you going?"

He ran past the unoccupied receptionist's desk and skidded to a stop at the closed door of the mayor's office. Looked back at Liv. She cold hear the murmur of voices inside. It was early for the mayor to be in his office. Maybe there had been a break in the case. But the other voice didn't sound like Bill Gunnison or A.K. Pierce.

"Come on, let's get to work." Liv reached for Whiskey's leash. Whiskey barked. The door opened. Ted looked out at them; Whiskey jumped up and put his paws on Ted's knees.

Liv rolled her eyes. All those obedience lessons and Ted was undoing most of them.

"Come in, Liv. I'm sure you'll be interested in hearing this." Ted gestured Liv in.

Liv was as surprised as Whiskey was disappointed. He dropped to all fours and whined. Ted bent down and distractedly scratched his ruff. Waited until Liv had stepped into the mayor's office.

There was a stranger sitting with the mayor. He stood as Liv entered. He was about five foot eight, with a delicately featured face topped by a black comb-over. He was dressed in a navy-and-gray plaid sports coat, khaki trousers, and a white button-up shirt finished off with a bow tie. Nothing patriotic about him.

She had no idea who he was. She was sure she'd never even seen him before.

Hopefully, he wasn't a tourist who had come to complain about something. Or from any county office that was looking to fine them for some minor infraction of the county code.

Ted cleared his throat. "Liv Montgomery, this is George Grossman."

Liv shook hands with the man. "How do you do?"

The mayor looked ill at ease, so she turned to Ted for more information.

Ted raised an eyebrow at her. "Mr. Grossman has just informed us that he is the new owner of Gallantine House."

Chapter Twelve

....

"What?" Liv blurted, but quickly covered her lapse. "I mean, so nice to meet you. I didn't know Gallantine House was for sale."

"Well, not me personally," Grossman said as he leaned over to shake her hand. "I represent Onyx Historical Housing Conservancy. We locate historic homes that have museum potential but that have fallen into, shall we say, less-than-pristine condition. We either buy them outright, completely furnished, or fit them out with appropriate artifacts from our permanent collections."

Mayor Worley popped up from his desk chair. "I was just explaining to Mr. Grossman that Gallantine House is leased to the town for ninety-nine years for use during the month of July for the reenactment. And that we hope that his organization will continue to honor that lease." His smile was polite, tight with no sign of teeth.

Grossman chuckled. "And I've been telling your mayor that I can't promise anything. That is up to my board of directors. I'm just here to catalogue the contents of the house and make a detailed record."

"But what about the reenactment?" the mayor asked.

Liv watched Grossman's jaw tighten. "What I saw Friday night was not a reenactment. Totally without merit. A travesty of historical accuracy. Though the fireworks were good."

The mayor turned an apoplectic red. "But—"

"Mayor Worley. As we are all aware, there was never a battle in Celebration Bay during the Revolutionary War or any other war. There were never any British ships blown up by patriots on the lake. Certainly not with any pyrotechnics like the ones we saw Friday night.

"And even if there had been, Henry Gallantine wasn't even in residence during the time of the supposed battle, much less standing on the roof waving a lantern. He was being tried in a general court-martial for treason."

"Of which he was later exonerated," the mayor said.

"Of which he was exonerated," Grossman agreed. "Though it was never actually proven he was innocent."

"Well, of all the—" Mayor Worley snapped his mouth closed, seemed to lose his train of thought, and cast an agonizing look at Ted and Liv.

"Well, we'd like to welcome you to Celebration Bay," Liv said, since the other two had been struck mute.

Grossman turned his attention to Liv. Sensing a possible ally?

"First I would like to know where Henry Gallantine is," Grossman said.

You and the rest of the world, Liv thought. She wondered if his board would still be interested in buying after they learned about the murder and that Henry was either dead or a possible suspect. Traitor, murderer. History repeating itself in a twisted sort of way.

"And have him tell us why he didn't inform us of his intent to sell," added Gilbert Worley.

For some reason both men were looking at Liv, the mayor
desperately, Grossman as cool as a cucumber.

"When we met with Mr. Gallantine to go over the plans
for the reenactment," Liv said, "he didn't mention he was selling." She finished with a look at Ted, who had also been there.

"Just so," Ted said, almost as if he were bored by the
announcement. Which couldn't possibly be the case. If
Grossman didn't honor the lease, they would have to find
new grounds for the reenactment, which would probably
fall to Liv and Ted, which meant she could kiss the rest of
her summer good-bye. And where would they find a place
as perfect as the Gallantine lawn?

"Well, someone must know," Grossman said. "I was supposed to meet him Saturday to sign the papers. But when I
arrived, the police informed me that the house was a crime
scene. And Gallantine was nowhere to be found."

"So you haven't actually signed the contract?" Ted asked.

"No, but it was virtually agreed to, dependent on whether
the house is actually salvageable or not. And I do have this
letter of authorization from Gallantine himself, allowing me
full access to the house and grounds for my inventory."

At this, Ted cut his eyes toward Liv before looking at
Grossman directly. "Perhaps you should talk with the sheriff, Bill Gunnison."

"I have. He said the house and grounds are still a crime
scene, but that I could have access to the downstairs if
accompanied by a representative of the town."

Liv got a sudden sinking feeling.

"Mr. Grossman." Mayor Worley was finally galvanized to
action. He came around his desk. "I really don't know what
more we can tell you at this time. No one has seen Henry
Gallantine since last week. Perhaps he has confused the time
or the day. I'm afraid you'll just have to wait for his return."

Grossman didn't deign to answer but gave the mayor a
look that brooked no argument. His diminutive appearance,
the bow tie, and the comb-over were deceiving. He might

not beat out anyone in a physical fight, but Liv had no doubt he wielded a lot of power in other ways.

"And your real estate agent doesn't know where he is?" asked Liv. If said agent was Janine, they could stick her with him. But not even Janine would sell Gallantine House out from under them, even for what had to be a huge commission. She might put on airs, but she was a Celebration Bayite to the bone. Wasn't she?

"We didn't use an agent. Gallantine knew I was interested. He was going to have his lawyer present to make certain all the t's were crossed and the i's dotted. Once my board okays the deal, we're prepared to take occupancy immediately."

Ted raised his eyebrows. Liv bet he'd be making a call to Silas Lark as soon as they got back to the Events Office.

Whiskey took this moment to shuffle over and sniff Mr. Grossman's pant leg.

Grossman looked down. "Ah, a West Highland white. Which breeder?"

"Actually he's a rescue dog."

"Terrible, people who don't care for their pets. This fellow looks in decent shape." He leaned down and took Whiskey by the muzzle, an indignity that he rarely tolerated, except from Liv or Sharise at the Woofery.

Liv half expected Grossman to pull back Whiskey's lips to look at his teeth.

Whiskey immediately backed away and bared those teeth.

Mr. Grossman brushed his hands together. "The sheriff assured me that the Mayor's Office would have someone who would accompany me on my inventory. Not an ideal way to work, but I understand the necessity under the circumstances." He finished the statement looking at the mayor, clearly expecting him to come forth with a volunteer.

And all eyes turned to Liv.

"I'd love to. It sounds fascinating, but I have a meeting with Bayside Security at nine. In fact, I'd better run. So nice to meet you." She practically dragged Whiskey out of the office.

"I have to take shorthand," Ted said, and followed her out.

As soon as Ted closed the Events Office door behind them, Liv began to fire questions at him. "Did you know about this? Is it possible that Henry would sell without informing anyone?"

"Whoa. Not until we've had sustenance," he said. "Shoo. I'll get the supplies."

Liv went into her office, while Ted and Whiskey went through their morning routine.

"Who's my favorite dawg?" Ted crooned.

"Aroo-roo," Whiskey answered.

"Dawg," Ted repeated.

Liv sighed and drummed her fingers on her desk while she waited for it to end. At least it wasn't "Yankee Doodle."

And while she drummed, she thought. A gardener is killed during a heavily attended reenactment. The owner, who should have been on the roof instead of the gardener, goes missing. Leo Morgan actually—probably—saw the killer, but can't identify him—yet. And the new owner, who no one has ever heard of, shows up demanding to take residency.

Suddenly things were moving at a breakneck pace. Her chances for a vacation receding just as quickly to slim-to-none.

Ted came in with the tea tray, the pastries, and the newspaper.

Liv grabbed for it. It wasn't the *Clarion* but the *Plattsburgh Press-Republican*. Disappointed, she scanned the front page to make sure they hadn't made the headlines.

At least Chaz was back and semi-functioning, though not nearly up to his usual snark. Still no edition of the paper, but Liv had hope. She wondered what he'd think of Gallantine's decision to sell.

"I'm afraid your coffee isn't very hot. Want me to nuke it?"

Liv shook her head. "Never tastes the same." She reached for a slice of cinnamon bread.

She managed one bite before the outer door opened and they heard footsteps across Ted's office.

"Gilbert," Ted said and pulled the paper from his muffin. "We're back here, come on in," he called without even turning around.

The mayor came in.

Ted took a big bite of muffin just as the mayor said, "What are we going to do?"

Since Ted's mouth was full, the mayor turned his question on Liv.

Liv gave Ted a look that said *Thanks a lot.*

Ted just chewed his muffin.

"Well," Liv said, "if it's true that this Onyx Conservancy has made an offer on the house—and we only have Mr. Grossman's word for it—we'll have to renegotiate with him."

"With the way he just insulted the reenactment?" The mayor turned away as if he planned to storm out of the room at the very idea of negotiating with Grossman. But he turned just as suddenly back to Liv.

Ted swallowed. "Gilbert, you're giving me whiplash. Pull up a chair and let's discuss this rationally."

The mayor spotted an extra chair by the wall, dragged it to the desk, and sat down.

"Care for a bear claw?" Ted held out a napkin. "Sorry, we only have two plates."

"How can you think about eating at a time like this?" The mayor distractedly took the napkin and reached for one of the pastries. "How can this happen?" He waved his pastry in the air. "Our own historical society wasn't even interested in buying it."

"Oh," Liv said. "So Gallantine had tried to sell before this?"

"No, but Janine thought it would be better if the town controlled the mansion, since Henry is letting it go to wrack and ruin. She approached the historical society. No interest there at all.

"Not that Henry would sell it even if there had been. His family has lived there for generations. And now of all times to have a stranger show up and says it's practically a done deal. And Henry isn't even around to say yea or nay." He chomped down on the bear claw, sending a rain of icing particles down his shirtfront.

"And where the heck is Henry?" he continued. "Why didn't he give us any warning that he was planning to sell?"

"If he was about to sign a contract, they must have been talking about this for months," Liv said. "There would have to be inspections, the lawyers must have been involved. Do you know who Gallantine's lawyer is? Silas Lark by any chance?"

"Daniel Haynes," Ted said and sipped his tea.

"The general?"

"One and the same."

Liv laughed.

"What can you possibly find humorous in this situation?" Worley said.

"Just two fine revolutionary families still doing business together after all these centuries. I'm always amazed at the ties that bind this town together."

"The good people of Celebration—"

"Save it, Gilbert," Ted said, and reached for his tea.

"You'll have to talk to Daniel, then," the mayor said impatiently.

"Lawyer-client confidentiality," Ted said.

"This affects the whole town," the mayor countered.

"He won't talk," Ted said. "But when property goes on the market, even privately, you can bet the real estate community knows about it."

Mayor Worley put down his pastry. "You think Janine knew about this?"

Ted shrugged, but Liv caught the momentary gleam in his eye. "I don't know, but someone in her office would."

"I'll give her a call right away." The mayor stood up, started to leave, reached back for his bear claw, and strode out of the office. Stopped at the door. "And you need to figure out what we're going to do about it."

"Maybe you should run for mayor," Ted said as soon as the door closed behind the mayor.

"Me? He was talking to you."

They both looked over to Whiskey, who was happily gnawing on a flag-shaped treat.

"As good a candidate as any. And it does have a certain ring to it. 'Whiskey for Mayor.'" Ted grinned.

"Can you imagine what Hildy Ingersoll would do with that one?"

"Lovely," Ted said, and took another bite of muffin.

"Do you think Janine really knew about the pending sale?" Liv asked.

"I have no idea, but I'd guess no. If she did, she would have hustled herself into the deal, and if she didn't, she'll be hopping mad. Either way, it won't hurt anybody for the mayor to ask her."

Liv struggled with a smile. "Except maybe the mayor."

"At least it might stir up things between those two. Help push the *blumen* off the *rosen* so to speak."

"Why does Gilbert let her boss him around? What hold does she have over him?"

"Beats me. Her charming personality?"

"Ugh," Liv said. Janine was another Celebration Bay native who liked to cause trouble, but in a quasi-sophisticated pencil-skirt-and-high-heeled way that was usually aimed at Liv.

Liv took a sip of her latte and made a face. "Lukewarm."

"Mine, too. Shall Whiskey and I make a desperate-for-a-latte run?"

"In a minute, but first . . . someone must have known Henry Gallantine was planning to sell his mansion."

"I hadn't heard a thing. Scout's honor."

"Hmm. If you didn't, it's pretty certain that no one else in town did."

Ted shrugged. "You flatter me."

"Nope. Just calling it like it is. But what about Hildy? She's there every day, right?"

Ted nodded.

"She would be upset if she knew her job security might be coming to an end."

Ted nodded.

"And she was surprised that Rundle was on the roof instead of Gallantine."

"Yeow. I'll never figure out how your mind runs in several directions at once while keeping the strands untangled. You think Hildy may have killed Rundle thinking it was Gallantine?"

Liv leaned back in her chair. "Sounds totally absurd, doesn't it?"

"Not totally. But she'd definitely be out of a job if he was dead."

"True. But she might know what was going on about the sale."

"Are you volunteering to spend the day with Grossman watching him photograph tchotchkes?"

Liv screwed up her face. "I'm really busy." She opened her laptop.

"Don't look at me. Hildy doesn't trust men."

"Really?"

"Really. Looks like it's you. Besides, we could use someone on the inside."

"I suppose. Though I'm not sure Hildy will even let me in after yesterday."

"I heard." Ted attempted to hide his smile. "Why don't you finish organizing your notes for our meeting with A.K., and Whiskey and I will make an emergency coffee run."

"Sounds good, but first come look at this." She hadn't

pulled up her meeting notes but had searched for the Onyx Historical Housing Conservancy.

Ted came to stand behind her. "Nice, tasteful. 'Dedicated to the preservation of neglected . . .' Sounds legit."

"It does. I wonder if we might have better success with someone else in their organization. One that isn't as anti-imaginative-battle-reenactments as Grossman." She clicked on Who We Are, where photos of the board of directors were usually posted. There was only one photo displayed.

"Whoa," Liv said.

Ted leaned closer. "Well, well, well. It seems that not only does George Grossman represent Onyx Conservancy, he *is* Onyx Conservancy."

A few minutes later, Ted and Whiskey left for the Buttercup, and Liv pulled up her spreadsheets for the Independence Day weekend. Looking further into Onyx's legitimacy would have to wait. She needed to prepare for that night's meeting. The committee heads would turn in written reports the following week. Tonight would be mostly verbal reporting. A few energetic committee heads would have completed reports, but this weekend had been too busy. The reenactment, the murder, the parade, the return of Chaz Bristow, the Leo situation, and now the possible sale of the reenactment site had put her and probably others way behind schedule.

She stopped mid-thought. Had she really just lumped murder in with the other events of the weekend? That could not be good, to take something so awful in stride. And what was she going to tell the committee heads tonight?

She knew no more today than she had Friday night at the police station. Maybe A.K. could fill her in on the nonconfidential aspects of the case. At least enough to assuage the residents' fears. Murder was definitely something they did not want to schedule into the upcoming festivals.

Attendance to the town's activities was skyrocketing. That was a good thing. But a lot of aspects of the organization of the events were lagging way behind. At the end of less then a year, Liv was at the point where she was actually considering taking on support staff if the council would approve the salaries. Just someone to do paperwork and make phone calls would free Ted and her up for more hands-on work.

She also needed to consult A.K. about the security situation. She knew his people were efficient and effective. Up to a point. She needed to hire more of them, but they were expensive.

The town was certainly making more than they had been when Liv arrived last September. But some of the trustees had taken a wait-and-see attitude. They didn't want to get overextended only to see the economy drop off again.

Liv wondered just how much the council was willing to allocate to the Events Office.

Ted returned with their drinks, and Liv stopped thinking or planning long enough to enjoy her latte. She was just finishing it when A.K. arrived for his meeting with her.

Liv felt a little rush of adrenaline as he stepped through the door. She quickly wiped her lip in case she was sporting a latte mustache and dropped her cup into her wastepaper basket before she stood to greet him.

He always startled her: tall, strong, intense. Today he was wearing a black T-shirt that stretched across his well-developed chest and hugged his biceps in a way that made Liv stop to enjoy the view.

"Come in and have a seat. Would you like water or . . ." She didn't have anything else to offer. Maybe she should consider keeping stores of coffee and tea for meetings.

"No, thanks." His deep voice rumbled across the desktop at her, catching her off guard like it always did.

Seemingly unaware of the effect he had on her, he sat down and opened a leather briefcase. He pulled out several manila folders, which he pushed across the desk to her. He brought out a similar set of folders, which he kept.

The first thing she saw was the fee they owed him. It made her gulp. Not that she hadn't been aware of it before, but once overtime was added to it, it barely left her enough to pay for the day-to-day operations and the smaller upcoming events that would need less security.

But they would need security. She turned the page. A breakdown of the duties and hours of each operative. One thing about A.K. Pierce—he was thorough in everything he did. Well, at least everything she knew of.

She nodded. "Good." She closed that folder and reached for another. A report of crimes committed and crimes prevented. Which ones the police were involved in and which ones the agency had deflected.

It seemed like a lot to Liv, even after all the events she'd organized in the last nine months. In her former career, the police only had to be called when some dignitary's car was towed for parking in a no-parking zone, or the bride or groom's brother, cousin, best man, friend—or, occasionally, sister—got snockered and started a brawl.

Taking care of a whole town was a new experience: pickpockets, random fights, shoplifting, petty thefts, panhandling, fender benders, accidents that might become potential lawsuits, not to mention the standard injuries, illnesses, and episodes of normal groups of people.

"This looks impressive," Liv said. "Just out of curiosity, how many of the incidents go unreported or unnoticed?"

A.K. thought about it. "Generally ten to thirty percent. Sometimes people don't notice their wallet missing or the dent in their car until they get home. Those trickle in after the fact, if they choose to report them to the authorities. Some are never noticed or reported."

"That seems like a fairly wide range."

"Depends on the event. The more contained, the easier it is to patrol." He shifted in his seat and leaned forward, resting his weight on his forearms. "For example, when we're escorting, say, a public figure—rock star, athlete, politician— we have a tight target. We get the random crazed fan or drug overdose. Occasionally a death threat, but the whole event is easier to cover, close to a hundred percent secure."

Liv pulled her attention away from his arms and nodded. "But in a less-controlled event it's higher."

"Yes, and when the event meets in several different venues, sometimes simultaneously—or runs several days and nights, as this past weekend did—the odds are that you will miss a good amount of minor infractions." He frowned at her. "It doesn't matter how many security people you hire. Stuff happens. It's human nature."

Liv swallowed, resisted the temptation to push her chair farther away. He was impressive. And she was a little intimidated—even while she was slightly attracted to him and not guilty of any crime. "And murder?"

He gave her one of his fleeting smiles. "Like I said, human nature."

Liv guessed he was right. But it seemed so depressing to take murder in your stride. She hadn't forgotten his words when they'd found Leo crouched against the parapet on Friday night. He thought Leo had killed Jacob Rundle.

But he didn't know Leo. Well, she didn't either, really, if it came to that.

"Can I ask you something?"

One of his eyebrows quirked, a physical reaction, she thought, rather than a thoughtful one. "Do you still think that Leo Morgan killed Jacob Rundle?"

"You know, Ms. Montgomery—Liv—I'm a fair man. I can even be sympathetic on occasion. But I look at the facts, what I see, hear, smell. What I saw that night was a frightened young man holding a bloodied bayonet near a man who was killed with a bayonet. No one else around. We didn't pass anyone coming to the roof. My men didn't see anyone leaving the house. There may be another explanation, but the most valid one at this point is that we caught him before he had time to flee."

"But he wasn't trying to flee."

"Not when we finally saw him. It would be a natural reaction to being cornered. Fight or flight or . . . fright. Like a trapped animal." He held up a hand before Liv could protest. "I'm just saying that's a possibility. Not that it is what actually happened. But based on the evidence in situ . . . I think the police have a decent case."

Liv was afraid he was right. And if they thought they had the murderer, how hard would they look for the real one?

Chapter Thirteen

....

Mayor Worley was waiting in the outer office when Liv
saw A.K. to the door. Liv smiled in passing and hightailed
it back to her office.

Gilbert was right on her heels. Behind the mayor, Ted
lifted his hands in a gesture that said he was not responsible.

She'd barely made it back to her desk before Gilbert said,
"I just got off the phone with Hildy Ingersoll. I told her you
would be accompanying Mr. Grossman on his tour of the
house."

"Me? But I have the roundup meeting tonight."

"This is more important. I told him you would meet him
at the mansion at ten thirty."

She glanced at the time. Her meeting with A.K. had taken
exactly an hour. That gave her half an hour to plan the meeting for tonight and then get over to Gallantine House, which
was a good ten- to fifteen-minute walk.

The mayor rushed ahead. "He wasn't happy, but since

Bill had the good sense to tell him he had to be accompanied by a town official—"

Liv opened her mouth to say she wasn't exactly an official. She needn't have bothered.

"Purely to cover our legal responsibilities." He sucked in air. "God forbid the man should fall or have a heart attack. Or worse, if something went missing."

Hopefully the mayor hadn't mentioned that last possibility to Mr. Grossman when he'd been explaining the rest. He'd practically just accused him of stealing. That should make for a fun afternoon.

On the other hand, Liv wouldn't mind taking a good look at the inside of the mansion. Her curiosity was piqued. Besides, it would give her a chance to further observe the crime scene surroundings and get to know Hildy a little better. Woman to woman, not sheriff to witness.

"And you can take the opportunity to convince him to keep the town's lease in operation."

"He seemed pretty anti–Battle of the Bay."

The mayor wrung his hands. It was becoming a habit with him lately. And there was increasing gray in that shiny hair of his. Politics was taking its toll on the Celebration Bay mayor. "If anybody can convince him to honor our agreement, it's you."

"Thank you, I think." Liv glanced at the clock on her computer screen again. *Twenty-five minutes.*

"Well, I'd better get a move on." Liv stood.

"Thank you. Be sure to tell him how important it is to the town and how the reenactment would be good for the museum, too."

"I will."

"And you'll let me know how it goes as soon as you get back?"

"Of course."

"And—"

"She knows exactly what to do," Ted called from the outer office.

"Right, well. Okay, then." And with a final, quick scrub of his hands, he hurried away.

As soon as the door closed behind him, Ted broke into a wide grin.

"Thanks for the vote of confidence," Liv said drily.

"Go forth and investigate. And I really do want to know everything. You can censor it for the mayor."

Liv checked the battery life on her iPad mini and returned it to her bag. "Might as well get some work done while I'm there."

"Or jot down some notes about the crime scene?"

"I won't be going to the roof if that's what you mean. I can't imagine Mr. Grossman would need to go up there." She paused. Smiled. "But you never know."

She grabbed her bag and, after a quick cleanup in the ladies room, she started for the Gallantine mansion.

Liv wasn't sure how it happened that she had become the town "official" to get stuck spending the day with a museum photographer who hated their battle reenactment.

She really needed to be prepared for tonight's meeting. It would be hard enough just keeping it on track once the news of the murder got out. And she was sure it was already out and being embellished as the day went on. And everyone would want answers and reassurance from her.

She didn't know why, but since she'd become the town's event coordinator, the town tended to look to her to solve a multitude of things, some that were unassociated with events. Like listening to disputes, solving murders. Not that she could do much about either. Still, they sought her out, like people who told their innermost secrets to bartenders.

Trouble was nothing new to Celebration Bay. The locals enjoyed a good argument almost as much as they enjoyed a good tractor pull, a spirited fistfight as much as a spirited charity auction. And even though some people—Janine, to name one—swore the town had never had a murder until Liv moved there, Liv knew it wasn't true.

Not content to believe the word of her neighbors, Liv had looked at back newspaper reports and even at county records. It seemed to Liv that the residents of the area had been committing crimes like every other community in the country.

The crimes just hadn't attracted much notice, because the town hadn't been a successful event town until the last few years, during which attendance had nearly doubled.

Liv would just have to remind everyone of that when they asked their questions tonight. For there would be questions, there always were, and there would be heated arguments, especially if Janine was there to incite their emotions.

It had grown muggy in the few hours she'd been inside, but at least the walk toward the lake sent an occasional breeze her way. Most of the town was close enough that she didn't really need her car most of the time, but it was times like today when she contemplated buying a bike, maybe a mountain bike.

Within a few minutes she had reached the brick wall that surrounded Gallantine House. The street was clean and the vendors were gone but George Grossman was there, waiting by the front gate, camera bag and tripod hung over one shoulder.

"I hope I haven't kept you waiting," Liv said. "The mayor just asked me to join you."

He gave her a sour look and opened the iron gate for her to go through.

Not friendly, but at least a gentleman. Liv wondered how long that would last once he confronted Hildy. They walked up the brick walk to the front door, and Grossman rang the bell.

Hildy met them with a scowl and an extra tightening of her lips for Liv. "Come on in. Don't suppose I can keep you out. Don't mess things up and don't break anything. Come on, I can't leave him alone for a minute."

Him? Had Henry Gallantine returned? Now there would be a welcome event. He could clarify why Rundle had been on the roof, could deal with George Grossman, and Liv could return to the duties she was paid to perform.

Hildy pushed the heavy front door closed, then hurried past them into the front parlor with efficiency if not grace.

The front parlor was a large square room with high ceilings and was filled with exotic furnishings. Gallantine had a penchant for the Orient in a thirties-movie way. A camelback sofa and two chaises were upholstered in red velvet and finished with gold braid and tassels. A wing chair was covered in a satiny fabric depicting peonies and golden dragons. A pair of swords hung on the wall above the mantel where a row of Fabergé eggs stood between two ceramic urns. There was a gap between two of them, and it took Liv a second to remember Hildy saying one of Mr. Gallantine's fancy eggs had been stolen. Had anything else been stolen while they all had been searching for a killer?

And how would they know if more was missing? Dark carved furniture, chairs, tables, curio cabinets, and bookshelves filled the space. And every surface was crowded with objets d'art.

Liv felt a momentary sympathy for Hildy, who must have to dust each individual piece, as well as all the ornately carved furniture.

A tall man, dressed in jeans and a loose madras sports coat, was leaning over a table of curios. He straightened when they entered, and Liv saw that he was holding a porcelain figurine.

He was tall and slightly overweight, late thirties, Liv guessed. Light brown hair receded slightly from his forehead and his chin was covered by a puffy goatee that made Liv want to reach for a razor.

"Put that back," Hildy said, and strode forward.

"Relax," the man said, and turned back to the table to put the figure down.

Then he saw Liv and George Grossman, and Liv immediately saw his guard go up. It was a small change in his posture, a little narrowing of the eyes, but Liv dealt with people all the time, and she didn't trust this one for a second.

He smiled, turning on the charm. "I'm Frank Gallantine. And you are?"

For a second Liv just stared. Then she remembered the name. Henry's nephew, the one who hadn't returned the sheriff's call. The one with the gambling problem. She wondered if Bill knew he was here.

"*She's* supposed to be here and *you* are not." Hildy shoved her fists onto her hips and glared at him.

"You must forgive Hildy. She's never been one for manners."

Or housekeeping, Liv thought. Every surface was covered in a fine layer of dust.

"Not for the likes of you."

Ignoring the housekeeper, he shook hands with Grossman, then Liv, holding hers a little too long, which Liv thought he meant as a compliment. It just made her want to bring out the Purell.

"I'm afraid my uncle isn't here at the moment."

"We know that," Grossman said, not bothering to hide his annoyance. "Do you know where he is?"

"No. I came the moment I heard he was missing. Poor man, I hope this halfwit who killed Mr. Rundle hasn't killed the dear old man, too."

Hildy snorted.

"No one has been taken into custody," Liv informed him in her most officious voice. "Have you spoken with the sheriff?"

His smile slipped slightly before returning firmly to place. "Not yet, though I fully intend to. And I'm afraid I must ask you to leave . . . in view of the situation. Hildy will see you out." Another smile. He didn't come anywhere near lord of the mansion. More like a street thug.

"It's you that will be leaving," Hildy said. "I don't know how you got in here, but you're getting out now. Mr. G said I was not to let you in. Though I don't know how I could keep you out when you sneak in like the thief you are."

"Now, Hildy. You know that isn't true." He leaned over to Liv. "Hildy's always been a little jealous of me." He sighed. "Very well. But, Hildy, it won't do to be so mean to me. Not in view of—" He stopped, sighed indulgently. "Very well. I'll see the two of them out when I go." He smiled and gestured Grossman and Liv toward the door.

Liv had no intention of leaving and neither had Grossman. He pulled his authorization letter out of his pocket and waved it at Frank. "I'm here by appointment. I have this authorization letter to prove it. So if you will excuse me I'll start setting up my equipment." He didn't wait for an answer but carried his equipment across the room.

"Now, wait just a minute," Frank began, but Hildy cut him off.

"He has a right to be here. You don't," Hildy said. "*I'll* see *you* out, and if I catch you trying to sneak back in, I'll call the sheriff."

"Hildy, you can't really keep me out. I am the heir after all." Frank Gallantine, who Liv was already thinking of as Frankie G, winked at Liv, as if saying, *What can you do?* "Nice to meet you, Ms. Montgomery. I'll let myself out."

He sauntered across the room under Hildy's alert gaze. But not alert enough. As Liv watched him go, she noticed a bump in the pocket of his sports jacket. She automatically turned to the table where he'd been standing; the figurine he'd been holding was gone. Only the clean circle in the dust remained, marking the spot where it had been.

So the nephew wasn't just obnoxious; he really was a thief. And a brazen one at that. Was it possible that he was Hildy's thief and not the teenagers like she'd thought? Evidently he knew how to get in without the housekeeper knowing about it, and he most certainly knew how to sneak things out.

Hildy finally remembered they were in the room. "A piece of work that one. Mr. G gave him and his mother everything they wanted. They always wanted more."

And if Henry Gallantine was dead instead of just missing, they might have it.

The housekeeper seemed to recollect herself. "I suppose it's okay to let you go on and do your picture taking. Mr. G didn't tell me any different. Didn't tell me you were coming back at all. Just don't make a mess. I got my work to do, and I can't stand here watching you."

She frowned at Liv. "You just make sure nothing gets broke. I'm holding you responsible."

"Thanks, Hildy."

Hildy just grunted and left the room.

"Formidable woman," Grossman said.

"Yes, she is," Liv agreed.

"That nitwit is Henry Gallantine's nephew?"

"Apparently."

"I wonder if he really is the heir." Grossman began setting up his gear, and Liv wandered over to the window to look out, partly so Grossman wouldn't think she was hovering over him and partly because she wanted to call Bill.

She'd just give him a heads-up that the nephew, Frankie G, was in town. She deliberated on whether to tell him about the theft or not. She hadn't actually seen him take the piece, but he had been holding it, then it was gone, and there was that bump in his pocket. Pretty damning.

But she didn't want to make any accusations that might raise alarm and send Frankie running for cover before Bill had a chance to investigate him thoroughly. If he was pocketing things from this house, what else was he helping himself to? And how far was he willing to go to get it?

The sound of a vacuum drowned out that thought as well

as any possibility of having a phone conversation. She'd have to wait for a more opportune time.

Liv sat down at a round Queen Anne side table in the window alcove to tweak her presentation for the committee meeting that night, but soon her eye wandered out to the lawn.

The bleachers had been removed. She'd have to send a special thanks to the cleanup crew. They'd done an excellent job. The lawn was as pristine as it ever was, except for a few gouges and trampled grass where Daniel Haynes's horse had reared up as the general gave the order to attack. Thank heaven it hadn't been a cavalry unit.

Grossman moved from place to place, taking long shots, close-ups, and making notes in a spiral notebook. Occasionally, he would pick up some chest or box to study it more closely.

The first couple of times, Liv held her breath, wondering if he had authorization to snoop as well as document. Once she looked up to find him picking up a lamp of a ceramic Chinese guardian figure and turning it upside down to look at the base. The lampshade started to fall, and Liv had a horrible vision of the antique ceramic breaking into hundreds of pieces. But somehow he managed to save both the lamp and the lampshade and put them back on the table intact. Another time she caught him kneeling on one knee, studying the stones of the fireplace, which seemed like an odd thing to be doing, since the fireplace was hardly a furnishing.

The man was beyond thorough; it was going to be a long day. She went back to her meeting agenda. But her mind soon wandered back to the night of the murder.

The patriots moving silently onto the lawn. Rufus's group from the left copse of trees and Roscoe's from the right. She couldn't see Roscoe's position from where she was sitting; it was in the trees behind the house.

And the general. He must have been waiting on horseback behind the house.

Had Haynes or one of the patriot soldiers seen anything

suspicious? Like a man jumping from the roof? Or were they too busy playing at war to notice? Surely Bill had asked.

A "hmmph" from across the room interrupted her thoughts. "Just look at this." Grossman pointed to where two crossed swords hung above the fireplace.

Liv looked, but she had no idea what was wrong with them. They were polished. There was even a brass plaque below them. Clean and already documented. "What's the problem?"

"Props—from a movie." The curator made a sound as if something nasty was caught in his throat.

"Really?" Liv said, not knowing what reaction he expected.

"Must have been one of the movies Gallantine was in. *Treasure Island.* Really. Fakes hanging here on the wall above a collection of Fabergé eggs and two Sèvres urns." He huffed out a disgusted sigh.

"I saw part of it last night. I thought he was really good."

"What are you talking about?"

"The movie, *Treasure Island.*"

Grossman darted her a look that made her shrug and go back to studying her computer screen. She worked for a while, dividing her time between her agenda, watching Grossman, and staring out the window.

The reenactment had been spectacular until that SOS signal. So what if it was historically inaccurate? It was entertaining and it was authentic-ish.

The general appearing on horseback between the trees and silhouetted by the lake and night sky had been pretty effective. The soldiers swarming down to the water and jumping in boats to row out to the British ships. The way the boats were rowed toward the ships, then fanned out to disappear from view, with perfect timing, as the night fell into darkness and the first fireworks appeared.

She didn't want to lose this venue. It was perfect.

She needed to find a way to approach Grossman about leasing the property back to them for the reenactment, somehow convince him that, although it was inaccurate, it was educational. Heck, they would even put a disclaimer in the program.

She wasn't optimistic. The man was a fanatic about the truth. But time was running out, and she hadn't even approached him.

When he folded up the tripod and moved into the back parlor, Liv grabbed her mini and followed him. He set camera and tripod up again and began the same process of long shots and detail shots. At this rate she would be here all day and maybe tomorrow, too.

"Can I help in any way? I'm supposed to be expediting your visit."

"Oh, and I thought you were making sure I didn't make off with the family silver."

It was now or never. "Actually, it was to persuade you to continue Mr. Gallantine's agreement with the town to use the grounds for the reenactment each year."

Grossman snorted. "I believe you heard my opinion of your 'reenactment.'" The last word dripped with air quotes, even though Grossman's hands were busy with his camera.

"But does it really do any harm?"

Grossman straightened. "It didn't happen. By performing this mock battle, the town is perpetrating a lie. Among others."

"It's a celebration."

"Of a man who may or may not have betrayed his country?"

"I thought he was exonerated."

"After he died and some numbskull in the Continental Congress convinced the others to restore the family's good name. That's what power and influence can do."

That seemed a particularly harsh view of the matter. These historians took their work very seriously. As they should. She understood that mentality and respected it. She was the same way herself. "You think he really was a traitor?"

"If you must know, yes, I do. And I plan to right the historical records."

"Why is it so important?"

He looked at her, incredulous. "Because I'm a historian first and museum curator second. And I think there's evidence that will prove me correct."

Chapter Fourteen

·····························

It was after four o'clock when Liv looked up from her iPad to see Grossman standing at the bay window looking out. He'd taken hundreds of photos, knocked on panels, opened and closed doors, but Liv drew the line at watching him daydream. It was time to call it a day.

She came to stand beside him, looking out to where he was looking. He seemed oblivious to her presence.

Was he merely daydreaming? Or calculating uses for the lawn when the museum took over? Liv bet his plans didn't include the Battle of the Bay reenactment.

She was just about to ask if he was close to finishing when he said, "I'll think I'll stop for the day," and abruptly began collecting his equipment.

He left immediately, not bothering to thank Hildy or Liv, or offering Liv a ride back to Town Hall, just raised his hand as he left by the front door.

That was fine with Liv; it was only a few blocks, and she wanted to have a minute with Hildy alone. More than once, Liv had noticed Hildy coming to the door to the parlor, looking in, and leaving again. And Liv imagined she had made more trips than Liv was aware of. She took her duty of protecting all things Henry Gallantine seriously.

By now, Liv was sure that Grossman had no intention of honoring Gallantine's agreement with the town. In fact, he seemed intent on destroying the family name. Which didn't make sense now that she thought about it. Onyx must think people would flock to a museum of a traitor as well as of a hero.

Of course they would, Liv thought. *Look at the torture museums, the wax museums: criminals drew the crowds.*

This is not what she envisioned for Celebration Bay. And she needed to make sure that Henry really understood what the Onyx Historical Conservancy was planning. If they could only find him.

Maybe Hildy knew. Maybe she would tell Liv once she heard that Grossman intended to prove Henry's illustrious ancestor a traitor.

So when Hildy stood at the door after seeing Grossman out, Liv, instead of following him, said, "I thought he would never leave."

Hildy's expression said she didn't know why Liv hadn't left with him.

"I wanted to talk to you about something."

"I'm busy."

"It's important. About Mr. Gallantine's ancestor."

Hildy narrowed her eyes until they were black slits.

"What about him?"

"Could you give me a cup of tea? It was a long day and I'm parched. I hope it didn't disrupt your work too much. I know it did mine. But now I'm glad I came."

Liv hoped her confiding tone and the little bit of question she'd left in the statement would open the taciturn housekeeper's mouth. And also that, if she didn't mention being found trespassing the day before, Hildy would forget all about it.

"Well, it did, and if he thinks he's going to make himself at home here, like that no-good nephew, he can think again."

"Good. The only reason I agreed to come was because the sheriff didn't think Mr. Gallantine would want him in here alone."

"He got that right at least. Is that what you wanted to say?"

"There's something else."

Hildy gave her a long look. "I guess I can give you some tea." Without another word, she started toward the kitchen.

"Thanks." Liv followed and sat down at the kitchen table while Hildy put water on for tea and got down two mugs.

"Well, what do you have to say for yourself?" she asked, turning around.

"There are two things really. I thought I should say something. I don't want to be overhasty, but I think I saw Mr. Gallantine's nephew pocket one of the little figurines on the table he was standing next to."

"Why that little— Turn my back for one minute and he's helping himself. Never was no good, that one. Next time he tries to get in here, I'll meet him with my shotgun."

"Maybe you should call the sheriff and let him handle it."

"Bill Gunnison? I've been telling him people have been stealing things for the longest time. If it isn't the no-account nephew, it's them teenagers. They're all robbing Mr. G blind. And now this museum man, saying he's gonna buy the house and the furnishings."

"I can't believe Mr. Gallantine would want to sell this beautiful old house," Liv said. "It must have been in his family for years."

"Years and years. All the way back to the colonial period." Hildy plopped tea bags into two mugs.

"So how on earth did Mr. Grossman talk him into selling?"

"He didn't. Leastways he hadn't when he left from his last time here."

The teakettle began to whistle. Hildy poured water into

the mugs and put one down in front of Liv and placed another on the opposite side of the table. She placed an empty saucer between them—Liv guessed it was for the tea bags, since Hildy hadn't offered milk or anything to eat—and sat down.

"I wonder what made him change his mind?"

Hildy dunked her tea bag several times while she frowned at her cup. She looked up suddenly.

"I don't know. I'm not sure he did. Last time that museum man was here . . . he was picking up things like they were already his, asking Mr. G impertinent questions. I don't know how Mr. G stood it." Hildy lifted her tea bag out of her mug and swung it over to the plate, where it landed with a splat. Then she leaned forward. "It was all I could do not to toss him out on his ear."

And Liv bet she could. "Good for you."

For the first time ever, Hildy smiled. The smile quickly turned back to her habitual frown. "What I don't get is why Mr. G didn't send him packing."

Liv made sympathetic noises.

"Everything's out of whack around here. Mr. G's not been acting like himself lately. He always goes to his sister's for summers, beats me why. She's a money-grubbing little so-and-so. But he does. He doesn't even like going. Says it's his duty. Mr. G has a strong sense of duty. Only this summer he seemed like he couldn't wait to go. Real excited like."

"That sounds strange."

"Don't know why this time was any different from all the other summers. Does the same thing ever since he moved them out of here. But that's like Mr. G. Good and generous, and everybody taking advantage of him.

"I don't know what got into him this time. I asked him about it, but all he said was he had plans. Wouldn't tell me what, just acted all secretive, but like it was a good thing."

Liv wondered if she'd told this to Bill, but she wasn't about to ask now that Hildy was talking. She'd clam up for sure if Liv mentioned the sheriff.

"And he gave Grossman that letter?"

"I guess so. The week before he goes, he tells me that while he was gone this museum person would be back to take an inventory of the house and . . . and . . . I forget the word, but make sure all his stuff was real. Well I coulda told them that. Mr. G didn't like fake things—or people."

"What about the swords over the fireplace? Mr. Grossman said they weren't authentic."

"A lot he knows. They were the actual swords used in Mr. G's movies. If that ain't real, what is?"

"Maybe he meant historically."

"I'd like to know just what business is it of his?"

So would Liv. "You know he came to the mayor when you wouldn't let him in the first time. And good for you. You don't know what kind of people you might be dealing with."

"That's what I told Bill Gunnison; didn't do no good. I tried calling that dang lawyer, but he didn't call me back yet. He's another one. Too busy playacting at being some fancy general that died hundreds of years ago to take care of people who pay him."

"Daniel Haynes? I thought just about everybody in town used Silas Lark."

Hildy shook her head. "Mr. G did at one time. But when Daniel Haynes set up his shingle, Mr. G said that the old families should stick together. Like Silas Lark isn't just as good as them, even though his family's only been here since the Depression."

And Liv had thought it was strange when BeBe, who had lived in Celebration Bay for over twelve years, was still treated like an outsider. Silas's family had lived here for almost a hundred years and still didn't measure up to the DAR.

"But I'll tell you right now, that man's not coming in this house again until I hear from Daniel Haynes. And you can just tell him that."

"I don't know if I'll see him again. I don't have time to

run around after somebody that's snooping where they don't belong." *Like Chaz and me.* "And I don't blame you not wanting to stay in the house with a stranger roaming around. Especially when Mr. Gallantine isn't here. Where do you think he could be?"

Hildy shook her head slowly. "I can't figure it out. He never leaves until after the reenactment."

Liv nodded. "You thought it was him on the roof the night Jacob Rundle died."

Hildy scowled. For a minute Liv wasn't sure if she was going to throw her out or burst into tears. "He always gives the signal. I had his favorite sandwiches packed up for the drive. It's always the same, year after year."

Hildy stood up and Liv was afraid that Hildy was ending the conversation, but she merely got a tin off the counter and offered Liv a cookie from it.

Hildy sat heavily in her chair. "I just don't understand."

"What?"

"What Jacob was doing up on the roof. It just don't make sense."

"Maybe Mr. Gallantine asked Jacob to stand in for him for some reason."

"Never," Hildy snapped. "Mr. G never liked him. Don't know why he kept him on. Always putting his nose where it didn't belong. Then, last week, Mr. G and him had a terrible fight. Mr. G had come downstairs and found him in the parlor. Had no reason to be there. Talked some nonsense about the electricity. He fancied he knew things like electricity and plumbing as well as gardening. Full of beans, that one.

"Anyway, I could hear it all the way down the hall, where I was cleaning. Mr. G said he was not to come inside the house anymore, and he'd fire him if he did."

"Do you know what the fight was about?"

"I wasn't listening, if that's what you think."

"Of course not." Liv backed off. She didn't want to

alienate the woman. She might have been the last person to
see Henry Gallantine before he disappeared.

"Hildy, nobody can find Mr. Gallantine. He's not at his
sister's. They can't find his car. Do you have any idea where
he could be?"

"No." And then Hildy did start to cry.

Even after all the abuse Hildy had doled out indiscrimi-
nately, Liv felt sorry for her.

"Did they fight a lot? Did Mr. Gallantine have a temper?"

The tears stopped abruptly. "If you're thinking he killed
Jacob—"

"No, of course not," Liv said quickly.

"He's like a lamb most of the time. But he does get broody.
Just sits in his chair like he just didn't give a hoot for living.
But he don't usually yell like he was doing to Jacob." Hildy
took a cookie and dunked it into her tea. "I was afraid he was
going to give himself a stroke, the way he was carrying on."
She slid the soggy cookie into her mouth and chewed.

"Was he ill?"

"No, just excitable. These movie-people types. Never
grew out of it, Mr. G, even though he hadn't had a part in
forty years at least. Used to have videotapes of his old movies from when he was a boy. Had them all changed over to
DVDs. Sometimes he'll pull one out and watch it.

"Sad, a man of his age, just watching and laughing like
it wasn't some dumb movie that nobody remembered."

"Leo said sometimes he watched the movies with Mr.
Gallantine."

"Don't know why Mr. G took a liking to that boy. Guess
cause Leo never grew up either. Two of a kind, though Mr.
G has his wits about him."

Hildy snorted. "Playing games and looking for treasure.
Put notions into that boy's head. There ain't no treasure, just
some crazy rumor that Mr. G kept alive just to make himself
feel important, even though everybody who ever saw his
movies had long forgotten him. It didn't do no harm, I guess.

Until he started filling that boy's head with ideas. And look where it got him."

"Where?"

"That boy was after Mr. Henry's money, and after how kind Mr. G had been to him. I heard him say so that night in the kitchen when he killed Jacob. I think he meant to kill Mr. G. Didn't know it was old Jacob until it was too late."

Liv stared at her.

"Maybe he killed both of them." Hildy pushed herself ponderously to her feet. "I hope he isn't dead. He's not always the easiest to deal with, but I'm used to him. But I'd never work for Mr. G's sister if she comes to live here. I'd rather some museum got this old place than her and that son of hers. Though, what I'm going to do I don't know. I'd best get back to work now. But, Ms. Montgomery, you oughta be careful with that Charlie Bristow. Always had a way with the girls. None of 'em could ever say no." She nodded wisely.

"Thanks, Hildy, I will be." Liv said, taken aback at the woman's concern. She looked in her bag, pulled out her business card, wrote her cell number down. "Here's my number. If you think of anything, need help, or just want to talk, whatever. You can reach me at this number."

Hildy, looking somewhat abashed, took it.

"And, Hildy. Try not to worry. We don't know that Mr. Gallantine is dead."

Hildy looked at her like she was crazy. "Well, if he ain't dead, just tell me where he is."

"I can't, Hildy. I wish I could." Liv stood and carried her cup over to the sink. A flash of movement outside the window caught her eye. She looked out. Looked more closely. Someone was out there, and she thought she knew who it was.

She also thought that if Hildy found out, she'd be running for her shotgun.

"I'm sorry, Hildy, I have to go. I'll let myself out." Liv grabbed her bag.

"I don't mind," Hildy said, and began to amble toward the front door.

It seemed to take an eon for them to get to the door. And then for Hildy to close it behind her. But it had given Liv time to make a decision. No way was she going to risk Hildy and her shotgun by walking around to the back. She went out the front gate and sprinted down the sidewalk.

She didn't think twice when she came to the driveway where Chaz had led her to the gate into the Gallantine estate. It was full steam ahead.

It was hard to tell where she and Chaz had tramped though the shrubs to get to the wall. Things had already begun to grow over in the few days since the fireworks. But when she came to a place that looked more accessible than the rest, she slipped in between the bushes. Within a few feet she came to the stone wall that surrounded the Gallantine estate.

It was easy to see the door from here, because the ivy was torn where Chaz had pulled it apart. She pulled at the vines, clearing the doorway. The ivy would grow back; ivy always did. She started to lift the iron latch and realized the gate wasn't fully closed. Chaz must have left it open so they would be able to get out again. She pushed the gate inward, just enough to stick her head in and make sure no one was on the other side.

Chaz hadn't left the gate open. And Liv wasn't the only person sneaking back onto the property. Resting up against the brick wall was a tripod and camera case. Mr. Grossman must have thought they would be safe here while he was . . . What could he possibly be doing that he had to sneak around instead of asking to be let in the yard?

Liv left the gate open in case she needed to make a quick getaway, and began to slowly make her way toward the house.

To her left was a clothesline of clean towels. Hildy must have done the wash that morning. The laundry blocked Liv's view of the kitchen. And Hildy's view to this part of the lawn.

Which was a good thing. Liv had just worked hard to win a little bit of Hildy's trust, and she didn't want to jeopardize it by having Hildy catch her snooping around the estate again. On the other hand, she wanted to know what the Onyx curator was up to.

She'd just take a quick look and would quietly let herself out again.

She skirted the turret, where they'd climbed to the roof. Kept her back to the wall of the house and inched along the rough stones until she came to the corner of the house. She peered around the side.

She didn't see Grossman anywhere. Actually, it was hard to see anything though the leafy trees.

She scooted along until she was beneath the ledge where the ghost must have landed after his disappearing act. At least, she thought that was the ledge. The house was an architectural nightmare, with ledges and small roofs jutting out all over the place.

She stepped away from the house and looked up. There was the window the killer hadn't climbed through to get back inside. But there was another ledge three feet below it and to the right. And another to the left, a little lower.

She bet it would have been fun to climb as a teenager, like Chaz and his buddies had done. How many boys had taken that rite of passage and jumped from level to level until they were safely on the ground? How many broken legs and collarbones had it taken to impress the girls? And who had made the same leap only three nights before, after killing a man?

Between the house and the woods, the lawn was trampled and churned up where Daniel Haynes had sat on horseback, waiting for his cue to begin the attack.

What if he'd looked up? He might have seen the killer make his escape. At least he might have seen him in the split second when the murderer had jumped to the ledge, arms spread wide, then disappeared. After that, he would have been hidden by the ledge. He only had to wait until the attack began, and then leisurely climb down to the ground.

A movement down at the water's edge brought her back to her main purpose for skulking about the grounds. George Grossman had stepped into the opening between the trees. If he looked around, he would catch Liv looking back at him.

She made a mad dash across the swath of lawn to the trees, threw herself behind one, and peered out just as Grossman turned to retrace his steps. Liv stepped behind the tree and pressed herself against the rough bark. Waited a few seconds and carefully looked out again.

Now he was looking into the opposite stand of trees. His back was to her, and Liv took the opportunity to move closer to the lake.

What was he doing? Why all the stealth? Liv supposed the museum might use the grounds for something, like the Women's Club held events in the manicured garden of the club building. But why not just ask to see the property again?

He disappeared from view again, and Liv kept edging toward the water. He might be on an innocent recce, but Liv didn't think so. There was something not on the up-and-up with this guy. And since she'd come this far, she was determined to find out what he was up to.

As Grossman stood there, another man appeared. Liv recognized that madras jacket even at this distance. Gallantine's nephew and the museum man? Definitely something spurious going on.

They'd acted like they'd never met before when they'd shaken hands a few hours ago. And Grossman hadn't been out of her sight more than a few minutes the entire day. Had they planned this meeting?

The nephew quickly looked around. Liv plastered herself to a tree, heart pounding. She peeked out again just as he took Grossman's elbow and led him back out of Liv's sight line.

Liv took the chance to move even closer, though she felt

rather silly, jumping from tree to tree like a cartoon character. What would she say if they caught her? What would they say? She'd make sure to take the offensive.

And if Frankie Boy got violent, she had no doubt that she could hold her own against him. She'd taken out Cliff Chalmers one night, though it had been more of a case of him tripping into her fist. But, whatever worked. She'd spent good money on those self-defense lessons.

Little by little she narrowed the distance between them until she could see them standing in front of the derelict boathouse. She didn't think it was still in use. It should have been torn down years ago. It was an accident waiting to happen.

They didn't go inside, but stood facing each other. Then, abruptly, they shook hands and Grossman walked away. He was leaving. And coming right toward her.

Liv lunged behind a bush and held her breath while he passed by barely four feet away. She held perfectly still until she could only see his back darting through the trees.

She turned her attention back to the nephew. But he'd disappeared, too.

She had no choice but to stay where she was, surrounded by scratchy branches, and listen. He could be anywhere, but surely she'd hear him before he saw her.

But what she heard was a door creaking on rusty hinges. And when she got up the courage to look out of her hiding place, she saw that the door to the boathouse was open.

Frankie Boy must have gone inside.

Liv crawled forward and waited to see if he would reappear or if he had a boat there and would take off on the lake. After a good five minutes, he hadn't left by water or by land. The boathouse wasn't that big. What was he doing?

She began to get impatient, worried about her agenda for the evening meeting, but not willing to leave until she saw what he was up to.

When he finally came out, he was carrying a small suitcase, and Liv could guess what might be inside.

Of course. It hadn't been the teenagers at all. She bet there was loot in that suitcase and he'd been storing pieces there until he had enough to . . . sell? Is that what he'd been talking to Grossman about? It didn't make sense if Grossman was planning to buy the mansion and its contents.

Unless Grossman had also seen him pocket the little figurine and decided to confront him. Maybe that was why he left so suddenly. He'd seen Frankie when he'd been looking out the window.

This was definitely turning into a job for the sheriff. And she'd call him as soon as it was safe to leave. He would yell at her, but he might be able to stop Frankie before he got away.

She watched as he padlocked the boathouse, picked up the case, and walked away in the same direction the museum director had. But Liv was farther away now, and she just waited until she figured he'd had time to get to the gate and leave.

Still, she was careful as she backtracked to the gate, stood still listening before she stepped from the safety of the trees, then cautiously let herself out.

Chapter Fifteen

....

There was no sign of George Grossman or Frank Gallantine.

The whole thing was getting crazier and crazier, Liv thought as she walked back to Town Hall. Henry Gallantine missing, Rundle dead, Henry's nephew helping himself to Henry's possessions, Grossman insisting he owned Henry's mansion and intending to prove Henry's ancestor really was a traitor, Henry filling Leo's head with tales of treasure, Grossman and the nephew in league together.

And Liv still had to finish her report for the committee meeting roundup tonight. Well, there was one thing she could take care of while she was walking back to town.

She called Bill.

His voice mail picked up the call. "It's Liv. I've been at Gallantine House accompanying Mr. Grossman from the Onyx Conservancy, who is doing an inventory preceding his purchase of the property. Thanks a lot for insisting he have a public official go with him. That official was me.

"I met him there, and when Hildy let us in, Mr. Gallantine's nephew was in the parlor. I'm pretty sure I saw him pocket a figurine off a display table before Hildy kicked him out.

"Now I'm on my way back to the office, but I saw the nephew and the museum guy just meet down by the lake. After Grossman left, the nephew went into the boathouse and came out with a suitcase. Don't know if it means anything, but if you hurry you might catch him. There's more, but—"

She heard a ping. Her time had run out, which was just as well. She'd give him the details at the office, where he would no doubt be waiting for her.

Where I'll have Ted to run interference. Because she was pretty sure Bill was going to blow a gasket over her spying on the men at the boathouse.

She hadn't gone half a block when sweat began to trickle down her back. Inside the thick stone walls of the mansion, it had been cool. Out on the street, the humidity was high and even the breeze off the lake didn't do much to make her walk comfortable.

Her stomach growled. It was after five and she hadn't eaten since Dolly's pastries that morning. If she hurried, she'd just have enough time to take Whiskey home, grab something to eat, and hurry back for the meeting. Which left her no time for her final preparations. But at least she might avoid having to face Bill on an empty stomach.

She needed to start concentrating on the meeting. She wanted to be super prepared tonight. There were bound to be questions about the demise of Jacob Rundle.

She passed the *Clarion* building and, though she tried not to look, she did. It looked just as deserted as it had before, not that it was ever a hotbed of activity. Still, she was a little worried about Chaz. He never wanted to get involved, but he always did, and he always complained about it. And he'd helped with Leo. She knew she could count on him in a pinch, but she could tell something was eating at him.

She wished she could help, but Chaz wasn't one for sharing. Nor evidently was Henry Gallantine, nor Ted, who entered into every scheme or plan or idea with enthusiasm but never gave any information about his own past.

She, to her discredit, had actually done a search on Google for Ted and found nothing, an occasional mention in reference to Celebration Bay and its festivals, but no personal information. Of course, a lot of people didn't have Facebook pages or websites. But until she'd moved to town, she hadn't known anyone who didn't.

Chaz was another story. She'd done plenty of research on him—strictly for purposes of information gathering of course—and he had a long trail of investigative reporting before he'd dropped out and moved back to Celebration Bay to take over the paper. After that, there had only been a few fishing articles until those articles about the kidnapping trial.

Losing that case must really be bugging him. For a few minutes when they were climbing around the roof of Gallantine House, he'd seemed like his old self, but it ended as soon as they'd gotten into Bill's cruiser; he clammed up, and she hadn't heard from him since.

Of course, it had only been one day, but usually he'd be right back, comparing notes with her. She would see him tonight; he was bound to be on hand to report the outcome of the meeting for the *Clarion*.

She passed the rectory and saw Leo sitting on a bench in the side yard. He was slumped forward, and at first she had a horrible moment of panic. She crossed the street to take a closer look. But when she got nearer she saw that he was just slouched forward breaking off pieces of a twig and dropping them on the grass at his feet.

"Leo?"

He jumped and cowered back. And that's when she saw the dark bruise around his eye.

"Oh, Leo."

"Got in a fight," he mumbled.

"I can see you did. What happened?"

"I didn't start it. Boy said I killed Mr. Gallantine. I didn't kill nobody. Killing is a sin."

"Of course you didn't." Liv sat down beside him. "When did this happen?"

"After school, when I was going to the bus. Missed the bus. Had to walk back here."

"What are you doing sitting here? Did Pastor Schorr put something on that bruise?"

"He's not here."

"Do you know when he'll be back?"

Leo shook his head.

"You don't have a key?"

He shook his head.

"Maybe he's over at the community center."

He shrugged.

"Want me to walk you over and see?"

He shook his head. "Can't go if you fight. Pastor don't want fighters."

"Well, it wasn't your fault, was it?"

"Don't matter. Supposed to turn the other cheek. I hit him back."

And good for you, thought Liv. But she said, "Why don't I call over there and tell him you're home."

"Don't have a telephone."

"I think I have his cell phone number." Liv scrolled through her contact list until she came to Schorr's entry and the several numbers she had for him. One of the convenient things about technology. Hundreds of numbers at her fingertips.

He answered on the first ring.

"Phillip Schorr."

"Hi Phillip, it's Liv."

"Have you seen Leo? He didn't show up at the community center, and the kids that go to summer school say he wasn't on the bus. I've called his house—"

"He's at the rectory." Liv stood and walked away from Leo. "It seems he was in a fight at school."

"I was afraid that might happen. Is he okay?"

"He's got a shiner, but other than that he seems all right."

"Tell him to come on over to the center; I can't leave for another hour at least."

"Well, he seems to think you don't want him at the center . . . because of the fight."

"Oh Lord. You never know if you're getting the right message across to the kids or not. Can I talk to him?"

"Of course." She handed the phone to Leo.

He listened for a minute and handed it back. "He says I can come to the center."

"Can you—?" It was nearly six, only two hours until her meeting. No time for her to take Whiskey home. If she walked Leo over, Sharise would be closed by the time she got back, and Whiskey would have to have dinner compliments of the Quickie Mart. On the other hand, she didn't want to risk any more trouble for Leo tonight.

"Why don't I walk you over."

He nodded.

While they walked the two blocks to the community center, Liv called Ted. "I'm running late."

"I'll say. Not to worry. Whiskey and I have taken our pre- and postprandial exercise—twice. We've both eaten dinner and we even left you some."

"You are the best assistant ever. I owe you big-time." She hung up.

Leo shuffled quietly beside her, his head bowed, his hands in his pockets. He seemed totally defeated. It must be challenge enough for him just getting through each day, and then to have something like this happen. It just wasn't fair.

"I was over at Mr. Gallantine's house today."

He glanced over. "Did he come back yet?"

"Not yet, but I saw Hildy."

"She don't like me."

"Well, I think she just doesn't like anybody."

"That's what Mr. Henry says." He pushed shaggy hair out of his eyes with both hands.

"You and Mr. Henry are good friends, though."

"Yes ma'am. We play games and watch the movies. He used to be a movie star." He broke into a smile. "He looked funny."

"You must miss him."

Leo nodded. "I wish he'd get back and tell them about the ghost. Nobody believes me. They think I don't think right. But I do. Kinda."

"Of course you do. Have you seen the ghost . . . other than the other night up on the roof?"

"No. Not up close."

Liv's attention pricked up. "But you've seen him at a distance."

"Every year when he signals with the lantern."

Liv repressed a sigh of disappointment. "Mr. Henry told you the ghost knew where the treasure was?"

"He didn't have to. The ghost knows where the treasure is because the ghost is Old Mr. Henry, who got the treasure."

"Ah. But Mr. Henry, the new Mr. Henry, likes to talk about the treasure?"

"Oh, sure." Leo frowned, bit his lip. "He used to talk about it lots. We'd looked for it, just like pirates. All over the house. Sometimes we even dug in the yard."

And what did that mean? That Gallantine really believed there was a treasure, or that he'd entered his own second childhood?

"We found lots of stuff, but we never found the real treasure. Then he stopped wanting to play. Said it was a stupid game and not to think about it anymore. Then he taught me how to play checkers instead." He stopped on the sidewalk. "Checkers is okay, but not as much fun as looking for treasure."

"No. I can see where it might not be, but I don't think Mr. Henry would want you looking for the treasure without him."

"No. He said not to look anymore. He sounded kinda mad. That it was like some lady's box. I forget her name, but she's like the radio. But bad things happened when she found it."

A lady like the radio? It took Liv a minute or two to figure out what he was talking about. "Pandora?"

"Yeah, her."

"Why do you think he said that?"

"Don't know."

They'd come to a block of old houses and businesses, several of which were unoccupied. The community center was set back from the street down a wide drive. It was a one-story wooden building with few windows but a wide cargo door. Liv could just see the words *Auto Supply* beneath the new coat of white paint.

She followed Leo to a pedestrian entrance, where he held the door for her and she walked inside.

Pastor Schorr, wearing faded jeans and a T-shirt, was waiting for them at the door.

Leo hung his head. "I'm sorry, Pastor."

Schorr clapped him on the back, then pulled him into one of those buddy hugs men do, rough and fast. But it seemed to make Leo feel better.

"Thanks for bringing him over."

Several of the youths crowded around Leo. One of them was Roseanne Waterbury. She patted Leo on the shoulder and came over to Liv and the pastor, looking angry.

"It isn't fair," she told them.

"No," Pastor Schorr agreed.

"It was bad enough before, but now with Mr. Rundle being killed, it's worse." Her expression changed from anger to expectation when she turned to Liv.

Liv anticipated her question, but couldn't stop it.

"Can't you do something?"

Pastor Schorr looked surprised.

"You know the sheriff is working very hard to get to the bottom of this," Liv said.

"But you're helping him, aren't you?"

"Rosie . . ."

"Don't say you can't do anything, because I know you can."

"Roseanne," Schorr interjected. "I don't think you should put Ms. Montgomery on the spot like that. Everyone is sympathetic to Leo's situation, but it's a police matter."

"Sorry," Roseanne said, and walked away.

"Sorry about that," he said. "Rosie is a good and caring young lady. She's always been active in the church group and lately has become more involved with the center. She's been a good friend to Leo."

Liv watched Roseanne return to the group of teenagers clustered around Leo, so she didn't miss the look of appeal Rosie shot her before turning away.

"As you can see, this situation has impacted all of us. Especially the young people." Schorr sighed as he looked over the group. "Maybe he wouldn't have been up on that roof if he hadn't overheard that we might be losing the center." He visibly shook himself. "Not that I think he had anything to do with Jacob Rundle's death."

"Of course not."

Liv looked past him into the center. It was one large room with old couches, chairs, and tables clumped in groups around even older carpets, shags in orange and dirty gold. There was a Ping-Pong table and an old television, a microwave and an ancient refrigerator.

"Not much," Schorr said. "But it's an important place."

"I can see that," Liv agreed. There were over a dozen teenagers involved in various activities.

"And we have an adult program three mornings a week."

"And you oversee it all?"

"More or less." The pastor shrugged, smiled as he looked over the group. "They're my sheep."

By the time Liv left the center, it was well past six and she'd determined to help Phillip Schorr find a new, adequate, and affordable space. Just as soon as they wrapped up the

Fourth of July events, she'd approach the board of trustees for their input.

Not that she was so altruistic—or nosy, as some would say. She did care about having a place for young and old to come for help and entertainment, but she was also selfish enough to not want crowds of teenagers hanging out in the park with nothing to do and ripe for mischief.

They had plenty of those even with the community center open six days a week.

She speed-walked her way back to Town Hall. She was hot and her slacks and shirt were feeling limp and rumpled. Well, it couldn't be helped. There was no time to get home, cleaned up, and back unless she planned to go into the meeting only half prepared.

Unpreparedness was not an option.

Ted was waiting for Liv in his office with a sandwich and a can of seltzer. "Figured you didn't need any caffeine for the meeting tonight." He followed her into her office and put the food on her desk.

"You're probably right." Though one of BeBe's lattes was sounding really good about now.

"Anything to report?"

"Bunches, but I didn't have time to double-check the agenda."

"Not to worry. When you weren't back by five, I did it for you."

"You should ask the trustees for a raise."

Ted snorted and handed her a page off the top of a stack of papers. "The agenda. Good enough?"

"Absolutely. I thought Bill would be here."

"Bill?" Ted asked innocently.

Liv wasn't fooled. When you spent as much time together as she and Ted did, you learned to recognize suppressed amusement. "I guess he called?"

"Yep. In trouble, are we?"

"Is that the royal 'we'? Because I'm thinking I'd appreciate the company."

"Uh-oh, what did you do?"

"Nothing."

He got up and shut the door to her office. "Well, whatever nothing was, Bill called and said he was out following your tip, but he wants to talk to you after the meeting tonight."

"Gulp."

"Actually what he said was, 'Tell Liv not to even think about trying to sneak out without fessing up.'"

"Double gulp." Liv sank into her desk chair.

"Lord, girl. What did you do?"

Chapter Sixteen

Ted sat down across from her. "So spill."

She told him about the filching nephew, the less-than-forthright curator, their meeting in the woods, and the suit-case. "And Leo has a black eye. And Roseanne is mad at me because she thinks I won't help him."

Ted smiled. "A crusading spirit, our Rosie. Takes after her mother. And her father. But you can't blame her."

"I can't do anything to help Leo. Bill will have to find a way to protect him until he catches the killer." Liv sighed. "But Rosie didn't want to listen to reason."

"Because she looks up to you."

"Oh, great. That makes me feel worse."

"She'll get over it. I put Fred's traffic report and A.K.'s security report at the end of the meeting, along with Bill, who said he would like to say a few words. That way, if we keep moving things along at the beginning, we might make it through before the free-for-all over Jacob Rundle's demise."

Most of these wrap-up meetings were dull and boring but necessary. Liv was hoping for dull and boring tonight, though she wasn't optimistic. Nothing stayed dull and boring in Celebration Bay for long. A blessing and a curse. "I guess there's no way to avoid it."

"In Celebration Bay? I bet attendance tonight will be the biggest yet. No one will be phoning in their committee reports when there's murder to gossip about."

Liv groaned and hid her face behind her hands.

"You're tired. Eat your sandwich, and let's get ready to rock and roll."

Liv looked out at him between her fingers. "I think you enjoy all the hoopla."

Ted shrugged.

Liv waited for what he might say next. Something about how he enjoyed excitement because of . . . what? Something in his past, some kind of wish fulfillment? Her man of mystery was just getting more mysterious, and the less he said about himself, the wilder her surmises about his past became. Itinerant storyteller? CIA operative? Nuclear scientist? Armchair detective? Nothing would surprise her.

"Well?" she coaxed.

"Eat your sandwich," he said.

She ate her sandwich.

A few minutes before the meeting, Liv slid her laptop into her computer bag, gathered up her report folders, and pushed back from her desk. Whiskey, who had been snoring away ever since her return, opened his eyes, stretched, and got up.

"Sorry, big guy," Liv said. "We're not done yet. Go back to your nap."

"Arf." He padded over to her, and she leaned down to give him some attention. Something he was getting plenty of from everyone but her, it seemed. But starting next weekend . . .

"I'll try not to be too long. Stay."

Whiskey yawned and followed her to the door.

Ted was waiting for her by the door.

"Stay," she repeated, and went into the hall.

"Poor dawg," Ted said, and closed the door on Whiskey's pitiful yip.

"Give me a break. He's probably already back on his bed in doggie dreamland."

"We did have a rather energetic day today."

"Please tell me it didn't involve holes dug in someone's garden, chased cats, or stolen food."

"No, just all-around guy fun."

"I won't ask."

As it turned out, she didn't have time to.

The front door opened, and Fred and Dolly Hunnicutt came in. Fred and Dolly were a matching pair, both stocky and pleasingly padded, good-natured, helpful, and open-minded.

Dolly had come straight from work, her blue gingham dress relieved of its apron, and her honey-colored hair pulled loose from a granny bun. Fred, who managed the books for the bakery and served as the head of the town's Traffic Committee, was dressed in slacks and a striped short-sleeve dress shirt and tie and was carrying an accordion folder that probably held his traffic reports.

Fred waved and smiled at Liv, his nearly bald head catching the glint of the overhead lights.

They were accompanied by another man, who looked vaguely familiar. He was in his fifties, tall and lean with longish dark hair graying at the temples and a tapered beard streaked with white. And he was limping slightly.

Of course. Daniel Haynes, the descendent of General Haynes, leader of the patriot army, who played his ancestor in the reenactment, and one of the casualties of the evening. The general who'd sprained his ankle trying to get off his horse.

"Another successful weekend," Fred said as Liv and Ted waited for them.

"For the most part," she agreed.

"Liv, you know Daniel Haynes," Ted said, addressing the other man. "He plays his very illustrious ancestor every year."

"Yes, of course. Nice to see you. Your portrayal of

General Haynes was very moving." She decided not to mention the mishap with the horse.

They shook hands. Daniel Haynes had a firm grasp and a sparkle in his eye at her compliment. "I've done a lot of research into the role and what really happened that day."

She smiled. Daniel Haynes evidently believed his own mythology. No one rushed to remind him that the Battle of the Bay was pure fiction.

"Uh, not the battle itself." Haynes chuckled. "We all know the battle we present is a stretch of what really happened. But I have researched the period and the people involved, and the manner in which the battle would have been fought is quite historically correct."

"Well, it certainly is impressive," Liv said. "The planning and coordination it must take. How does everyone know when to start?"

Ted frowned at her. It was a stupid question coming from an event planner, but maybe Haynes didn't know that.

"We rehearse two nights a week all of June. Every piece must fit together seamlessly. Once Henry gives the signal, Rufus texts it to Roscoe and myself. I still don't know how Jacob Rundle ended up in Henry's place. Sad business. It just doesn't make sense.

"Is the mayor here tonight? I was hoping to catch him on another matter before we went inside, but I haven't seen him."

"He left earlier," Ted said. "I don't know if he's planning on coming back."

"Hmm. Maybe you know something about this rumor of some fella in town saying he was planning on buying the Gallantine estate and putting an end to the reenactments."

Word spread quickly in Celebration Bay.

"Well, I hope it isn't true," Dolly said. "We've done that reenactment for years. First we've heard of him planning to sell. And what are we going to do if we can't hold the battle there anymore?"

"Find another venue," Fred said.

"The reenactment has been held there every year since it began," Dolly said. "It would be such a shame to lose it. I can't think of a better place to hold it."

"That won't be necessary as far as I know," Haynes said. "I know that there was someone from this historical restoration group who talked to Henry earlier in the year. Henry wasn't interested in selling then, and I haven't heard since then that he's changed his mind.

"Though, Hildy called me to say that this curator, as he calls himself, was in the house this afternoon, and you, Ms. Montgomery, accompanied him."

"He had a letter of introduction. Bill said he had to be accompanied by a town official. The mayor sent me."

Ted grinned.

"That's what Hildy said. Well, she said you were there to prevent him from stealing anything. And that the mayor had told him he could have free run of the place."

Liv didn't answer. She had no idea what to say.

"Well, when Henry gets back I'm sure he'll explain everything," Dolly said.

"If he gets back," Haynes said.

Dolly looked at him in astonishment. "Why wouldn't he? He goes every summer to visit his sister and her family."

"Well, he isn't there now."

"How do you know?" Dolly asked.

"Because I have a little business I need to clear up with him. I *am* his attorney. When I called, she said he wasn't there and he wasn't planning to come this summer."

Liv started moving them toward the meeting room.

Haynes fell in step next to her. "I plan to meet this fella at the house tomorrow, take a good look at his letter of introduction. Sounds pretty smoky to me." He nodded brusquely. "Nice to meet you. I'd best be getting inside. Want to compare notes with Roscoe. I have a few suggestions of my own for next year." He strode off, tall, straight, and proud, touching on the arrogant, and with only a little limp.

Liv exchanged a look with Ted. Grossman had told them a lawyer was brokering the sale, but Haynes didn't seem to know anything about the arrangement.

"Pretty smoky indeed," Ted said, as if reading her thoughts.

"Don't mind Daniel," Fred said. "He takes his part in the reenactment very seriously. General Haynes actually led the troops supposedly betrayed by Old Gallantine. Gets on his high horse every Fourth. By August he's back to this century."

"There's no leftover enmity between the two after all their history, is there?" Liv asked.

"Nah, water under the bridge. Besides, General Haynes was given a hero's burial. If anybody was going to hold a grudge for centuries it would be the Gallantines."

"Which," Ted interjected, "has been known to happen in these parts."

"Oh, Ted," Dolly said, exasperated. "We're more civilized than that."

"Yes, we are, Dolly."

"What I don't get," Fred said, "is where Henry's disappeared to? And what was Jacob Rundle doing up on the roof instead of Henry?"

"Hush, Fred," Dolly said, as several other committee members came through the door.

Fred lowered his voice. "It's not exactly a secret he's dead and Henry's missing. You don't think that Henry killed him, do you?"

"Fred, the very idea."

"Sorry, Dolly, but it does make you wonder, doesn't it?" He patted her back and acknowledged the newcomers. "Good evening, Charlie, Harriett. Loved the concert in the band shell last Thursday."

Charlie and Harriett went ahead, and Fred ushered the rest of them through the door to the meeting room. Rows of tables and chairs were set up facing the dais where the mayor sat during town meetings and where Ted and Liv would sit tonight while the committee heads and select committee members each presented the results of the weekend.

It would be a long meeting, with reports from each committee, who would turn in full written reports during the next couple of weeks. Tonight was more of an info-gathering and idea exchange. Long, sometimes boring, occasionally argumentative, these roundup meetings invariably gave a better idea of the successes and failures of an event while memories were fresh and excitement still ran high among them.

To tell by the noise, Liv could already count the weekend as a success. Ted stopped to talk to someone, and Liv took her place at the front table, facing the others. Slowly everyone settled down and took their seats.

"Where *is* the mayor? Lying low so he won't have to answer questions about the murder?" Liv asked when Ted sat down beside.

He looked toward the door. "Dare we hope? Oops, I spoke too soon."

The door opened again, and Mayor Worley, looking preoccupied, ruffled, and like he wanted to be anywhere rather than at the meeting, walked in. The arm linked in his belonged to Liv's nemesis, Janine Townsend.

"So close and yet so far," Ted said.

"I am so not in the mood for Janine tonight," Liv said.

Janine was one of those middle-aged women who kept herself fit. Frosted hair hung in a face-framing cut. She was tall and thin and made sure she stayed that way by constant dieting, trips into Albany to the spa, and shopping for power suits for her career as a real estate broker.

Even with all that, she still managed to find time to ride roughshod over the mayor and throw a wrench into Liv's activities whenever possible.

Tonight she was wearing red patent leather heels and a navy-blue linen dress, accented with a string of pearls.

"Someone should tell her the Fourth of July is over," Ted said under his breath.

Liv smiled. Janine was being patriotic. Liv had learned to read people and what they were wearing a long time ago. It was a necessity if you wanted to survive in the event-planning industry.

Janine was obviously presenting herself as an upstanding citizen, a member of the Junior League and old society, with its traditions and attitudes. All the things Celebration Bay was not, but some aspired for it to be. The pearls gave her away.

Liv looked around the room. Dolly in her gingham dress from the bakery. Genny in polyester pants and a cotton blouse. Quincy Hinks, owner of the Bookworm, in light-weight trousers and a vest. Roscoe in khakis and a plaid shirt from one of the discount chains.

Not even Liv had dressed up for the meeting. She hadn't had time to change, but she would never have worn something so off-putting to the others.

The two of them came farther into the room, Janine propelling Gilbert to the front table, since there weren't seats on the dais for them, and making the three members of the children's play area move over. Gilbert shot one agonized look at Ted and Liv before lowering his head and staring at the plastic tabletop in front of him.

Things were not looking good for a quiet, boring meeting. Liv settled down, determined to push the agenda through with as little nonsense as possible.

The clock had just struck seven when the last stragglers hurried into the room, followed by Bill Gunnison and A.K. Pierce. Liv wondered if that had happened coincidentally or if they'd decided to meet ahead of time and compare notes. They moved to a table near Liv, and Bill gingerly lowered himself into a seat. At least his sciatica had waited until after the weekend to attack.

She turned on the table mic. "Thank you all for coming tonight. It was a wild and wonderful weekend. . . ."

Immediately after her opening remarks, Liv called on the first committee chairman to speak. She didn't want to allow any time for questions to be asked about the murder, the sale of the mansion, or the whereabouts of Henry Gallantine, or for Janine to start a yelling match.

And things went well—for two-thirds of the meeting.

Each committee member gave a preliminary report about various aspects of the weekend's event: vendors, bake sales, raffles.

Daniel Haynes stood for the reenactment report. "A wonderful evening," he said in the round baritone of a trial lawyer. "I'd like to thank a few people. The Elks for the use of their building for storage and changing areas. Miriam Krause and the ladies of A Stitch in Time for the repairs and upkeep of the uniforms."

He continued on, and Liv noticed Janine beginning to fidget. She glanced down at the agenda. Traffic was next, and then Liv would give the security report from A.K. and his team. A.K. Pierce was there, though he didn't need to be; Liv could have given his statistics. But she was glad to see him. And that made her wonder why Chaz *wasn't* there. He should have been there to report on the proceedings.

Haynes sat down to applause and a few shouts of "Hear, hear!"

And Janine made her move. "I would just like to ask how we think this was so successful when a man was killed in front of our eyes and the eyes of nearly a thousand tourists." She'd stood and delivered the question to the audience, then turned to Liv as if expecting an answer.

"Get 'em, tiger," Ted said under his breath.

Liv gave her back look for look. "I'm sure anything you need to know will be forthcoming from the Sheriff's Office." *Party of the first part* rang in her head. She could have used Chaz's nonsense tonight. She was dead tired, and it took everything not to lash out at Janine. That would be so unprofessional . . . but so satisfying.

"Well, if you ask me, it's about time you took some responsibility for all the murders that are occurring around here."

"Nobody asked you," came from the back of the room.

Liv was pretty sure it was Dexter Kent of Kent Landscaping and Nursery, who also was a member of the Fireworks Committee.

"Well, someone needs to be held accountable. And since we never had this kind of problem before Liv came to town, I can only believe—".

"Janine, give it a rest. We know what you think."

Janine shot an angry look toward the voice and then at the mayor, clearly expecting him to back her up.

He stood wearily. What on earth did Janine hold over his head?

"I think—" He cleared his throat. "I think there are questions that need some answers."

"And I suggest we have Liv answer them," Janine said. "It's all her fault."

The room erupted in opinions, yells, and catcalls.

Liv didn't bother to quiet them. Once they'd run down, she would do her usual rational argument about the success of the security team and the lowering statistics of violence with each new event.

But help came from an unexpected quarter. A.K. Pierce rose from his seat. *Like a colossus*, Liv thought.

The room became quiet.

"Whew," Ted whispered. "A marvel to behold."

"I believe you all were given a copy of the security report at the beginning of the meeting. We pride ourselves at Bayside Security on our efficiency and success rate. And to be able to accomplish this with a very low-key presence."

There was a smattering of applause.

"That's all well and good, but—"

He smiled coldly at Janine. "And your county police always do an admirable job of crowd control."

Liv saw Janine's hand clench. *Don't do it, Janine*, she thought.

But Janine couldn't help herself. "Ever since she's come here—"

"Some people," A.K. said, "should worry less about the event coordinator and more about being sued for slander. Now I believe Ms. Montgomery would like to continue with the agenda in an orderly fashion."

Janine opened her mouth. Didn't seem to find what she meant to say and sat down rather quickly for a woman in a tight dress.

"Thank you," A.K. said in his commanding voice. "Ms. Montgomery?" He sat.

"Thank you, Mr. Pierce," Liv said, feeling a little overwhelmed. "Since you all have the statistics before you, I'd like to move to our last committee report. Fred, would you report on traffic, please?"

Fred stood. "Thank you, Liv. We hired ten extra . . ."

"Hmm," Ted said under his breath. "Looks like the tide has turned on Janine."

"Unfortunately, I have a feeling it will only encourage her to be more vindictive."

"Someday I'll tell you how she got back at her ex-husband." Ted sucked in air between his teeth, a sound that set off major foreboding in Liv's mind.

Fred finished his report. Liv thanked everyone for coming and reminded them that their written reports and financial tallies would be due by the following Monday.

Talking broke out as everyone collected their things and headed for the door.

Liv kept her fingers crossed that they would all make it to the street before they started speculating.

From the corner of her eye, she saw Daniel Haynes approach the mayor, and the two men left the room together, Janine following close behind them. And Bill hobbled more slowly after her.

A.K. came to stand by Liv's side until everyone had filed

out of the meeting room. No one stopped to ask her questions. Though she didn't need his protection, it was flattering and comforting to have a big strong man . . . *Gack*. What was she thinking?

She needed a big dose of a SoHo singles' bar to banish those kinds of thoughts. Besides . . . She made a cursory glance of the room. Chaz hadn't deigned to come. He often didn't, but usually he did manage to rouse himself to report the successes of the festivals.

She stamped down on the niggle of disappointment she felt. She turned to A.K. "Thanks."

He gave that quirk of eyebrow that on most people would be a shrug. "Shall I walk you out?"

She couldn't help but smile. "Part of the job description?"

"No. Because I'd like to."

Flustered, she nodded.

They started down the hall, Liv listening for sounds of conversation. She hesitated when they passed the mayor's office, but A.K. steered her away and toward her own office.

She unlocked the door and pushed it open for her but didn't come inside.

"Are you going to kibitz the meeting in the mayor's office?"

He didn't pretend not to understand. "I'll offer my services."

"And then you'll come and tell me what happened?"

A quirk of lips and eyebrow. Was it a smile?

"No."

Liv slumped in disappointment.

He touched her chin with one finger. "Buck up. I'm sure Ted will."

And he was gone. She hadn't noticed Ted slipping out behind Janine. A.K. had.

The man knew what he was doing. She'd hired the right security firm. She had no doubt. She just wasn't sure she could keep from succumbing to the power of their boss.

As the door shut behind A.K., Whiskey came padding

out from Liv's office, stopped at her feet, and looked up at her. He was ready to go home. So was she. But no way was she going to leave without talking to Bill and finding out what was going on in the mayor's office.

"Sorry buddy, just a little while longer."

It was twenty minutes later when she heard the outer door open and close. Ted was reaching for the light switch when she reached his office.

"Oh no you don't."

He nearly dropped his jacket, but recovered quickly. "I thought it was odd that you didn't lock up before you left."

"As you can see, I didn't."

"Waiting to pump me for information?"

"Yes."

"Good. Hang on for a second." He opened the outer door. Stuck his head out. Called, "Hey, Bill, she's in here."

Liv winced and went back to her office to face the music.

Bill hobbled in a minute later, followed by A.K.

Oh goody, thought Liv. *He's brought a friend.*

A.K. stopped just inside the door, crossed his arms, and leaned against the jamb.

Did he think she might try to escape?

Ted pulled up a chair, and Bill sat down. Ted perched on the edge of Liv's desk. A.K. stayed put.

Bill reached into his pocket, and Liv decided to take the offense. "So what happened in the mayor's office?"

Bill pulled out a voice recorder. Put it on the desk in front of her. Pressed the button.

"Every detail," he said, shifted his weight, and waited.

She told him about the way Grossman had acted at the mansion. How she'd talked to Hildy, and how she'd seen Grossman in the backyard when she put her cup away.

Then she told him about sneaking back into the yard, though she was careful not to call it sneaking. About how she'd made her way close to the boathouse. where Grossman and Frank Gallantine met.

As she talked, Bill's frown increased. Ted's eyes began to sparkle with amusement. Even A.K.'s lips once quirked up into a brief smile, which had the effect of making Liv forget what she was talking about.

She told Bill about Leo's fight and what he'd told her about looking for treasure.

When she finally wound down, nobody said a word, nobody moved.

She huffed out a sigh. "Well?"

No response.

"Doesn't it seem suspicious that all these people are suddenly interested in Gallantine's mansion? He disappears. Rundle takes his place. Rundle is murdered."

Still nothing.

"Rundle is murdered. Why? Because someone thought he was Gallantine? And why at that particular time?"

Okay, they were beginning to get her angry.

"Then who gave the SOS? A.K. said Rundle probably bled out in a matter of seconds. So who? The killer?"

Bill sighed.

"Or if not the killer . . . Leo? It was Leo, wasn't it? And don't tell me it's confidential," Liv said.

"You'd better tell her," Ted said. "You wouldn't like her when she's angry."

"Not funny."

Bill shook his head. "Leo did. Chaz taught him."

"Chaz?" Wonders never ceased. Not only had the less-than-enthusiastic—and these days downright unapproachable—newspaper editor taken Leo fishing more than once, he'd taught him Morse code. What other secrets were hidden deep inside the enigmatic newspaperman?

"Leo says it was so, if he needed help, Chaz could find him."

"Only Chaz wasn't at the reenactment," Liv said with an edge of disgust. She couldn't help herself. Not that Chaz could have prevented Rundle's death. He was dead by the time they'd reached the roof.

"He couldn't have reacted faster than you and Ted did."

"I know." But he might have been with Leo and prevented the teenager from becoming a murder suspect. She stopped, horrified at the turn her thoughts had taken. It wasn't Chaz's fault. But in one of those "aha moments," Liv began to understand why Chaz didn't want to get involved.

She'd caught herself feeling the same way earlier. Tired and wanting some downtime, a vacation free of worry and responsibility. Maybe that was what Chaz was after when he returned to take over the paper.

"Liv? Did you think of something?"

"No. Sorry. Does any of this help?"

"Yes. Now go on home. Get some sleep." Bill returned the recorder to his pocket and pushed himself to his feet. "Oh, and thanks for the heads-up about the nephew. We picked him up with a carload of stuff from Gallantine House."

"Did you arrest him?"

"No. He said it was rightfully his. We had to let him go. But we confiscated the goods until Henry returns."

"Well, that's something."

"Well, I'm for bed." Ted pulled on his jacket.

Whiskey padded over and stood at the door.

"I guess we'll be going to."

"Want a ride?" Bill asked.

"Thanks, but Whiskey and I can both use the walk."

The three men saw her out. She was too tired to even wonder what they talked about after she left.

She and Whiskey were both dragging by the time they walked up the driveway to home. Liv couldn't wait to get into bed. She fell asleep almost immediately, oblivious that the ghost would make another appearance before dawn.

Chapter Seventeen

....

Liv slept late the next morning. Post-event exhaustion was setting in—in spades. She needed a few days off, just to go grocery shopping. Get by the Woofery. Her stores of nutritional doggie food were getting low. The only people food she had came in cans.

She needed to do laundry, clean her little house. For the moment, food and coffee would suffice.

Summer had started in earnest, and both the Apple of My Eye and the Buttercup would be crowded. Several people left the bakery as she entered, and there was a line ahead of her. That was okay. Liv wasn't in a hurry this morning, but Whiskey pulled at the leash as they walked inside. Then Liv saw what had caught his attention. A small boy was standing with his parents, eating a donut.

"Don't even think it," Liv said.

Whiskey sat, calm but expectant. The kid saw him and slipped away from his parents to come closer. Whiskey was good with kids, something the rescue people had praised him for. They had been completely right. However, a kid with a donut might tempt his good manners.

"Elliot, you know you have to ask before you pet someone else's dog." The mother smiled at Liv.

Liv knelt down by Whiskey and took his collar. "It's fine," she said. "But he does like donuts."

The boy pinched off a piece and held it out to Whiskey, who took it delicately from his fingers. Friends for life.

The father paid for their purchases.

Liv stepped up to the counter. "Morning, Dolly."

"Morning. Whew, what a weekend. Have you, uh, heard anything more about"—she glanced over to the family, who had sat at one of the small tables and were obviously tourists—"the other thing?"

Liv had, but she didn't think this was the time or the place. Before she could answer, the door opened, setting off the little bell that announced a customer, and three men walked in. Local workers who were probably on break from dismantling the parade stand.

They already had their coffee and were laughing at something one of them had said.

"Hey, Ms. Montgomery, heard you found the body the other night."

Liv recognized Cliff Chalmers, one of the town rowdies, who Liv had run into before. Actually it was the other way around. She'd witnessed a fight, and when she came up to stop it, he tripped over her foot and happened to fall on her fist. Which meant the other two must be the Weaver brothers. Cliff was the ringleader, but the other two were always up for a fight.

Liv decided to ignore them. "Those muffins look good."

Dolly glanced to where the two parents had stopped eating and were paying close attention. Then looked at Liv.

"Why don't you guys go ahead," Liv said, and stepped aside. "I know you don't have long for your break." She gave them her evil eye. Executives had quailed beneath that look.

It seemed to have no effect on the laborers, except to make them crowd toward the counter.

Once there, they took their time about deciding. Liv saw the father edging forward. "Was there a problem at the fireworks? We came here because Celebration Bay advertises itself as a safe, family-friendly holiday town."

"And it is," said Dolly at her most jovial, grandmotherly self. "One of the patriot portrayers had an accident, that's all."

"If you call falling on your own bayonet an accident." Cliff laughed at his own humor. Liv really didn't like people who did that.

"Weren't no accident," one of the Weavers said.

Dolly shot a desperate look at Liv.

"Guys, can we move it? I have to get to work, and Dolly has other customers."

Of course they didn't take the hint. She hadn't really expected them to. She knew these guys, hotheads and troublemakers, especially when they were together. At least it was too early for beer; that's when they got really mean.

Nothing less than hitting them over the head and dragging them to the curb would stop them. And she was so tempted.

"Don't mess with Ms. Montgomery," the other Weaver said. "She licked you last time around."

The father picked up the little boy and steered his wife out the door.

Dolly came around the counter moving fast. "I'll deal with you three later." She opened the door and called out to the family. They stopped to talk, and Liv could see Dolly gesticulating and nodding back to the bakery.

Whatever she said seemed to have assuaged their fears, because the man smiled, Dolly smiled, the little boy waved good-bye, and they got in their minivan and drove away.

Then Dolly turned back to the bakery.

She opened the door with such violence that Liv was

afraid the bell would fall from the door. "And just what do you three think you're doing?"

"Trying to get something to eat on our break."

"Well, you can get it over at the—no, never mind. Better you should get it here and not stop anywhere else in town. And I'll thank you to keep your mouth shut about accidents and anything else that might scare people away."

"Heck, Dolly, we can't help if somebody run old Rundle through."

"Well, you don't have to talk about it. Especially in public."

"It wasn't somebody," said Cliff. "It was that halfwit, Leo Morgan."

The Weavers laughed.

"Guess that's why the ghost is after him."

"Okay, that's it." Dolly hurried behind the counter.

"I think I'll have one of those—" one of the Weavers began.

But he never finished. Dolly snatched up a broom and stormed around the counter. "I don't want to see you or your brother or friends in my bakery ever again. The only half-wits around here are you three. Now, get." She brandished the broom at them, and the three men practically fell over one another getting out the door.

"And don't come back." Dolly gave one more flourish and nearly knocked over BeBe, who'd come to see what the ruckus was about.

A small crowd was forming: some people that Liv recognized, others who were probably visitors.

Dolly, bun loosened and strands of hair flying, her apron twisted across her fulsome figure, turned to the crowd. "Sometimes these boys need to be taken in hand." She smiled at everyone, though Liv thought she looked slightly demented.

"It's Celebration Bay's promise to be a safe and friendly

destination town, and sometimes our young folks need to be reminded of that," Dolly announced.

A smattering of applause broke out, led by several of the locals.

Bless this town. Liv loved it, warts and all.

"Have a good day," Dolly said, and took a swipe at a piece of dirt on the sidewalk before going back inside.

BeBe and Liv followed her in. Liv closed the door behind Dolly. "You were magnificent."

"Mercy me," Dolly said, returning the broom to the corner and patting at her hair. "Those boys make me so mad. I'm afraid I lost my temper."

"I'll say you did," BeBe said. "I was coming to warn you about those three. They just left the Buttercup. I wish I had reacted to them as quickly as you. I just let them gabble on and hoped the steam machine drowned their voices out."

"Hopefully they won't come back. I don't need business that bad." Dolly yanked at her apron until it was riding fairly straight across her hips. "Now, what would you like, Liv? Oh right, muffins." Dolly added two more muffins to the bag she'd just filled before.

"These bear claws are nice. Oh, and I have some cinnamon bread. Should still be warm."

"Dolly, stop. That's more than enough."

Dolly looked down at the bag brimming over with muffins and pastries. "Oh dear, I'm just that discombobulated. Let me get you some fresh ones."

"They're fine," Liv said. "Just put them on my tab."

"But—"

"I have to get to work. I'm sure Ted will be delighted with the extras."

Dolly handed her the bag. Liv saw that her fingers were shaking slightly.

"Too much adrenaline," Dolly said.

"Me, too," Liv said.

"Well, come next door to the Buttercup. I'll give you some caffeine to calm your nerves."

Liv said good-bye to Dolly, and she and BeBe walked toward the door. But Whiskey sat down and refused to budge.

Liv gave him a look. "Dolly, do you have one of your famous treats for the dog?"

"Arf," Whiskey said.

"Oh dear, yes. You can see just how upset I am."

"Maybe you should come for a cup of coffee, too," BeBe told her.

"I wish, but I gave the rest of the staff off today, since they had to work through the weekend." She handed a cellophane bag with a leftover American flag dog biscuit in it.

Liv shoved it in her carryall, and she and BeBe went next door.

"Lord, summer seems to bring out all the vermin along with the tourists," BeBe said.

"I'm guessing they came in to tear down the judge's platform and will return to wherever they stay so we don't have to deal with them. Sometimes I think they just like to cause trouble regardless of how they really feel."

"I think you should call Bill and A.K. and tell them what's going on. Maybe they need more of a presence in town until this blows over." BeBe turned on the steamer, and for a minute they couldn't talk.

"Would you like some of these pastries?"

"Not after what I ate all weekend."

Liv sighed and stored the bulging bakery bag in her carryall while BeBe poured Ted's tea. "You know, the only food I ever carried around when I worked in Manhattan was maybe a granola bar. I never had time to eat it and would end up throwing it away once it crumbled into an inedible mess. I really need to start exercising."

"You do exercise."

"I mean serious, don't-put-on-thirty-pounds kind of exercising."

"Oh well, don't come looking for me when you start again." BeBe slid the tray of drinks over to Liv. The door opened behind Liv, and BeBe's face lit up.

Liv tried not to turn around, but she couldn't help it.

The man who had walked through the door was clean-cut and cute and was smiling back at BeBe in an even higher wattage than the barista's smile.

"See you later," Liv told BeBe, and gave her a look that said, *I expect every detail later.* She took her cardboard tray of drinks while the smiling new guy politely held the door for her.

"Thanks," she said, and stepped into the heat of the morning. Winter had seemed to last so long that she'd had a hard time imagining it ever being hot again. And never this hot, because she assumed there would always be a breeze from the lake, similar to the cutting wind in the winter.

Today there wasn't even a hint of a breeze, and the humidity was beginning to curl her hair. She could almost feel it frizzing like one of those old-time cartoons where the character's hair suddenly *boing*ed into springs.

Miriam Krause was waiting by the door to A Stitch in Time. "I heard Dolly was giving that Cliff Chalmers what for. I ran out to see, but I was too late. Isn't that just always the way?"

"Well, she did throw them out," Liv said. "But other than that there was not much to see."

"Maybe not. The Weavers aren't all bad, but you just never know when they're going to turn on you. Sometimes they're fine and sometimes they get just plain mean. Mostly when they're drinking and hanging out with Cliff Chalmers. He's just plain no good."

Liv knew it; she had seen them attack another man when they were drunk and spoiling for a fight.

"I wouldn't put it past them to be the ones responsible for what happened over at the rectory last night."

Liv had started to move away, but she stopped. "What happened?"

"Evidently there were a whole bunch of police cars there pretty late. Maeve Kingston lives nearby. All the sirens and lights woke her and her husband up, and he went out to see. Seems like 'the ghost' was looking in at the window. Gave poor Leo a fright.

"The police didn't find anything or anybody, but it sounds just like something those boys would do. The sheriff oughta talk to those three. They might know more about what happened to Jacob Rundle than they let on."

"How so?"

"Well, I've seen all their cars parked out at that bar on the county road. I drive by there on my way home from the store. Real rough types go there, so I've been told. It could have been some lowlife Jacob got involved with out there that killed him."

"I'll pass that on to Bill Gunnison," Liv said. She was suddenly in a hurry to get to the office.

"He better move on it, before they start roiling up trouble. They'll do it if they can. Just can't seem not to."

"I'll ask him to keep a close watch on them."

"You do that."

Liv smiled and started to walk away.

"Luanne Dietz over at Bay-Berry Candles saw you and Chaz Bristow in the back of the sheriff's car Sunday."

Liv's smile didn't waver. "He was just giving us a ride home . . . from church. I wore these high heels that hurt—"

"Chaz Bristow hasn't seen the inside of a church since he was a boy."

"I just happened to run into him outside the rectory. Chaz lives practically next door."

"Uh-huh. I just hope you two solve this soon. Don't want rumors scaring away business. Have a nice day. Tell Chaz we're all glad he's back." Miriam went inside, and Liv hurried down the sidewalk, head down, hopefully discouraging anyone else from stopping her to chat.

Things were not right in Celebration Bay, and Liv was worried. Even Whiskey seemed subdued as he trotted alongside her toward Town Hall.

Liv had coffee at her desk with Ted like always. She told him about the run-in with Chalmers and the Weaver brothers. Went into detail about Dolly and the broom, which Ted enjoyed immensely, before they both became serious again.

"Yeah, I heard about the rectory incident. Bill thinks it was a prank, but Phillip Schorr doesn't feel like he can keep Leo safe while he goes about his parish duties. And he doesn't want to leave Leo alone while he's gone. I guess he's been sitting at home doing what he can from his home office."

"Isn't there someone Leo could stay with permanently?"

"His mother won't take him back, if that's what you're thinking. And he hasn't finished high school, so he needs to be with someone who will see that he completes his schooling. Get him set up with the right programs to get some vocational training when the time comes."

"Have anybody in mind?" she asked hopefully.

"Not a one."

The telephone rang. Ted took it at his desk. A minute later he appeared at the open door to her office. "Speak of the devil, though that's really not appropriate, considering. It's Phillip Schorr on line one."

Liv took the call. "Good morning."

"Good morning. I guess you've heard about what happened at the rectory last night."

"Yes, are you and Leo all right?"

"I am, but the boy's pretty spooked. I kept him from school today. I wanted to ask a favor, if I might."

"Of course."

"Could we borrow Whiskey for a few hours?"

"Absolutely. He'd love to come."

"That would be wonderful. I can pick him up in a few minutes."

"No, no, I'll bring him over. I'd like to say hi to Leo anyway."

"Thank you."

She hung up. "Come on, buddy. Want to go see Leo?"

Whiskey thumped his tail, then stood up to give a full wag.

"I'm taking Whiskey for a playdate at the rectory. Do you think you can get the mayor to call an emergency meeting of the board of trustees for tonight?"

"Yes, but why?"

"I think they need to be brought up to speed on the Gallantine House business. The reenactment is a major event that is suddenly in jeopardy, and I want to act while Grossman is still around. And also I think they need to step up to the plate for the town's community center."

"I'm on it. Have a nice time."

It only took a few minutes to walk over to the rectory. When the pastor answered the door, Whiskey shot right past him to Leo.

Pastor Schorr sighed. "Animals are certainly God's creatures."

Liv could think of more than a few times when she'd been sure that Whiskey was the devil's spawn, mainly after forays into ripe garbage. Or when he decided that dragging a roll of toilet paper through the house was interior design. Or when . . . "Yes, they really are." And she imagined her feisty little-big dog with angel wings and a doggie smile.

Schorr led her back to the den where Leo and Whiskey were carrying on like old friends, which Liv guessed they were.

"Look who's here, Leo."

Leo looked up, scrambled to his feet. "Hi, Ms. Montgomery. Did you bring Whiskey to visit me?"

"I sure did, Leo. I was wondering if you could dog sit him for a little while."

"Oh yeah. Whiskey and me are good friends, aren't we, fella?"

Whiskey barked.

"Thank you so much," Phillip said as they left the room. "At least he'll have a little peace today. Though I don't know what to do about the nights. We could both move upstairs. I don't like leaving him completely alone, but the way things have been going, I don't really want to leave the downstairs vulnerable."

He pursed his lips. "That sounds awful from a clergy-man."

"It sounds like a very smart and caring clergyman," Liv said. "I think it was Cliff Chalmers and his friends last night. They said something about the ghost being after Leo. Bill is looking into it."

"Well, that somewhat relieves my mind."

"They seem like overgrown delinquents. They might throw a few punches, but I don't think they would resort to real premeditated violence. At least I hope they wouldn't."

She smiled at the pastor, saw the strain in his eyes. He was losing sleep and possibly losing his community center.

"I have an idea, if it's all right with you."

"I'm open to all ideas."

"What if I left Whiskey here to spend the night?" Liv felt a stutter of separation anxiety at the thought of Whiskey on a sleepover. "If you don't think he'd be too much trouble. He's slept away from home before, so that shouldn't be an issue." He'd stayed with the Zimmermans several times, and in Manhattan he'd been boarded more times than she cared to remember.

"And if he gets to be too much, I can pick him up. Just call my cell. There's a trustees meeting, so I'll be at work late."

"Are they worried over this latest business?"

"We're all a little concerned, but that's not what the meeting's about. Just routine board work. Actually, I've been feeling a little guilty for not paying enough attention to Whiskey, so you and Leo would be doing me a favor."

The pastor smiled. He was really quite charming. "Shall we tell Leo? I know it would make him feel safer."

"Whiskey's not only man's best friend, he's an excellent guard dog."

Leo was thrilled, and Whiskey seemed happy to stay at the rectory. Liv stopped by the Woofery and asked Sharise to deliver some dog food and supplies.

"Sure, I can send someone over in a few minutes. Is Pastor Schorr getting a dog?"

"Whiskey is having a sleepover with Leo."

"Ah. I heard the commotion over there last night. It's great to live so close to work; I just walk downstairs in the morning. But the downside of living in town and right around the corner from the pub is that I get some pretty loud drunks on their way home. Sometimes they hang out in the cemetery across the street and continue to drink.

"The church is constantly having to clean up after them. There were a bunch of them there last night, and it wasn't even a weekend. I wouldn't be surprised if they're the ones that went peeking in the pastor's window."

"Did you tell this to Bill?"

"To one of the officers. He wrote it down, don't know if he did anything about it. It's just speculation on my part."

"Maybe, but it bears checking out. I'd better run. Thanks for doing this."

"My pleasure. I'll put it on your account. Whiskey will be good for Leo. That boy loves animals. And I'm sure Pastor Schorr would enjoy the company. In fact . . ." Sharise trailed off. "I might just take them over myself."

Liv left after that. She took her time to stroll through the park toward Town Hall. It seemed like love was in the air. BeBe and the man with the smile. Sharise about to visit the pastor.

Liv considered feeling sorry for herself. But she never had time for love anyway, and with this festival and the murder, she wasn't about to take time off to look for it now.

Chapter Eighteen

....

Liv didn't love paperwork days, when bills had to be tallied, payments reconciled, requests for payments sent out. Successes and failures, efficiencies and inefficiencies were compared and analyzed. Files had to be organized and filed away.

And, in the case of her new job, where with any luck she would be doing repeats for years to come, they would have to be collated so that the following years would run even more smoothly, with even less need to improvise.

If they had a venue for next year for this particular event.

She would have to put a contingency plan in place immediately. Which is one of the reasons she had called a meeting of the trustees tonight. Liv wanted to give them a heads-up on the possibility of having to find a new site for the reenactment. And even worse, a site they might have to pay for.

And she wanted to introduce the idea of underwriting a building for the community center. They would probably balk at first. But it was used by all ages and ethnicities, by all denominations and no denominations. Surely the town should be contributing to its operation.

"Are we eating in today?" Ted asked, pulling her from her wandering ideas.

"Oh," Liv said. "Is it time for lunch?"

"It's almost three o'clock, and unless you're planning on going home and then turning around and coming back for the meeting, I say we eat."

"You're kind of crabby today," Liv said.

"Because I don't have my favorite dawg around to entertain me." He heaved a woebegone sigh. "I don't suppose you sing?"

"Don't look at me. I can sing so-so, but I'm not participating in any canine chorus."

Ted grinned. "Let's blow this joint and go out to lunch."

They both decided that it would take too much time to walk to Buddy's, their usual go-to place for takeout. They walked across the street to the Corner Café.

Mr. Salvatini greeted them at the door.

"Well, well. I haven't seen the two of you in quite a while."

"Liv is such a taskmaster, she never gives me a lunch break."

"Ha-ha." Mr. Salvatini turned his smile on Liv. "But worth it to work for such a lovely lady."

Liv smiled at the compliment and gave Ted a complacent look. Mr. Salvatini was an old-world gentleman who had emigrated from Italy when he was a young man. He'd come for a visit to family friends, but once he'd met their daughter, he decided to stay. He married Alda Tonelli the following year.

Together, they began serving lunches to workers out of a food truck. Over the years they raised four boys and built their business until they bought the Corner Café and turned it into one of the most popular restaurants on the square.

Though the décor was nothing fancy and the tables were set so close that you could see what your neighbor was eating, the Formica tables always had small arrangements of fresh flowers. The menus were printed on plastic-covered paper, and specials were written on a chalkboard displayed on the wall.

Good home-style food, handmade pasta, and bread baked each day on the premises kept people coming back for more. Even though it was nearly three o'clock, the little café still had occupied tables. Mr. Salvatini led them over to a table by the big plate-glass window.

"Today we have zuppa de pesce. Very good. And Alda has made her specialty, Lamb Shank Pietro." Mr. Salvatini smiled. "Named for our firstborn. And also a beautifully *picante* pasta primavera. Everything kissed by the sun in the garden and picked this morning."

"I'd come here just to listen to him describe the food," Ted said after he'd ordered the soup, the lamb shank, and the caprese salad, and Liv, the pasta.

Salvatini's descriptions of the food were delightful, Liv agreed, but the actuality was even better. Her pasta was covered with fresh zucchini, green beans, eggplant, onions, and tomatoes, all combined to perfection.

"Excellent," Ted said as he sat back from a plate that contained only a bone, picked clean. "Espresso?"

Liv nodded. The food was making her sleepy and content, not the best way to approach a board with bad news and a request for money.

Their coffees were brought by another Salvatini. One of the sons, medium height, a good-looking man in his twenties with glossy black hair and clear olive skin.

"Buon giorno, Nico. Como stai?"

"Good, Mr. Driscoll. And you?"

"Excellent, especially after this lunch. Give your mama our compliments."

"I will. But I actually came out because I may have some news." He looked quickly around. "Papa doesn't want me to get involved."

Liv remembered last December, when Mr. Salvatini had been so reluctant to confide information to the police.

"Well, by all means tell us." Ted had lowered his voice, but his smile was still in place, so anyone looking would think they were talking about the weather.

But Nico was not so good. "I don't know if this means anything, but twice that Jacob Rundle has come around trying to sell things to the kitchen staff. Watches, rings, phones. When Papa found out, he forbade anyone on the staff to deal with him. He was sure they were stolen."

Nico grinned. "Papa sometimes states the obvious." He shrugged in a "Who knows?" way. "Anyway, I thought it might be useful information considering what happened."

"Did you tell the sheriff?"

"God no, Papa would have a fit. No one knows why he is uneasy with the authorities. He is an honest man. It has to do with politics or something from when he was a boy in the old country. Who knows? But he said it was okay to tell Ms. Montgomery and you."

"Thank you, Nico. We'll pass it on," Ted said.

Nico nodded, duty done, and sauntered back into the kitchen.

"So, what?" Liv asked. "Do you think Henry Gallantine found out and lured Rundle to the roof to kill him?"

"It just doesn't sound like Henry. He's eccentric but not psycho."

"This is so frustrating." Liv twisted the lemon zest into her coffee. "If we just knew why Rundle was on the roof, we might be able to find out who killed him."

"Is that another case of the royal 'we'?" Ted asked, deadpan.

"Of course. Contrary to the growing belief, I don't know

anything about murder. I didn't solve any murders before or since I've been here. And, as usual, I don't have a clue." Liv took a sip of the strong espresso. "Ah, but this makes up for it."

The members of the board of trustees began arriving a few minutes before eight. Since it was a closed meeting, they met in one of the smaller meeting rooms on the first floor.

At eight o'clock, Liv and Ted walked down the hall to join the others. They had no presentations to make, no reports to give. This was entirely an opinion-gathering evening, which Liv hoped would mean a short meeting and an early night.

Roscoe and Rufus were sitting at the conference room table with a third member, Jeremiah Atkins, president of First Celebration Bank. Rufus Cobb ran a charming bed-and-breakfast a block off the square, and Roscoe Jackson was the proprietor of a quaint but useful general store on the east side of the park.

Ted and Liv sat down and the five of them chatted while waiting for the mayor.

Gilbert Worley walked in a few minutes later and closed the door behind him.

"Me and my . . ." Ted sang under his breath.

"No Janine," Liv said. "Dare we hope?"

"Sorry I'm late, but I was picking up phone messages. Chaz won't be joining us tonight. He said whatever we decide is fine."

"He doesn't even know what the meeting is about, does he?" Jeremiah turned to Liv. "Unless you know and told him."

"Not me," Liv said. They didn't need him, but she had to admit she was a little disappointed. Not that he did much but occasionally vote her way in a close vote, but the votes were often close. They wouldn't be voting on anything tonight, but she'd been hoping since their foray onto the roof of Gallantine House that he would bounce back to his old self and show up, even if he only came to sleep through the meeting.

"Shall we begin?" Gilbert asked, and sat down.

They all looked at one another. The mayor was never present without Janine tagging along. She wasn't a trustee and didn't have a vote, but she still managed to use the board meetings as a platform for her opinions—on just about everything. No one felt the need to ask where she was. Liv took that as a good sign.

"I'll turn the meeting over to Liv, then," the mayor said.

"Thank you, Mayor Worley. I asked for this meeting for two specific reasons, mainly for information gathering and as an opportunity for an opinion poll. As perhaps all of you know, a man approached the mayor the other day, a representative . . ."

When she'd finished giving them a detailed account of what Grossman had told the mayor and what she had learned from being stuck with him in the mansion for a day, she asked for questions.

"Can he do that?" Rufus asked, and chewed on his mustache.

"Not until Henry Gallantine reappears to enter into the contract," Jeremiah informed them.

"If Henry Gallantine reappears," Roscoe said, and slowly shook his head. "Where the heck is he? And why wasn't he where he was supposed to be?"

"I wouldn't be surprised if that museum person killed him," Rufus said.

Jeremiah gave him an exasperated look. "But why would he kill the gardener?"

"I don't know. Thought he was Gallantine, maybe."

"Why would he do that? If Henry is dead, he can't even bid on the property until after probate and then only if the heirs are willing to sell."

"Who are the heirs?"

Realizing she wasn't going to get any help from the mayor, Liv interrupted. "Gentlemen, the point is that we need to be prepared for the possibility of a sale. And begin looking at contingency plans."

"Might not happen after all," Rufus said. "Just be putting the cart before the horse if you ask me."

"Maybe Rufus is right," Roscoe said. "Maybe we should just wait and see."

The board of trustees was definitely of the head-in-the-sand, wait-and-see philosophy, but they generally listened to Liv's suggestions. Eventually.

"Let's just say the horse needs to be fed, groomed, and ready for the cart if we need it." She smiled at them, smiled at Ted, feeling pretty smug about her horse analogy. She was getting to be a downright small-town country girl.

Too bad no one even noticed. Chaz would have noticed and been sure to make some stupid remark.

"So, just to be on the safe side, I think we should start looking at alternative sites. If we don't need them, great, but we may need them for something entirely different in the future." She thought about saying "forewarned is fore-armed," but decided not to push her luck.

"I just wanted to apprise the board of the potential change. Just give it some thought, please."

They discussed possible venues and who should cover what territory and who should make what calls, most of it ending with Liv and Ted doing the work. Then Liv moved on to her second item of business.

"It's been brought to my attention that the town's community center is losing its lease on the property on Baxter Street.

"The Presbyterian church and fund-raising by the center have been responsible for the rent, which is two hundred dollars a month." Before moving here, Liv couldn't imagine even renting a storage space for two hundred a month.

"I'd like to suggest to the board that we look into either renting or buying a building to house the center. As of now, the center is used in the mornings by the senior citizens and in the afternoons by the teen group. It has the potential to accommodate numerous other programs and cater to all the citizens of Celebration Bay."

"That's all fine and good, Liv," Jeremiah said. "But how do you propose we underwrite this venture, and who's going to run it?"

"I'm thinking more along the lines of enlarging the programs and staff in increments. First, we just need to find an acceptable venue that can be accessed by everyone who uses the facilities."

"It sounds like a lot of trouble to me," Rufus said. "Why can't Phillip Schorr just run it in one of the rooms in the church?"

"He will if he has to, but since so many of the participants aren't Presbyterians, he would like to keep it in a neutral space."

Mayor Worley cleared his throat. "How much do you expect this to cost the taxpayers?"

One of the mayor's favorite questions. Liv had prepared for it. "As I see it, there are several options, including the possibility that someone could donate the building to the town for the express use of the community center. We could even name it after their family."

The men all nodded. They liked the idea of not having to raise money.

"There's always the bond route."

Gilbert Worley had started shaking his head before she'd finished the sentence. "People are just beginning to recover from the bad economy. They don't want to pay more taxes."

"And if they don't want the community center, they just have to vote against it. But there will need to be some way to keep the center afloat in the interim," Liv said.

"Or," she continued, "we could have a capital fund-raiser

and ask for donations until we have enough funds. Put one of those big thermometers in the square so people can see how close to goal we are. A constant reminder and an inspiration to give."

"Maybe we should look into it," Rufus said. "My mother-in-law goes on Tuesday and Thursday to do some kind of classes. I'd pay to keep her there." He blushed furiously. "I didn't meant it like that."

"We know what you mean, Rufus. And we completely understand." Roscoe tried to stop a laugh but only managed to splutter.

"It's not the worst idea, Mayor." Jeremiah folded his hands on the table, looking every bit the banker—and landlord. "A decent building and the right amount of collateral for the mortgage. It would be a service to the community."

Liv's cell vibrated. She slipped it out of her bag and glanced at caller ID, wondering who on earth would be calling her now.

Her landladies. They knew she was at a meeting; something must be wrong. Liv stood. "Excuse me, gentlemen. I'll be right back." She grabbed her bag and walked calmly outside to the hallway, where she swiped her finger across the phone and said, "Is everything okay?"

"No," said Miss Edna. "There's a brawl over at McCready's Pub. We just heard it on the police band."

The police band was the number-one evening entertainment for a good portion of Celebration Bay residents. "Oh dear, but what—"

"The sheriff is on his way over there and they've requested backup."

"But—"

"Now, you listen up. One of the perpetrators is Chaz Bristow, and I think you'd better get over there and do something."

Chapter Nineteen

....

Chaz in a brawl? And Bill on his way? He'd throw the book at him.

"Okay, we're on our way." Liv ended the call, though she didn't have a clue as to how she and Ted could help.

She hurried back to the meeting room, stuck her head in the door. "Sorry, I need to borrow Ted for a minute."

Ted rose and was across the room before she took a breath, and he managed it without even looking like he was hurrying. He stepped into the hall. Liv closed the door.

"That was Edna. There's a fight at McCready's. Bill is on his way to arrest Chaz." A bit of a stretch but the best shorthand she could accomplish.

"I'm on it. We'd better take the car. We might need to make a hasty escape." He opened the door to the meeting room. "Sorry, meeting adjourned." Then he took off down the hall to the back entrance.

"I'm coming, too." Liv only glanced at the closed door of the meeting room, then she ran after Ted.

For a man who must be well into his sixties, Ted could

run. He was already in his SUV and firing up the ignition when Liv, the trained runner, got to the parking lot.

Ted reversed out of the parking space and sped forward, slowing down just enough for Liv to jump into the passenger seat. As they turned the corner out of the parking lot, they heard sirens converging across the green.

It seemed to take forever to make the three-quarter round of the square. It was a balmy night, and people were out. A crowd had gathered across the street from McCready's, which was rarely a scene of trouble. And never on a Tuesday night.

A police cruiser blocked that section of the street. Ted merely stopped the SUV in the middle of the street and got out. Liv followed without questioning. Meese and several other officers were keeping the crowd at—hopefully—a safe distance across the street.

He saw Ted and Liv, and frowned, but Ted just nodded and practically shoved Liv past the police line. Meese made no attempt to stop them.

Halfway across the street, Ted seemed to realize that he'd brought Liv with him. "You'd better stay back with Meese," he yelled over sirens and the ruckus coming from McCready's as the door opened and a body was tossed out to the sidewalk.

"No way," Liv yelled back. "You've brought me this far. But what are you planning to do?"

"I'm not sure. But this is what you're going to do." He handed her his keys. "Go back to the SUV and drive it around the back to the alley behind McCready's. Wait for me. If I don't show, I'll text you and tell you what to do."

Liv took the keys and, without asking for more explanation, ran for the car. Once there, she backed the SUV to the corner, made a two-point turn, and drove around the block to get as close to the pub as she could.

She left the engine running, like her adrenaline. She had no idea what was so urgent. Chaz obviously was part of the brawl. It only surprised her that he'd bothered to get involved.

There'd been a night when he'd watched her apply a few moves she'd learned in her martial arts class to a couple of jerks while he stood in the doorway and watched.

And what was with her mild-mannered assistant? Ted rarely showed any sign of excitement or any extreme emotion. He was the calmest person she knew. But tonight he was moving at warp speed and was totally focused. She'd only seen that energy once before, and it had not boded well for the man who had been its object.

She let out a squeak a few minutes later when the back door opened and a body fell into the backseat. Ted slammed the door and ran around to the driver's side. He opened the door, and shouted "Move over!" as he climbed in, which Liv did with alacrity.

The SUV jerked into reverse, wheels screeching, and they backed all the way down the street, where they turned east and left the scene behind.

Chaz was slumped in the backseat, looking even worse than the last time she'd seen him. "Did we just break the law?" Liv asked Ted as they sped away.

He looked over at her and grinned. "Just a little bit."

The SUV slowed and they continued at a sedate pace to the *Clarion* office. Ted glanced over his shoulder and seemed to vacillate on what to do next.

"On second thought, do you have a first-aid kit at your place?" he asked Liv.

"I have first-aid supplies."

"Mind if we . . . ?" He nodded toward the backseat, where Chaz hadn't said a word, had not even whined, moaned, or groaned like he usually did at the slightest inconvenience.

"I guess not." She doubted if they could find first-aid supplies at the *Clarion* office, even if Chaz possessed any, and it seemed that going to Ted's was not an option. "Sure."

Ted made a U-turn in the middle of the street and, swinging several blocks out of the way to avoid the green, he sedately drove the three blocks to the Zimmermans' old Victorian. As soon as he pulled into the driveway, the lights to the Zimmerman sisters' Victorian popped on.

He drove all the way back to Liv's carriage house and got out of the SUV. While Liv unlocked her front door, Ted hauled Chaz's carcass out of the backseat. He smelled like a brewery, and she really wasn't excited about having him stinking up her house, but she was also curious as to why he'd been in a fight and why Ted had felt it necessary to whisk him away as if it was a raid at a gin joint in the twenties, not an altercation at the local pub.

Chaz managed to glare at her through one half-open eye as Ted dragged him past.

"I'll get some ice," Liv said, and hurried to the kitchen while Ted dumped Chaz on her less-than-a-year-old couch. "I'll make coffee, too."

"I'm not drunk," Chaz mumbled. "I'm wearing this booze."

"You may not need it, but we do."

She headed for the kitchen and put on a pot of coffee. *First things first.* Filled a plastic bag with ice cubes, gathered several clean dish towels, then detoured to the bathroom for first-aid supplies.

She didn't want to think about whether Chaz was really hurt or not. She soaked a washcloth in cold water and grabbed another towel and returned to the living room. Chaz was propped up in a seated position. Ted was standing over him, fists on his hips and looking like thunder.

"What the hell were you thinking?" He saw Liv and clamped down on what he was going to say next. But Liv had already heard him all the way in her bedroom. He was pretty angry at Chaz. But she didn't really understand why.

Chaz tried to get up but Ted pushed him, none too gently, back onto the couch. Liv put her supplies down on the coffee table and took a good look. Chaz's T-shirt was torn, blood had left a trail of splatters down the front. His lip was split, his eye was swollen and already turning black.

It turned her stomach, but she just said, "Lose any teeth, tough guy?"

"Too early to tell," he mumbled, or at least that's what she thought he said; his lip made everything come out without consonants.

Liv looked at Ted, realized he wasn't about to apply first aid, so she took the bag of ice, folded it into a towel, and placed it as gently as she could on Chaz's face. "Hold this," she ordered, and reached for the wet cloth.

She was dabbing at his mouth and was beginning to worry, since he wasn't whining or complaining like he usually did but was just sitting there like a lump, when there was a knock at the door.

"I'll get it," Ted said, and strode away.

Liv lifted her eyebrows at Chaz. He gave her a one-shoulder shrug. Maybe it hurt too much to raise both of them.

"Hope we're not intruding," said Ida as she and Edna bustled into the room.

"Heard it on the scanner," Edna explained. "When we saw Ted's SUV outside, we figured out what was going on."

Considering she had been the one to call her, Liv guessed that was an understatement.

Ida began taking things out of a basket she'd carried in: a plate of sandwiches, a plastic container of what looked like lemonade, a bottle of spring water, and a real first-aid kit with a red cross on the metal top.

Edna eased Liv out of the way and peered down at Chaz, shaking her head. "You are in trouble, young man." She took the cloth from Liv and made short work of cleaning the cut.

"I imagine the sheriff will be here shortly," Ida said. "We didn't snitch. But Bill is no dummy. Something you would do well to remember," she said, casting a disapproving look at Chaz.

"There seems to be some question as to the whereabouts of a certain participant," Miss Edna said. "And you . . ." She reached out and lifted Ted's right hand for inspection. "Really Ted, you should know better."

The knuckles were grazed. Liv stared at him open-mouthed. Ted had joined the brawl?

"Sometimes a man has to do what a man has to do." He turned on Chaz. "Especially when one of his friends is acting like . . . I can't even say it. There are ladies present.

"So, before Bill gets here, would you like to tell us why you got suckered into that? You're usually smarter."

They all stopped at the sound of another car pulling up outside. Chaz moved as if he might try to escape. Ted pushed him back to the couch.

"Stupid. Keep your mouth shut."

Liv blinked. Edna and Ida looked shocked.

Liv went to answer the door.

Bill was alone, but he wasn't happy.

He glanced at Ted as he came into the room. "I'll talk to you later." He stopped and looked down at Chaz, shook his head. "Fall down the stairs or step in front of the car?"

Chaz opened his mouth.

"Fell down the stairs," Ted said.

"I took Chalmers and the Weaver brothers and several others down to the station. They'll probably make bail before I get there. But you. You've got to promise me to keep a lid on your temper, or I'm going to lock you up. And that's going to look pretty bad, considering the recent past."

Liv was totally confused. What recent past? Had Chaz been in trouble lately? She didn't think he'd bother to do anything so energetic, unless maybe he'd forgotten to renew his fishing license.

She and the sisters stood like a silent chorus in the background while a drama that at least Liv didn't understand played out in her living room.

"Can you agree to that? No matter the provocation?"

"Sure. Can I go home now?"

"You better watch yourself or they're going to drag your sorry—you back to LA."

"Okay, fine. I'll behave. Can I go now?"

"Are you okay?"

Chaz nodded slightly.

"I'll drive you home."

Chaz pushed himself off the couch and pitched forward. He would have landed on the coffee table if Ted and Bill hadn't grabbed for him and lowered him back to the couch.

"He might have a concussion," Miss Ida said. "We'll take him home with us."

Bill looked skeptical; Ted, amused. The two men exchanged looks.

"Excellent idea," Bill said with what Liv thought was unholy glee.

"Thanks, but I can take care of—"

"Or you can recover in a jail cell."

Chaz started to get up again.

Liv pushed him back down. "Oh no you don't. Everyone is staying right here until you tell me what that was all about."

Bill didn't look happy but he didn't contradict her. "Well, since I have to question Ted anyway . . ."

"And Liv," Chaz said from behind the ice pack, which was beginning to drip.

"Me?" said Liv.

"Liv?" Bill asked.

Chaz grinned, or at least he tried to. His lip was too swollen to move, but Liv could see the grin in his eyes— eye—the one that wasn't swollen shut.

"She drove the getaway car."

Chapter Twenty

....

Bill groaned. "I wondered how you ended up here."

"I think you should arrest her." Chaz moved the ice pack from his eye to his lip.

"Oh, be quiet."

Bill looked to the ceiling, then at Edna and Ida, who had begun to fuss over Chaz.

"We'll stay," said Miss Ida, and sat down beside Chaz.

"Good idea, Ida." Miss Edna sat in the only other chair in the room.

Liv and Ted went to get coffee, mugs, and chairs from the kitchen.

Ida poured coffee while Edna passed around the sandwich plate. She didn't offer one to Chaz. Liv didn't think he could open his mouth wide enough to bite, much less chew.

Bill lowered himself to a straight-backed chair.

"Bill Gunnison," Miss Ida said at her strictest, "you should be taking something for that back."

"I will when I get home. And I'd be home if some people didn't start brawls in McCready's Pub."

Both sisters looked shocked and turned their disapproval on Chaz.

"It wasn't my fault," Chaz mumbled.

"What happened?" Liv demanded, no longer able to hold on to her impatience.

"I was in McCready's," Chaz said. "Minding my own business. Then the Weavers and that—and Cliff Chalmers came in. They started talking smack about the murder and Leo. They said he was staying at the rectory and they'd really scared the"—his one good eye roved around the room, pausing on each sister and giving Liv the creeps—"scared the expletive deleted out of him. They laughed and said they were going to do it again and did anybody want to go with them." He moved the ice pack back to his eye.

Liv shook out two ibuprofen from the bottle in her medicine cabinet and handed them to him. Handed two more to Bill, who swallowed them with a gulp of coffee.

Chaz did the same, only half the coffee dribbled back out of his mouth.

"Damn." He held up his hand. "Sorry, sorry." This was directed at the sisters, who were not at all fazed by his use of the word. Liv was sure they'd heard worse, but they had that effect on people. She'd seen them shut up grown men with a look or a word. Chaz should have sent them to McCready's. They would have made short work of the Weaver brothers.

"And?" Bill prodded.

"So I told them to cut the—to stop. Cliff said something I can't repeat, and I punched him. That's all."

"All? McCready's is a war zone. Tables and chairs overturned, glasses broken. Mike is fit to be tied. And who can blame him?"

"I'll pay for it. It was worth it."

"Was it? This breaks your bail agreement."

"Bail?" Liv blurted out in surprise.

"Bail?" gasped the sisters.

This time Chaz finally groaned.

Bill glared at him. "This yo-yo got himself arrested in LA for taking the law into his own hands like some latter-day Wyatt Earp."

Chaz leaned back on the couch and shut his eyes.

"Fortunately they caught him before he did any damage. He got off easy, considering."

"I just did what they wished they could do but couldn't."

"They fined him and sent him back here to cool his heels." Bill switched his attention to Chaz. "And stay out of trouble."

Liv slapped her forehead. "That's why you were holed up in your house. And I badgered you into helping me. Why didn't you just tell me?"

Chaz opened one eye. "That's what you think? You should know me better."

She did know him better. He wouldn't turn a blind eye while a friend was in trouble, for all his couldn't-care-less attitude. And she liked him better for it.

"Sometimes a man has to stand up for what he believes," Ida said.

"Thank you, Miss Ida." He moved the ice pack, and water poured down his shirt.

Exasperated, Liv took it away and carried it to the kitchen.

When she returned with a new bag of ice, everyone was talking at once. It sounded like a party.

"I think," Liv said, coming back into the room and shoving the ice pack at Chaz, "what we need is a strategy session."

"Liv," Bill began.

"You let her talk, Bill Gunnison," Miss Edna said. "She can go places and ask questions that you can't."

"Miss Edna, there's a killer out there."

"We're well aware of that."

"And my job is not only to catch that killer but to keep my community safe while I'm doing it."

"We know, Bill." Miss Ida reached over and patted his knee. "And you're doing a good job. So what do you know that you haven't told us?" She smiled sweetly at him. Turned to Liv. "Get out your lesson plan, dear."

Liv blushed. She'd kept the sisters' idea of a lesson plan for murder to herself.

"What's this lesson plan?" Bill asked suspiciously.

"Well," Liv said, once she realized no one else was going to explain, "it's like a spreadsheet. You know, just keeping abreast of what's happened and how and when, so we can better prepare for the next event, point to where we need to tighten security, fill in holes. Things like that. And—"

Ted made a minute shake of his head.

TMI—a telltale admission of prevarication.

"It's her lesson plan for solving a murder," Edna said. "You show him, Liv. He might learn a thing or two."

Reluctantly, Liv got her laptop and handed it over to Bill.

"It was our idea," Miss Ida said with a satisfied sigh.

Bill glanced at the screen. Pulled it closer. Liv watched his expression change as his eyes moved from column to column and back again.

He handed it back to Liv. "You have one of these for every incident we've had?"

Liv shrugged. "They affected the Events Office."

Miss Ida and Edna smiled proudly.

"Education at work," Miss Edna said.

Bill looked skeptical. "This is all speculation, you know."

"Of course she knows that, but what do you know?" Edna took the laptop from him and handed it back to Liv. "Go ahead, dear."

Liv settled the laptop on her lap and poised her fingers over the keyboard.

"Nothing more than you already know," Bill began. "Just what Leo, Ted, and Liv told us. Leo's prints are on the musket. No secret there. No other clues. Not a scrap of fabric or a fingerprint that doesn't belong. Whoever killed Rundle must have planned it in advance."

"Wore gloves," Miss Edna said.

"Dressed like the ghost so he wouldn't be recognized," Miss Ida added.

"Was familiar with the layout of Gallantine House," Liv said.

"Which," Ted said. "Would be just about any man and quite a few of the women who were kids here. After old man Gallantine died, the house sat empty for years. The roof was a popular hangout. Every kid with any imagination found the gate and the entrance to the tower. Then, when Henry came back, he let the tradition continue. There wasn't anything to vandalize. Some graffiti that the rain eventually washed off. Bill and I hung out up there."

Chaz raised a finger.

"Chaz did, too," Liv interpreted. "Among other things." Miss Edna and Miss Ida pursed their lips.

Chaz hung his head, though Liv suspected it was so they wouldn't see his reminiscent smile.

"But it could also be someone not from town, but who had visited," Liv said.

"The nephew," Ted said, suddenly taking an interest in the conversation.

"Who I saw helping himself to a figurine, and who was seen carrying a suitcase out of the boathouse."

Chaz made an indeterminate noise.

Liz glanced over, but it was impossible to tell what he was trying to say. His face was contorted, but it was so swollen, not to mention also turning black and blue, that it was even harder to read.

"We don't even know that something has happened to Henry," Bill said. "Or that Frank's even a suspect, though . . ." He glanced at Liv. "You do make an interesting supposition."

Chaz groaned.

"Put that ice pack back on your face," Miss Ida said. "And let this be a lesson to you about fighting in bars."

"And George Grossman conveniently shows up saying that he's authorized to buy the Gallantine mansion," Ted added.

"I don't believe Henry would sell his house. Piddle," Miss Ida said.

"Who is zhee?" Chaz slurred.

"The guy from the historical housing conservancy," Liv said once she had interpreted his question. "He said Henry had agreed to sell the house to him. He must have showed him around the house."

"Henry loves that house. Why would he do that?" Edna asked.

No one knew.

"Actually, how do we know Grossman's telling the truth?" Liv asked. "We just have his word for it."

"The woman has a devious mind," Chaz mumbled.

"And," Bill added, "Daniel Haynes—who is Henry's lawyer and who, according to Grossman, had brokered the deal—denies knowing anything about it. Though you'll be glad to know, Liv, he has put a stay on Grossman's letter of authorization until Henry's whereabouts are known."

"That's great," Liv said. "I hope it applies to the nephew, too. Not only is he robbing the house, we just learned today that Jacob Rundle had been selling what we think are stolen goods."

"Where the heck did you learn this?" Bill asked.

"Got a tip," Liv said.

"At lunch," Ted volunteered.

"Huh," said Bill. "We caught the nephew red-handed, thanks to Liv, though don't make a habit of spying on suspects."

"I—"

"Don't bother to deny it. Funny that he should show up

two days after his uncle disappears and Rundle is killed," Ted said.

"Seems funny to me, too," Bill agreed. "Said he came for the fireworks and to pick up some things his uncle had given him—the goods."

"What about him meeting with Grossman?" Liv asked as she typed. "Did he say anything you can tell us?"

"Said that he'd caught him trespassing, there was something that wasn't right about Grossman, and we should look into it."

"The nerve of the guy," Ted said. "Catches a trespasser while he's stealing from the house himself. Did you look into it?"

"I've got somebody on it."

"Seems like a lot of sudden interest in Gallantine House," Miss Edna said.

"Especially since that sister and her son never gave Henry the time of day until now they think he might be dead," Ida said. "Let him visit a few weeks each summer and ignored him the rest of the year. And after all he did for them."

"What did he do for them?" Liv asked.

"Just sent money to her and to his father the whole time he was working in the movies. Even after his mother went a little around the bend."

"I didn't know that," Bill said.

"We used to see Hildy Ingersoll at the interfaith get-togethers and she was on the Toys for Tykes Committee, the Shut-In Visitation Committee, and a few others. She used to visit the old Gallantine housekeeper before she died. She told Hildy that the checks came to old Mr. Gallantine regular as clockwork." Edna sighed.

"That was before Hildy lost her husband." Ida said. "After that she just lost her zest for life. Never got it back." She shook her head and for a second seemed far away.

Thinking about her own loss? Liv wondered.

"She just turned bitter. Didn't come to the meetings anymore, didn't see her friends. Just dropped out of everything but working for Henry Gallantine." Ida *tsk*ed. "We should give her a call, Edna. Be better friends."

Edna nodded solemnly.

Liv looked over to Chaz to see if he was at all interested in what they were saying, but his eyes were closed again. "But why kill the gardener? Do you think they were really after Henry himself?"

"Good question," said Miss Edna.

Ida patted her chest. "How do we know that the culprit didn't kill Henry, too?"

"True," Edna said. "No one has heard from him, have they?"

Bill reluctantly shook his head. "But we're looking."

Liv wondered how many times he'd had to say that since Friday night.

"Is he a suspect?" Edna asked.

"Just a person of interest at this point."

"No leads?" Liv asked.

"Not yet." He pushed to his feet and almost straightened up. "And now I have things to do."

"Bill Gunnison," Miss Ida scolded. "It's the middle of the night."

"Crime waits for no man," Bill said with resignation. "Come, ladies. Chaz and I will walk you home."

"I'll walk them home," Ted said. "I haven't had the pleasure of a late-night stroll with two such lovely ladies in the longest time."

"And we haven't had two young men fighting over us in a dog's age," Edna said wryly.

"But it is nice," Ida said.

Ted offered his arm to both ladies, and they said good night. "You go on, Bill. I'll come back for Chaz when I'm done. I'll take him home. You couldn't get him off the couch much less up his stairs with your back."

Liv wasn't sure Ted could, either. But she'd go with them

and help if she had to, because she had no intention of letting Chaz bed down on her couch.

Bill looked toward Chaz. "You sure?"

"Yes, I'll see that he gets home. But, Bill, what are you going to do about Leo's safety?"

"I have a squad car posted outside for tonight, but I think I should put Leo in protective custody. Reverend Schorr can't keep him. With the mood of some of the people in town, it wouldn't be safe for either of them."

"What does protective custody mean exactly?" Liv asked. "Jail?"

"I hope not. Leo is eighteen; I'll try to find a safe house through social services. Just until we close this case."

"And if you don't?"

"I have to." He glanced toward Chaz again. "Keep him out of trouble if you can."

"We'll try." Liv walked Bill to the door, then out into the summer air. "Can you tell me what Chaz did to get himself arrested?"

"Threatened a suspect in a murder trial in LA."

"The banker?"

Bill nodded. "Chaz is convinced the man arranged to have his own wife kidnapped, paid the ransom, then killed her. There wasn't conclusive evidence, even though Chaz, as well as the police, followed the case for several years. The prosecutor didn't prove it."

"So he took things into his own hands," she said. "What would he have done if they hadn't stopped him?"

Bill shrugged. "Hopefully his good sense would have prevailed. It's not something I want to think about. He's very lucky. Like he said, he'd just done what most of the law enforcement involved in the case wished they could do. Some cases just work out that way."

Liv shivered in the cool night air. "Do you think this case might be one of them?"

"I sure as heck hope not."

"Bill?"

Bill stopped at the door. "Yes?"

"Janine isn't right, is she? That murders never happened here before the festivals got so big."

"Of course not. We've always had murders and manslaughters, they just didn't get much attention. We didn't have so many tourists or the publicity we get now. So don't even think it's the Events Office's fault. We had them. Same as any town."

"So you think our security program is good enough?"

"Yep. You just keep doing what you're doing. Now, get some sleep."

Feeling slightly uneasy, she closed the door behind him. Was he just reassuring her? Or was he giving her free rein to investigate?

She went back to the living room to clear away the dishes and wait for Ted to come retrieve the sleeping newspaper editor.

"You need to make sure they explain to Leo what's happening."

Liv screeched and almost dropped the coffeepot.

"I thought you were passed out."

"I wish." Chaz straightened up. "You can't just shuffle Leo around like he's a piece of furniture. He'll get confused." Amazing how he suddenly could make himself understood.

"Maybe you should have told Bill that while he was here."

"He wouldn't listen to me right now. He'll listen to you."

"I understand your point, but you can't expect Pastor Schorr to fend off that bunch of hooligans. I think the church probably frowns on their preachers getting in fistfights."

"Not the Weavers. The killer."

"But Leo didn't recognize him. He thought he was the ghost."

"But the killer doesn't know that."

"He might come after Leo, just in case?"

"I would." He winced. His words were getting sluggish

again. The cut in his lip had reopened. She should probably get more ice, but she wanted to question him while she could still understand what he was saying.

"But where will he be safe if they don't put him in custody?"

"Somewhere."

"I realize you're not at your best right now. But can you be more specific?"

Chaz closed his eyes. "Not at the moment."

When Ted returned from the Zimmermans' and he and Liv had poured Chaz into the front seat of Ted's SUV, Liv went back inside and straight to bed. Pulled the covers up, and relaxed for the first time in days.

She closed her eyes, but her brain wouldn't shut off. She'd forgotten to tell Bill about Pandora's box. It might have some bearing on the murder. Leo said they'd suddenly stopped looking for the treasure. Pandora's box, Henry had told him.

Something that would cause trouble if it were opened. Gold? Greed was a popular motive. Or some kind of document, the other possibility. But if it were a document and proved Old Gallantine's innocence, why would he have called it Pandora's box?

But if it had proven his guilt? It wouldn't change anything. Centuries had passed. Did anybody really care?

Stupid question. In Celebration Bay? They could argue over anything. But Liv couldn't see them turning against Henry Gallantine because his ancestor had sold out a troop of patriots. They'd either ignore it and carry on as before, or merely change the presentation to include his perfidy, and have a great time doing it.

Ted had told her that at one time they'd reenacted his hanging, but had gotten so many complaints from parents of frightened children that they had stopped after the first portrayal.

Maybe Henry would feel a little embarrassed, but would people really hold it against him in everyday life?

Of course, some might. Every town had a few.

And she noted with another yawn, she'd just inferred herself into a mental corner.

Why was the gardener dead?

Unless . . .

Just as she fell asleep her cell phone rang.

Chapter Twenty-one

....

At first she considered letting it ring. It was after one o'clock. Then good sense reared its ugly head. Late-night, or in this case early-morning, calls were either wrong numbers or emergencies.

Please let it be a wrong number. She reached for her phone. It was a local number, but one that she didn't recognize.

"Hello?"

"Ms. Montgomery?"

"Yes. Who is this?"

"You said to call no matter what the time."

"Hildy?"

"Yes, you need to get over here right away."

Liv sat up. "What's happened?"

"I can't tell you. Please come."

"Hildy, are you in danger? You should call nine-one-one."

"No, not now. If you won't come . . . I shouldn't have bothered you. But don't you dare call the police."

"Wait. I'll come. Five minutes."

It was closer to seven minutes by the time Liv dressed, got the car out of the garage, and drove across town. She deliberated about calling Bill. But she didn't think Hildy had lured her out in the middle of the night for some nefarious purpose and would be waiting with a kitchen knife.

The woman sounded frightened and distraught. Not in danger now. Hopefully that meant the danger was over. And hopefully not because Hildy had used the kitchen knife on whatever or whoever the danger was.

She pulled up to the front of Gallantine House in darkness. No porch light. No lights from any of the windows she could see from the street. And Liv was sorry that Whiskey was still at the rectory and she would be doing this solo.

She pressed Redial.

Hildy answered immediately. "What?"

"I'm outside. Why is the house dark?"

"Just is. I see you. Turn off your car lights. I'm coming to the front door now."

Liv turned off her car lights. Put her keys in her hoodie pocket, just in case she needed to make a quick getaway. Checked her other pocket for her small canister of Mace. And hurried up the brick walk.

As soon as she reached the porch, the front door opened and Hildy motioned her inside with a frantic wave of her hand. And practically fell against the door as soon as Liv was through.

Hildy, dressed in an old full-length bathrobe, her hair in pin curls tied up in a nylon scarf, scowled at her.

"What is it, Hildy?"

"He ain't dead." Hildy lumbered past her toward the parlor. Liv followed; she didn't have much choice at this point.

Two table lamps were all the light in the room. The curtains were pulled across the windows, preventing the light being seen from the street.

A man was kneeling by the fireplace; another sat on the

floor, head between his knees and a white towel pressed to the back of his head. It seemed to be a night for ice packs.

They were both barely silhouetted by the two lamps.

"She's here," Hildy announced from behind Liv in a voice that made Liv jump.

The kneeling man rose. She recognized him immediately, though the light exaggerated the planes and valleys of his face. He looked older than the last time she'd seen him. Medium height, hair graying at the temples, a Hollywood face—lined with age and worry? An aging matinee idol, dressed in pajamas and a silk bathrobe.

"Mr. Gallantine," Liv said. "We've wondered where you were."

"So I've been told. Hildy, please see to Mr. Grossman."

"Grossman? What's he—? Have you called the EMTs?"

"No. No one, including Mr. Grossman, wants that." Henry walked over to an old-fashioned drinks cart. "Would you care for a sherry or a brandy?"

Liv nearly laughed out loud. Had she stepped into an old movie? A locked-room mystery? "No, thank you. But go ahead."

She even sounded like she was reading a script. She pulled herself together.

Grossman was struggling to get up off the floor. Hildy leaned over and hauled him to his feet.

He stumbled and grabbed a side table for support, jostling a wooden box that sat open on top of it. *Just like a miniature treasure chest from a pirate map.*

Hildy grabbed his arm, maneuvered him past the table, and dumped him onto a wing chair with the admonition not to bleed on the upholstery.

And that's when Liv saw the rectangular opening in the wall where a section of wainscoting had been. A secret hiding place. Pirate chest or Leo's Pandora's box, it was just large enough to house the chest that was now sitting open on the table.

Could this really be the reason someone, possibly one of the three people in this room, had killed Jacob Rundle? If an evil twin had jumped down from the rafters, she wouldn't even have been surprised.

Liv hoped she wasn't about to be in really deep trouble.

Henry Gallantine poured out two brandies and carried one to the museum curator.

"Would anyone like to tell me what happened here?" Liv asked. "And why Hildy called me and not Bill Gunnison?"

Hildy scowled at her, then at Henry. "Go on and tell her before they come knocking down the door. You know they will. Nothing stays quiet in this town."

Henry sighed. Gestured for Liv to sit down on the over-stuffed couch.

"Hildy told me about Jacob Rundle," he began in a soft, mellow baritone. "I had no idea he was dead. Though I'm afraid it is all my fault."

Liv stiffened. Was he about to confess?

"As you know, I always give the signal for the Battle of the Bay to begin." Henry grimaced.

"Only, this year, something came up, and I wasn't able to be here. Since I—well, to tell the truth, it's a delicate matter, and I didn't want to make my absence public knowledge. . . ."

What in this day and age could be a delicate matter? Prostate problems? Even the general had to abandon his post for an emergency pee. A disgruntled lover? Something financial? A little nip and tuck? Or merely an alibi for the time when a murder was committed?

Henry stared into his brandy, seemingly lost in thought.

At this rate Liv would have to go straight to work from here. Though she took his sense of timelessness as a good sign that he wasn't about to murder them all.

Grossman looked out from under his makeshift bandage.

"And what are you doing here?" Liv asked.

He made a movement that Liv supposed he meant as a shrug.

"Not good enough, Mr. Grossman. Daniel Haynes forbade you to be on the property until Mr. Gallantine's return." She switched her attention to Henry. "Did you give him permission to be here?"

"Not I."

From across the room, Hildy shook her head.

"So he was trespassing?"

Hildy nodded. "And not just trespassing, but breaking and entering."

"I didn't break and enter—" Grossman's sentence broke off in a moan.

"Breaking and entering," Hildy repeated.

"No. The door was unlocked."

Hildy's mouth opened in outrage. "Not by me."

"Now, Hildy," Henry began.

"Don't 'Now, Hildy' me. He broke in."

Sensing an impasse, Liv jumped in with another question. "Did you hit him over the head?"

Hildy turned her outrage on Liv. "I did not, but if I'd known he was in here snooping around, I'd have got my shotgun after him."

"My protectress," Henry said with a wry smile.

"Well, somebody's gotta look after you."

"And I appreciate it, Hildy. I too would like to know why you are here, George."

Grossman took a sip of his brandy. "You know why."

"I understand your impatience with the sale in abeyance, but really, was it necessary to search my house in the middle of the night?"

"Yes, if you must know. And if you hadn't hit me over the head, I would have had my proof and been out of here with no one the wiser."

"Your proof?"

Grossman clamped his lips together.

"You mean it wasn't about cataloguing the contents but about finding proof? Proof of what?" Henry put his snifter down. "You were not really interested in the purchase of Gallantine House?"

"Of course I was—am—the research is just a personal hobby of mine."

"Well, I might as well tell you. The house is no longer for sale."

"What? We had a handshake deal."

"Yes, well, circumstances have changed, and I no longer intend to sell."

"Onyx will not be pleased with this."

"I'm sorry you went to all this trouble, but there it is. You can take it up with my attorney when you're feeling better."

Henry sat there with his brandy at his elbow, his legs crossed at the knee, looking comfortable, charming, and so at ease.

His movements and demeanor were so polished and inappropriate to the situation that Liv had to fight the urge to yell, "Take two!"

The sophisticated landlord, the bumbling thief, Mrs. Danvers in pin curls just itching to pick up her shotgun. All they needed was a thunderstorm and the real murderer breaking in with a pistol in his hand.

That image was a little too real for Liv and she pulled her exhausted mind back to the problem at hand.

"So you broke in here to steal the chest that's on the table?" She'd tried for serious but ended up sounding like the clueless detective in the same movie.

Grossman remained stubbornly silent.

Exasperated, Liv blurted, "Will someone tell me what's going on? A man has been murdered. Someone masquerading as the ghost is tormenting Leo. Grossman here broke into the house. Did you hit him over the head?"

"Certainly not," Henry said. "I heard a noise down here

and came to see who it was. I found him sprawled on the floor. And the safe empty."

The safe wasn't very safe as it turned out.

"So if neither Hildy nor you hit him, who did?"

"I haven't the foggiest," Henry said.

"Whoever it was, he got away with whatever you had in that chest."

Henry chuckled.

Liv's patience began to fray. She was tired, body and mind, and she was sitting here with three potential murderers who were carrying on like they were acting in a comedy of manners.

"See what I mean?" Hildy strode across the room and stood next to Liv. "I told him the police would be looking for him. They were asking all sorts of questions. They think you killed Jacob and if you don't stop playacting, they're going to arrest you."

For a second Henry's urbane façade slipped. "I didn't kill Jacob. I—I was called out of town."

Hildy fisted her hands on her hips. "That don't cut it. When did you go, and can you prove it?"

Henry looked at the tips of his bedroom slippers.

"Well?"

"Out of town."

"Where out of town?"

Henry's head hung even lower. He mumbled something.

"Where?"

"Los Angeles."

"Los Angeles? What kind of business would you have there?"

Liv sat back. Hildy was a better interrogator than a housekeeper. She'd missed her calling.

But Henry turned recalcitrant. The body language of a trained actor. Arms crossed, lips tight. He didn't want to tell. And why would that be?

Something to do with business or "the business"? He

hadn't been in the movie business in decades. Was he planning a comeback after all this time?

"Mr. Gallantine."

"Call me Henry, please." Followed by his charming, sophisticated smile.

"Henry. This is serious. A man has been murdered. Leo Morgan is being hounded by someone dressed up as the ghost. Some people are even blaming him for Rundle's murder. Everyone here needs to start telling the truth."

"Hildy told me about Leo wanting to ask the ghost for the treasure." He smiled. "A very altruistic thing to do, no matter what Hildy says."

"Plain stupid thing to do, filling that boy's head with stories, and look where it led."

"Yes, well, perhaps you're right about that," Henry said, looking properly chastised, as a small boy might. Or an actor.

Was he playing them all? Had he really murdered Rundle and then left town for LA? It should be an easy thing to check.

"You really need to explain this to the sheriff. The sooner he can check out your whereabouts, the sooner you can be eliminated from the person-of-interest list."

Henry chuckled. "I noticed that you managed not to say 'suspects.'"

Liv caught Hildy's eye.

"See what I have to deal with?" the housekeeper said.

"Do you think I could have some aspirin?" Grossman, looking very pale, mumbled from the wing chair.

"Lord spare me." Hildy stomped away to get it.

"I think I must confess," Henry said. "I wouldn't have Leo hurt for the world. He's my best bud." He smiled sheepishly. "The only person who takes the same delight in . . ." His face fell, and for a minute he looked like a tired middle-aged man. "On reliving my life. I wouldn't jeopardize his well-being for the world. Yes, I think it's time to call the sheriff."

"No." Grossman put up a hand.

Henry looked from him to Liv.

Liv handed him her cell phone. She felt a little qualm about waking Bill in the middle of the night, but she didn't see that she had much of a choice.

Henry took it, held it. "What are we going to do about him?" He flicked his eyes toward Grossman, who had once again buried his head in his hands.

"Let Bill handle it. He did break in, right?"

"No, I didn't. The door was unlocked."

Liv looked at Henry for confirmation.

Henry nodded. "Hildy isn't the most fastidious of house-keepers, but her husband, Albert, was a gem. Gardener, landscaper, could fix anything with an engine." He glanced toward the door. "I couldn't not take care of her."

"So Rundle wasn't always your gardener?"

"Heavens, no. He was the handyman. And not a very good one. I let him live over the garage because he was such a stock character that I thought he would be entertaining. That was a big mistake. By the time I realized that, I couldn't figure a way to gracefully get rid of him." He stopped. Looked startled. "That didn't come out quite the way I meant it."

"I'm relieved," Liv said.

Hildy returned with a bottle of aspirin and a glass of water, which she begrudgingly shoved at Grossman.

"I suppose Gunnison will have to check my alibi?" Henry asked.

Liv nodded.

He hesitated then, looked at the phone, and Liv was afraid he was going to hand it back to her.

"He's number six on speed dial."

"I'm a little old fashioned. You'll have to do it for me."

Liv took the phone, pressed six, and handed it back to him.

"That's it?" he asked.

Liv nodded.

"Hmm." Silence while they all waited. "Bill? Henry Gallantine here."

The conversation was brief. Henry handed Liv her phone. "He's coming over."

"I hope you know what you're doing," Hildy said. "And what are we going to do about that one?" She shot a thumb over her shoulder, not deigning to look directly at George Grossman.

Grossman leaned forward as if he thought he might actually get away before Bill arrived.

"Sit," Liv ordered.

He sat, though Liv had a feeling that it was not because of her voice of authority, but because he was too dizzy to stay on his feet.

They all sat except for Hildy, who had taken a sudden urge to start dusting.

"Hildy, I think the sheriff will want to see the scene as it is right now," Henry said.

"Then I'll be in the kitchen until he gets here." Hildy marched off.

Henry sighed. "I've offended her. Very temperamental. But she's a fixture." He sighed. "Just like me."

After that no one spoke.

It was a long twenty minutes before the doorbell rang and Hildy showed Bill Gunnison into the parlor. She'd changed into a housedress and taken the pins from her hair. Bill looked like he'd slept in his uniform.

He took one look at Liv and threw his head back to look at the ceiling, or more likely the heavens, which were probably beginning to lighten by now.

"I won't even ask," he said to no one in particular. He strode over to Henry, who rose effortlessly from his seat.

"Sorry to disturb you at this ungodly hour. I hope my absence hasn't caused the police force too much bother."

"Could you please tell me where you were from Friday last until now?"

Henry gestured for Bill to sit, which he did, next to Liv, saying to her, "I'll talk to you later."

Henry sat. Sighed. "I was called to Los Angeles on business. Since I would have to miss the reenactment, I asked Jacob Rundle to take my place. He knew what to do, and I rehearsed him several times before I left."

Bill pulled a voice recorder off his utility belt and looked a question at Henry, who waved his approval.

Once the recorder was on and Bill had given the date, time, and speaker, Henry continued in a fuller, rounder voice than he'd used before. "As I said, I was called away. I agreed to pay Jacob an extra hundred dollars to give the signal."

Hildy gasped. "As if you don't pay him enough."

"Academic at this point, I'm afraid."

"And you have someone who can verify that you were with them for the time between Friday night and Saturday morning."

"I have plane tickets and hotel receipts, and there are those people with whom I met while I was there. If you must have their names."

"I'll need those names before I leave." Bill turned to Grossman, who was trying to make himself invisible and not succeeding.

"And you are here because?"

"Because—"

"Because he's a burglar and a thief," Hildy said.

"Thank you, Hildy. I'll get to you in a moment."

Hildy *hmmph*ed and stood a little away from the group, a guardian figure of imperious proportions.

"Now, Mr. Grossman, you were saying."

"I had a gentleman's agreement with Mr. Gallantine for the sale of his property. On which he has since reneged."

Bill glanced at Henry, but Henry's mind seemed elsewhere.

"As you know, I came to inventory the property on Monday. Ms. Montgomery was with me and she can attest to the fact that I didn't steal a thing." '

"But you did meet with Henry's nephew," Liv said, then clapped a hand over her mouth.

Bill narrowed his eyes at her but merely turned back to Grossman. "And did you meet this other Gallantine?"

Grossman sputtered. He must not have realized he'd been seen. "Yes, but quite by accident."

"And how did this chance meeting come about?"

"I was . . . I decided to take a walk by the lake, and he was down at the boathouse and we said hello. We'd met up at the house earlier. Then I continued on my walk."

Liv wasn't satisfied with that explanation, but it seemed that Bill was.

"And why are you here tonight?"

"The next day the lawyer, Haynes, I think his name is, told me that I was not allowed in the house. Which was absurd, because it had all been arranged. Which I pointed out. But he said that, since no one knew where Mr. Gallantine was, he would have to rescind permission."

He turned to Henry. "There has been one obstruction after another. I acted in good faith and have been thwarted at every turn."

"My apologies. But you must understand that, without directives from me, Daniel Haynes had no other choice."

"A damned inconvenience."

"You didn't have a chance to rob us on Monday, so you broke in tonight."

"Hildy, please," Bill said.

"I know. I'll be quiet, but get on with it, Bill Gunnison. Some of us have work tomorrow."

Bill took a deep breath. "Did you break into this residence?" He paused to name the address again. "Tonight?"

"No. The door was unlocked. I came in."

"At one o'clock in the middle of the night?"

"Hildy, please."

Hildy glared at Bill, crossed her arms, and began to tap her foot.

Liv was tempted to join her. This was taking forever.

"And why did you do that?"

"I just told you. I couldn't get in during the day."

"Let me rephrase that," Bill said politely. "Would you rather answer these questions down at the station?"

"Okay, okay. Monday, during the inventory, I discovered quite by accident what I thought might be a priest hole. The wood sounded hollow."

And why were you sounding the wood if you were taking inventory? Liv wondered.

"And how did you discover this hollow-sounding panel?" Bill asked.

"I was merely ascertaining whether the wainscoting was covering plaster or some other substance."

Lame excuse, thought Liv.

"And was that part of your inventory?"

"It was part of my inspection, which included the inventory."

"So why didn't you explore it at that time?"

Grossman's eye flitted from Bill to the carpet.

Having a little trouble coming up with a reasonable excuse for breaking in? Liv yawned. After all the excitement, she was beginning to get a little punch-drunk. She really wished Bill would move this along.

"I didn't know at the time that I wouldn't be allowed back in."

"So you decided to take matters into your own hands?"

They were seeing a lot of that tonight. First Chaz, now Grossman. Liv stifled another yawn.

It seemed to be catching. Bill yawned, then Henry. It was ludicrous.

"Mr. Grossman. I suggest you move this along or I will finish questioning at the station."

"All right. I decided to come back here tonight and have a look. I have to return to Schenectady tomorrow—well, today, actually. And I didn't want to leave without seeing what was behind that panel."

"Did you expect to find something?"

Again he deliberated.

"The treasure perhaps?" Henry asked.

"Yes. It's a hobby of mine. The Revolutionary War. I'd heard of the treasure and I was curious."

"Why not just ask?"

"Who? Her?" He cast a caustic look toward Hildy. "And besides, with Mr. Gallantine here out of town, I thought I'd better get to it before it was too late."

"Too late for what?"

"Well, when I was down at the lake, Henry's nephew told me he knew where Henry kept the treasure. Not a treasure in the usual sense but a document or documents, primary sources of that period. He knew where they were kept and offered to get them for me for an exorbitant sum."

Henry shook his head and rested his forehead in his hand. "Stupid young man. Gambling problem. He would hustle his own mother. Probably has. He's certainly helped himself to many of the things in this house."

"What do you mean, 'before it was too late'?"

"Only that he had other people interested in them and he'd hate for them to fall into the wrong hands. I didn't have any idea what he meant by that. And I wasn't about to pay what he asked, so I decided to look for it myself." He shrugged.

"But your plans were thwarted?"

"I had just gotten the box out and on the table when someone hit me from behind. And that's all I remember until I woke up and Henry was standing over me."

"Did you knock him out?"

"Not I."

"And I came in after Mr. G found him," Hildy volunteered.

"So some third party hit you?"

"I suppose."

Slowly they all looked at Liv.

"I didn't even know about it until Hildy called me and asked me to come over."

"We'll get to that later."

Bill's threats were beginning to pile up. Liv guessed she'd be facing the music pretty soon. But, hopefully, after she'd had a few hours of sleep.

"So an unknown assailant?"

"I guess."

"And where are the papers now?"

"I don't know. Before I could open the box, I was knocked out. Whoever it was must have the papers. When I came back to consciousness, the box was empty."

"Was it empty?" Bill asked Henry.

"Most certainly."

"And you're sure you don't have them?"

Grossman spread out his arms. He was wearing a short-sleeve sport shirt.

Across from Liv, Henry Gallantine looked so innocent, she knew he was holding out on them.

Chapter Twenty-two

"Henry, did you or Hildy take any papers or anything else from the box on the table?"

They both shook their heads.

"So whoever hit Mr. Grossman must have taken the papers or whatever else was in the box?"

No one answered.

Finally, Henry leaned forward. "Sheriff, as far as I know, the box was empty to begin with."

Grossman surged out of his chair. "You mean I got hit over the head and questioned by the sheriff over an empty box?"

"I'm afraid so. If only you'd asked, I could have shown you."

"You weren't here."

Henry shrugged. Liv could almost hear him say, *C'est la vie*.

This was all getting too bizarre. Henry definitely knew something he wasn't telling. But questioning so far had not elicited any real information from him.

What was he hiding? Or was he just enjoying the game?

Liv had totally lost patience with the two men. All she

wanted was to go to bed. But what were the chances of getting out of here before Bill grilled her, then yelled at her for interfering?

"Mr. Grossman, where were you last Friday evening between the hours of four o'clock and eight o'clock?"

Grossman nearly levitated out of the wing chair. "Having a light dinner at the inn, and then I came to the reenactment."

"And if I ask at the inn, they will attest to that?"

"Yes. I signed in to my room."

"And after that?"

"Like I said. I went to the reenactment."

"And did anyone you know see you?"

"Sheriff, at that time I didn't know anyone else in town."

Bill stood. And so did Henry Gallantine.

"I'll ask everyone in this room not to leave town without informing me of your intentions. You, Mr. Grossman, can come with me."

Grossman's face flooded with horror. "I thought you said I wouldn't have to go to the station."

"I said you wouldn't have to answer these questions. Breaking and entering is a serious crime. I am holding you until bail can be posted."

"Sheriff, is that really necessary?" Henry asked. "I really don't think I should press charges. I reneged on our agreement, not the gentlemanly thing to do."

"Henry, you don't seem to understand that, until proven differently, you are all persons of interest in the death of Jacob Rundle. This is not a game."

"I didn't kill him," Grossman said.

"Well, Mr. G didn't kill him." Hildy glared at Bill. "And don't you look at me that way, Bill Gunnison. I didn't kill the man."

At that point, Bill seemed inclined to take them all out to the station, but Liv reminded him that would leave the house unguarded and the "unknown assailant" might return to look for whatever they were looking for in the first place.

"Everybody stay put." Bill walked away from the group and spoke into his phone, then came back to where the others waited. "I'm pulling a unit off their patrol and posting them outside. For your safety, Hildy. And to prevent anyone else from breaking into the house. They should be here in a few minutes."

"What about Mr. G?"

"I'm taking Henry and Mr. Grossman back to the station with me to sign their statements. By the time they finish, maybe Henry will call his lawyer to post bail for Grossman here."

"And you, Ms. Montgomery, are going home to bed where you should be now. I'll talk to you later."

"That means I'm free to leave?"

"Don't you start. Just get out of here."

There was a knock at the door. Bill beat Hildy to answer it. Two officers stepped inside.

Bill gave them instructions and herded the two men and Liv into the foyer.

"Hildy, are you sure you'll be okay?" Liv said over her shoulder as Bill nudged her out the door.

"I'm just fine. But you better not let anything happen to Mr. G, Bill Gunnison."

Liv walked beside Bill as he escorted Henry and Grossman to his cruiser. Grossman looking like he might bolt if given the chance. Henry took solemn, measured steps. His head hanging down like an already convicted man.

Beside her, Bill gritted his teeth.

It was all an act. Henry Gallantine was enjoying the attention.

Liv drove home almost too tired to think. A man dead, people disappearing, breaking and entering, looking for treasure. She just didn't get it. Not at all. She yawned as she drove past the *Clarion* building. She didn't mean to even glance that way, really didn't mean to slow down, and really, really didn't mean to stop in front of it when she saw the lights on.

But she was no dummy. Okay, maybe a little bit of a dummy, but there were only three reasons she could think of for the lights being on at—she looked at the car clock—three thirty. Either he forgot to turn out the lights when he went to bed, he had company and they'd never gone to bed, or he was doing research.

Not wanting to butt in if it were either of the first two, but curious to see if it was the third and if it had anything to do with the murder of Jacob Rundle, she sat with the engine running. Turned it off. Sat some more, and finally picked up her cell. It rang four times before he answered.

"What?"

"Is that how you always answer your phone?"

"Only when it's the middle of the night and it's you."

"Thanks. In that case, I'll just go home."

"Aren't you home?"

"No, I'm parked outside your house."

"Aw, am I being stalked?"

"Not by me, anyway. What are you doing?"

"Is this phone sex?"

"Stop it. I've had a long night. And I just wanted to know if maybe on some whim you were doing research on the ghost business."

No answer.

"Or if you are otherwise engaged?"

"Have you been watching Doris Day movies again?"

"Not Doris Day. I've been at Gallantine House."

"Hell."

"Is that a yes or a no?"

"It's a maybe. Why were you there and in the middle of the night?"

"Henry is home. Grossman broke in and someone hit him on the head. Bill has taken them both to jail. And there's still a killer loose."

"I'm opening the door."

Liv hung up and opened the car door. And, just because she was tired and paranoid, she locked the car behind her.

Chaz was waiting at the door when she reached the porch. She couldn't see his face in the early morning light, but he no longer smelled of beer.

He closed the door behind her and led her back to the "office," a pigsty of papers and used coffee cups.

His laptop was open, and there was a Dick Tracy screen saver on his desktop.

She turned around and saw his face.

She grimaced. "Nasty."

"You should experience it from my side. So bring me up to speed."

"The speed at this point is molasses. Unless Bill is investigating a line that we don't know about."

Chaz sat at the desk, rested his fingers on the keyboard, and raised both eyebrows—the only parts of his face that actually worked the way they should—at Liv.

"The police have been searching for Henry's car and his whereabouts. Henry showed up tonight, and his car, I imagine, is in his garage. The museum curator breaks into Henry's house to steal a treasure chest—yes, it's small but it looks just like a movie prop, probably is a movie prop—from behind a secret panel in the wainscoting. But an unknown assailant knocks him over the head but doesn't steal the chest.

"Only the chest is empty. And according to Henry, it was empty before the assailant broke in, after Grossman broke in. Only Henry refuses to press charges. So Bill took them both to the station."

Chaz had been typing, but he stopped and laughed. "It sounds like a zany, madcap comedy."

"Only a man is really dead."

"There is that. Are you sure Henry isn't putting you on? He lives in an alternate universe, stuck somewhere between reality and all those movies he made. Sometimes he has trouble separating the two."

"Or he doesn't want to," Liv said. "He really seems to be enjoying this. You don't think he would kill the gardener and make his escape in one of his delusional moments?"

"He always was the good guy, the underdog. I don't see him killing anybody, even someone like Rundle."

"Nobody liked him, did they?"

"Rundle? What was there to like? He was a drunk, took delight in hurting the weak, and an ex-con. All rolled into one."

"Henry said he was such a good stock character that he kept him on just for entertainment."

"Sounds like Henry."

"So do we even have a motive in this mess?"

"Would it be futile for me to say to leave it to the police?"

"You aren't." She pressed a key on the desktop computer, and Dick Tracy vanished, revealing a primary-source search engine. The computer beside it was opened to a site that Liv thought neither of them had legal access to, and on the laptop were the beginnings of a list Chaz had started before she'd arrived.

"That's because I've fallen off the no-news wagon. I blame you."

"Sorry." Liv pulled up a chair and sat down next to him. "If you'd rather not get involved . . ."

"A little late now."

"I'm sorry. I really am. I don't want you getting in any more fights."

He stopped to look at her for a long moment. An intense, serious look she'd never seen from him, and which he ruined a second later. "Aw, I didn't know you cared."

"Well, actually, I do, a tiny, teensy bit. And I don't want you getting all upset about things."

"Hon, listen to me. My pig. My farm. Just don't get covered in the—mud."

"I won't as long as you don't end up being the bacon."

He broke out in a real laugh. "That's the hottest thing you've ever said to me."

"Right. Show me what you got so far."

He sighed. "I'm guessing that request isn't continuing with this fascinating foray into double entendres, but getting back to work?"

"Work," she said, aware that she might be blushing. Fortunately the light wasn't all that great. Maybe he wouldn't notice.

He reached across her and scrolled up the document on one of the desktops. "The story of the Gallantine trial and exoneration has been around Celebration Bay so long that it's unrecognizable from the actual facts. As much actual fact as was even known in seventeen-something."

He glanced at her. "You do know there wasn't really a Battle of the Bay?"

Liv nodded. She was already reading the document. After a couple of paragraphs, she looked up. "So someone did warn the British of an attack very similar to our battle?"

"Yes, only farther down the lake. And strangely enough, both Daniel Haynes's and Henry Gallantine's ancestors were both in that troop of patriots. Though the horse is a twenty-first century embellishment."

"And no signal from a roof?"

"Nope. Someone tipped off the British to the placement of the American army. The Brits struck at night, two days before the planned attack, and decimated the encampment, taking camp followers with them, including some wives and children."

"Ted said a group of men who were going to draw up a freedom document of some kind were killed."

"Maybe. There was a group bivouacking with the troop that night. I haven't gotten that far."

"Okay, so what do you have?"

"Gallantine came under suspicion because he was a courier between the various generals. One of those generals was a Haynes."

"That's really true, both their ancestors were in the same troop?"

"Not so unusual. Families are still here from the original colonization."

"Wow."

"Now, here's a little tidbit I dug up. Just a footnote in the action."

He typed something into his laptop, and a list of troops came up. There was an asterisk by one of them. Chaz moved the cursor to point to it.

"I don't recognize that name," Liv said. "Is it important?"

"That's the thing about following a lead. You never know until you get there. But in this case . . ." He clicked on a download from what appeared to be a genealogical site. "Here's the same name. Now watch." Another page. A family tree.

"Where do you find this stuff?"

"If I told you—"

"You'd have to kill me. Ted tells me the same thing." She stopped as a sudden thought that had nothing to do with revolutionary wars intruded. "Do you know what Ted did when he lived away from Celebration Bay?"

"Do you think you could stay on one subject at a time?" Liv sighed. "Okay. So, what is it?"

"Hezekiah Jenkins, married to Elisabeth Cummings."

Liv yawned.

"Am I boring you?"

"No. I'm just sleep-deprived. Go on."

"Elisabeth was one of those killed in the melee. She'd come to bring Hezekiah woolen socks. She never got a chance to give them to him."

"Oh, that's sad."

"It gets worse. Hezekiah was also a courier. When old

Gallantine was hung, everyone thought there was an end to it."

"But he was exonerated," Liv said.

"Yes, and this is where history and fiction get twisted together. Some said it was the influence of the Gallantine family, who were very rich, as you can tell by the mansion, and politically savvy enough that they convinced one of the higher-ups of his innocence.

"Yippee hooray for Celebration Bay. But what got lost in the retelling is that a traitor was still out there. They needed to find him, and if that wasn't possible, they needed a scapegoat."

"Go on. I'm getting a nasty feeling."

"Haynes came under suspicion for a while. But the Hayneses were also a prominent family, so that inquiry didn't lead far. But Hezekiah Jenkins, self-made man, owned a small fleet of ships and was heavily in debt. He was hoping to restock his coffers from the war.

"However, before he got too far down that road, the powers that were decided he was the real traitor, stripped him of his property and reputation. He escaped before they could arrest him and headed west, where he eked out a life in the wilds of Pennsylvania. His wife dead, his young son orphaned. The rest of his family was left destitute and shunned by the community."

"And?"

"And guess who's his descendent."

"I'm afraid to."

Chaz scrolled down, circled the cursor around the screen several times. "And where she stops . . . is right here."

Liv leaned forward. Blinked. Blinked again. *George Grossman.* "Holy cow. But do you really think he would hold a grudge for something that happened so long ago?"

"I just follow the lead."

"I wonder if he knows."

"You could ask." Chaz grinned at her.

"All right. It's pretty obvious. He probably came across a mention of the 'treasure' in his research. And came to see if it exonerated Hezekiah."

"At Gallantine's expense."

"But again, why kill the gardener?"

"Unless he thought he was killing Henry."

"That's so crazy. Look at Haynes and Gallantine, they're friends."

Chaz shrugged. "They're both nutcases."

"And killing somebody for something that happened over two centuries ago isn't?"

"It's not any stranger than any other possibility. Anyway, research is an equal-opportunity employer. You can't just wait around for someone to blurt out, 'Ooh, ooh, me. Me. I'm the murderer. Come arrest me.'" He gave her a sideways glance. "Okay, maybe you can. But it's really unscientific, not to mention dangerous.

"Oh, don't look so glum. Your way works, too." He stretched, and Liv was waiting for him to casually drop his arm across the back of her chair, but he didn't, just went back to typing. "All right, I showed you mine, now show me yours." He waited, fingers poised over the keyboard.

"Let's see. Rundle is an ex-con. Or did you tell me that?"

"You are tired. Yes. Grand theft auto."

Liv yawned again. "Well, he'd moved on to smaller things. Watches, stuff like that, some of which he probably lifted from Gallantine House and who knows where else. Hildy said Henry and Rundle had a big fight and Henry told him if he ever caught him in the house again, he'd fire him."

"Are we sure that was about stealing?"

"No. Hildy didn't seem to know, and I didn't want to force her confidence; she's a little prickly."

"That's one way to describe her."

"And the nephew has definitely been helping himself to the family heirlooms, too. Bill picked him up with a suitcase full of loot."

"And you know this how?" Chaz asked. "Bill doesn't usually share."

"He got a tip."

"From you?"

"Yep."

"God, you'll make me gray before my time."

"I'm sure you'll look very distinguished. But it wasn't my fault. The mayor made me go sit with Grossman while he did his inventory. When we came in, the nephew was there. Hildy sent him packing, but not before I saw him lift a figurine off one of the tables and slip it into his jacket pocket."

"And how did this lead to a suitcase full of loot?"

"We-e-ell."

"Liv?"

"At one point, Grossman was staring out the window to the lawn. He might have been daydreaming, but I don't know. He left abruptly after that. I talked to Hildy a bit, and I asked her if she'd make me a cup of tea. So we went back to the kitchen—"

"Wait. You had tea with Hildy Ingersoll?"

"Yes. I thought she might want to talk to someone sympathetic."

"And did she?"

"Yeah, a bit. Anyway, I went to put my empty cup in the sink, and I happened to look out the window, just like Hildy was doing the other day when we were there. Only I'm not nearsighted, and I saw Grossman down by the lake. I decided it wouldn't hurt to just take a look-see."

"Hildy went with you?"

Liv shook her head. "I thought it best not to involve her, so I left the house and went back in the way you'd showed me.

"And I saw Grossman and the nephew meet by the boathouse. Grossman left, and Frank went into the boathouse and came back with a heavy suitcase. I'd seen him lift the figurine earlier that afternoon, ergo . . ."

Chaz started to rub his face with his hands, thought better of it, and shifted the laptop so Liv could see. "Is there more?"

"Not really, but I did take a look around beneath the ledge."

"When will I learn?"

"Anyway," she said, gritting her teeth, "at the reenactment, all the right flank were in full view of the back of the roof and the ledge where we think the ghost escaped. Maybe not full; the leaves are pretty thick this time of year. But Daniel Haynes and his horse were waiting for their cue right beneath it.

"If anyone at all had looked up during that one split second, they could have seen the killer and prevented his escape."

"If wishes were horses."

"Unless it happened when Haynes left to answer a call of nature."

"Are you kidding me? We lost an eyewitness to a nervous bladder?"

"A strong possibility."

"Then what?"

"I called Bill and told him."

"Finally an intelligent move. I gotta make some more coffee."

"Good idea. I need the caffeine. Be sure to wash the pot. Just as a favor to me, please?"

Chaz grumbled but took the coffeepot back to the kitchen. Liv stretched. Stood and leaned over to touch her toes. Her eyes were gritty and her head hurt. Maybe she'd call Ted later and tell him she was sleeping in tomorrow. Or leave a message on the office phone. He'd check it first thing. She sat on the couch, reached into her bag, and made the call. She leaned back on the cushions, closed her eyes, just for a minute while the coffee brewed.

* * *

"Wake up."

Someone was shaking her. "What?" Liv sat up and opened her eyes. Smelled coffee. "That was fast." She sat up. Blinked. Saw the black-and-blue face of Chaz Bristow. And saw something else.

The lamps had been turned off but the room was light. She looked wildly around. Found the window.

No. It couldn't be true. She was on Chaz's couch covered by a light blanket. And it was daylight. "Holy cow!" She pushed the blanket away.

"I was going to let you sleep, but I was afraid that Ted might send out an alert, and I didn't want to have to explain if he asked me why you were going to be late. And I really didn't want to confess that you were here all night and I didn't get lucky." He handed her a cup of coffee.

She took it. Sniffed and tried a sip. "This is terrible."

"That's because it's left from last night."

The coffee sloshed in her cup. "Oh no, and my car's parked outside."

"And just steps away from the rectory. What will people say?" Chaz's mouth quivered. In the morning light it looked even worse than it had the night before. Then his body started vibrating. "Don't make me laugh or my lip will open up again."

"It would serve you right. Why did you let me fall asleep?"

"I couldn't stop you. You were like a little sleeping beauty. Zonked right out without warning."

"Oh, shut up. Did you learn anything more?"

"Nothing earth-shattering." At that he broke into a laugh. "Sorry."

Liv gritted her teeth. "Your lip's bleeding."

"It was worth it to see your face."

"You know it's really juvenile to get in a bar fight. What possessed you?"

"I was sick of listening to them laughing about scaring Leo and making all sorts of accusations just to get everyone riled up."

"So you decided to take the law into your own hands?"

"Why not? It's the only way the law gets done."

"I get that you're pissed at the legal system right now. But did getting in a fight change any of that?"

"No. But, hey . . ."

"You just needed to beat someone up."

"Pretty much."

Liv shed the blanket completely and stood up. Fished under the couch for her shoes.

When she stood up again, Chaz was grinning.

"Now what?"

"Nothing, just thinking."

"Well, don't." She folded the blanket and put it on the couch.

"Do you know you snore?"

"I do not."

"Well, maybe it's more of a purr. Kind of sexy."

Liv looked to the ceiling. "Don't you ever give up?"

"I plead the fifth. Hey, where are you going?"

"Home."

"What's your hurry?" He followed her to the front door. "Don't you want to try sneaking out the back door?"

"Ugh. I can do without your snarky suggestions." She yanked the door open and looked quickly around. Which was ridiculous. She wasn't even guilty of anything, except maybe stupidity.

"A little late for regrets." He pulled a tragedy face.

"Ugh. I'll expect to hear from you later, with complete reports of what you've found out."

"Thanks for last night," he yelled after her. "I'll call you."

She heard his laughter as she jumped in her car and drove away. She doubted if he heard her reply.

Chapter Twenty-three

Liv peered out the window of the carriage house. No sign of the Zimmerman sisters. For a second, she considered driving to work. That way she wouldn't have to face her friends, because somebody was bound to have seen her car at Chaz's, make certain assumptions, and tell everyone in sight.

But she needed coffee, big-time. And besides, she had to face them sometime, and the sooner she did, the sooner she could explain what she'd been doing there and clear her reputation.

Which was a pitiful thought. She didn't care about clearing her reputation; she didn't have a reputation, but she wouldn't mind getting one. But not with Chaz; he just couldn't be trusted to take things seriously. What the heck was she thinking? She didn't want anything serious.

She wanted coffee. Out of habit, she reached for Whiskey's leash, remembered that he was still at the rectory. She probably should have picked him up on her way home this morning. She'd call Phillip as soon as she got to the office—after coffee.

She set off at a brisk pace, not looking left or right. Barely got to the sidewalk before she heard, "Yoo-hoo, Liv."

That didn't take long. She didn't stop, but called out, "Late for work," and waved to both sisters, who were standing on their front porch, smiling indulgently at her.

She speed-walked to the square and was building up a sweat by the time she reached the door of Apple of my Eye.

She took a breath and put on a smile.

"Morning, Liv." Dolly was looking as jolly and friendly as ever; then again Dolly might be counted on to be sympathetic. She didn't have a totally spotless past herself.

"Morning, Dolly." Liv leaned over the case to peruse the pans of breads and pastries.

"I have raspberry turnovers today. And I sent a peach cobbler over to Ida and Edna this morning, I told them to make sure to save you some. It's yummy, if I do say so myself. Where's Whiskey?"

"He's on a sleepover at the rectory."

"Keeping Leo company? That's a good idea. Quincy Hinks saw your car at the newspaper office this morning on his way to work."

"It's not what you think."

Dolly's eyes widened. "You mean you weren't investigating?"

"No."

"Oh. Do tell." Turnovers forgotten, Dolly leaned over the counter.

"Not that either. Okay yes, we were doing some research. Not exactly investigating."

"That's all right. We know the two of you will get to the bottom of it."

"Gotta run, Dolly. I'm really late."

"Oh, Ted can hold down the fort until you get there." She put two turnovers in a bag and handed it over to Liv. Then handed her another bag with Whiskey's doggie treat.

BeBe was waiting for her at the coffee steamer.

"Don't even say it."

"Don't make me withhold caffeine to hear all about it."

"I'm late, but in a nutshell, Henry Gallantine came home last night. Hildy called me to go over there. I don't know why she called me."

"Was that before the fight or after?"

Liv huffed out a sigh. "Is there ever a time when anything goes unnoticed in this town?"

BeBe shook her head. "You just have to learn to live with it. And go on doing what you want to do."

"It was after the fight. Then, after I went to Gallantine House, I drove past the *Clarion* office. The lights were on, so I went to report Henry's return to Chaz, who it turns out had been doing research on his own, so we started looking at connections, and I fell asleep on his couch while he was making coffee. Really terrible coffee.

"I didn't wake up until this morning. That's all."

"Learn anything?"

"Just some history, Revolutionary War history. But there's definitely some six degrees of separation in this town. And in its visitors."

They were quiet while BeBe steamed the milk for Liv's latte.

"Have you solved it yet?"

"No, I'm hoping Bill will. But I think we may have narrowed down the suspects."

"I hope I don't miss it all."

"I hope I do. Gotta run."

She practically ran to Town Hall and actually sprinted down the hall to the Events Office.

"Is my favorite dog still at the rectory?" Ted asked, taking the drinks and bakery bag from her.

"Yes. I'll call Pastor Schorr as soon as I get some caffeine in my system. Sorry I'm late."

"Liv, it's not even ten. Chill."

"Henry Gallantine is back in town."

"I heard. I talked to Bill."

"So you know about Grossman breaking in."

Ted nodded. "You had a busy day and night yesterday."

"I guess you also know I was at the *Clarion* office all night."

Ted turned to get the tray, but not before Liv saw him stifling a smile.

"Yes, Chaz called me to say you'd be late."

"He what?"

Ted chuckled. "Come on, I need my breakfast."

Liv filled Ted in on what they'd learned about Grossman.

"So we seem to have a lot of suspects here." He took a bite of turnover and chewed thoughtfully.

"Has Bill said anything to you besides what we already know?"

"He said he was going to talk to the LAPD as soon as it was late enough to verify Gallantine's whereabouts. If it checks out, I guess that lets Henry off the hook."

"Anything else?"

"They fingerprinted the musket and got a handful of different prints as well as some encrusted peanut butter; some soldier must have been eating his dinner during one of the reenactments."

"So the musket was one of the reenactment ones?"

"Yep. At least, evidence points that way," he added portentously. "One is missing. It wasn't checked out and it wasn't returned."

Liv felt a rush of excitement. "And who had access to them?"

"Just about anybody who walked into the Elks' storage room. That's where they're kept between battles."

The office phone rang, and Ted went out to answer it. He came back a few minutes later. "That was Phillip Schorr. He just dropped Leo off at school. He and the counselor decided it would do more harm than good to keep the boy out of school any longer. I hope they're right."

"You don't think there's real danger, do you? It was Cliff Chalmers who scared him by peering in the window."

"Yeah, I guess. Anyway, he said he'll drop Whiskey off in a few minutes."

Liv and Ted had just finished their morning "munch and crunch" session when Phillip Schorr came in with Whiskey.

Before Liv could yell, "Drop the leash," Whiskey had dragged the pastor through the outer office to Ted.

Fortunately, Schorr was laughing when Whiskey pawed at Ted and they began their yodeling routine.

"Sorry," Liv said. "They've got me trained to let go of the leash when Ted opens the door."

"Not at all. It's an experience to witness. I want to thank you for letting us keep him for the night. No incidents to report. Leo was very much comforted. Sometimes a pet is as good as a prayer." He smiled. "Or perhaps a pet is a form of prayer. Or the answer to a prayer. Sharise brought over supplies. She stayed awhile, and the upshot is that she's asked Leo to work for her two days a week after school. I think that will be an excellent job for him."

"That's great."

"Yes it is. He is really wonderful with animals; you should have seen him and Whiskey together. He has a special gift. And with a little training . . . this could be a very good thing. Thank you."

"Whiskey does have a way of making things better—I mean, not whiskey but—"

Pastor Schorr laughed. "I know what you mean. I hope any parishioners who drove by yesterday, with the three of us in the yard playing fetch and Leo and I calling out, 'Here Whiskey,' at the top of our lungs, will be as understanding."

"Do you think his mother will take him back after this is all over?"

"That I'm not sure about. But we'll think of something. Maybe find a foster-type family who will give him a room and a place in their hearts."

Someplace close to the Woofery, Liv thought, since Leo didn't seem to have a car.

"Well, I'd best be going. Catch up on some parish business while I have the morning to myself."

After he was gone, Whiskey went to sleep on his bed in the corner of Liv's office. Ted went to the post office, and Liv began plugging the committee figures into her Fourth of July spreadsheet.

Liv spent extra time studying A.K.'s security report. This report was more detailed than the one she'd made public at the roundup meeting. This showed the positions of his staff members, the areas each was responsible for, and the various patrol routes.

There had been two men at the entrance to Gallantine House, and they'd never left their post. There had been two traffic volunteers posted at the front gate, who directed people to entrance gates farther along the lawn.

Whoever had gotten onto the roof had to have either been in the house, known the "secret" door, or been part of the army that had been bivouacked in the woods before the first arrivals.

Stop it, Liv. Not your job. Filling in these numbers is your job. Planning the next event is your job.

But speculation kept encroaching into her best-laid plans, which slowed down her efficiency, which was why she was still working when the phone rang late that afternoon.

Ted came into her office. "That was Phillip Schorr. Leo didn't come to the community center. Phillip went home, but he isn't there either. He wondered if he came here. I told him no. You haven't heard from him?"

"No." Liv started to get up.

"Don't panic yet. Phillip is calling around."

"Do you think he might have gone over to the Woofery? He might be excited about having the job and just got confused about the day."

"Phillip already called there, too."

"Maybe he went to see Henry Gallantine? He might have heard something at school about him being back."

"Good thought. I'll tell Phillip to check with Hildy."

Ted came back a minute later. "He's calling Henry." He sat in his usual chair across the desk from Liv. Sighed.

"What?"

"I'm trying to remember the old days when life was dull around here."

Liv felt irrationally hurt. "You're beginning to sound like Janine. Do you miss those days?"

"Not once. And looking back, it's amazing I didn't murder her before you ever got here. I take it back, life was not only dull but continually exasperating. You have no idea how you've turned this town around."

Liv had some idea, but it hadn't been just her. Everybody was putting forth their best efforts for the most part. "I think someone said, 'It takes a village.' And this village has enthusiastically jumped on board. They just needed some organization."

"And effective publicity and marketing. And new ideas. Not to mention expanded venues and—I won't go on, or you might ask for a raise and throw the mayor into a tizzy."

"I'm very happy with what I have," Liv said. "Now, if we could tighten security just a bit."

"Not going to happen. I'm afraid this might be as good as it gets. And if you look at the stats, crime and accidents are way down from before."

"Except the biggest crime of all. But they are good. And I suppose it's nearly impossible to stop a murder when it's personal, as all of the recent ones have been. Right? They were all personal and not caused by the events?"

"Right."

"What did you do for security before I came?"

Ted grinned. "Fred and his orange-vested traffic-control team. Two cruisers and four patrolmen borrowed from the county."

Liv shuddered.

"So, you see, my dear: Crimes could have been happening all around us and chances are they went unnoticed. I must say, this Bayside team is good. No telling what they've stopped before it had a chance to happen."

"Well, when you put it that way."

They went back to work.

Pastor Schorr called a few minutes later to tell them Leo was indeed at Henry Gallantine's.

"One crisis averted," Ted said.

"Let's hope it's the last."

By late that afternoon, they had entered every report into the Battle of the Bay and Fireworks file.

Liv clicked out of the program. "I say we're done here."

"Yes. And I'm sensing a weekend off as next on our agenda."

"Sounds good to me. When did we last take a whole weekend?"

Ted tapped his forehead and frowned. "Too long ago to count. And after that, you're taking two weeks off, and after *that* you're giving me two weeks off. Then it starts all over again."

"Sounds like a plan." Liv pushed back from her desk and stretched.

Whiskey, recognizing a cue that work was about to wrap up, got up from his bed and came over for some attention.

Liv's cell phone rang.

"That's the last call and we're going home," Ted said.

Liv looked at caller ID. This time she recognized the number. "Not again. I wonder what it is now. I should never have given her my number." Liv swiped her phone and answered.

"Ms. Montgomery. I don't know what to do. You've got to come quick."

Liv was sure Ted could hear Hildy's screech through the phone, but she turned on speakerphone anyway.

"Hildy, slow down. What's wrong?"

"They're going to kill each other!"

"Who? What's going on, Hildy? Is Leo okay?"

Her question was answered by a scream, and the phone went dead.

"Let's go," Ted said, while Liv was still looking at the phone. "We'll take my car."

"Shouldn't we call Bill?"

"From the car." He ran from the room. Whiskey shot past her and followed Ted out the door.

Liv could only grab the leash and try to catch up.

Chapter Twenty-four

....

They raced to the employees' parking lot at the back of the building. Ted beeped the doors and the three of them scrambled in. Ted was backing out of the lot before Liv even got her seat belt on.

"Call Bill and tell him to meet us there."

Liv hit her speed dial; it went to voice mail. She left a message, told him about the call, and that they were going to the Gallantine House. "Meet us there." She hung up. "Now what?"

"You'd better call Chaz, we may need backup."

Chaz answered after the fourth ring, sounding sleepy, as usual.

"Focus," Liv practically screamed into the phone. "Ted and I are on our way to Gallantine House. Hildy called hysterical, there's some kind of altercation, Leo is there. Meet us there."

He hung up on her.

She shrugged at Ted. "He hung up on me."

Chaz's Jeep was screeching to a stop when Ted pulled his SUV to the curb outside the Gallantine mansion.

"That was fast," Liv said as they ran toward the door.

"That's because I'm good," Chaz said.

And she could see it. He was in reporter mode. And something else. Someone else. Someone who cared about the kid inside.

Hildy was waiting at the door. "Oh Lord, thank you. I don't know what he was thinking. They're all in there."

She hurried toward the parlor, not even looking askance at Whiskey. Ted, Chaz, and Liv followed close behind. They all stopped in the doorway.

Whiskey rushed past the housekeeper into the room and made a beeline for Leo, who was sitting on the floor with his back against the couch.

Liv was hit by a heavy sense of déjà vu: Leo crouched against the parapet and Jacob Rundle lying dead on the roof.

Whiskey climbed onto his lap and licked his face, which Leo buried in Whiskey's fur.

Henry's nephew stood off to the side, holding a heavy brass candlestick, but Liv couldn't tell whether he was planning to steal it or use it as a weapon. Either way, he wasn't going anywhere. Ted, Liv, and Chaz were blocking his only means of escape.

Seated, stiff-backed in the wing chair, was George Grossman, his arms raised as if to ward off a blow.

Daniel Haynes, dressed in a sport shirt and slacks, and Henry Gallantine, in a satin smoking jacket, were standing face-to-face in front of the fireplace. Both red-faced and angry.

"Oh my God," Ted said. "He's gathered all the usual suspects."

"You're not getting away with this again," Haynes cried, and before his astonished audience he grabbed one of the *Treasure Island* swords off the wall and brandished it at Henry.

Henry was out of reach of the other sword, but he jumped nimbly out of the way. "You fool. There are witnesses this time."

"What do I care for witnesses? Justice will be served." Haynes lunged. Henry took a step back.

"Justice? *You?* Talk of justice?"

Daniel lunged again. Again Henry jumped out of the way. Daniel began slashing at the air as he pressed Henry farther and farther back.

Haynes had backed Henry almost to the wall when Hildy wailed, "Somebody stop him."

Ted and Chaz looked at each other.

"A couple of nutcases," Chaz said.

"Agreed," Ted said. "But Liv doesn't want any more murders this month."

"She's no fun."

Liv stared at the two men in disbelief. Were they just going to stand there and let Daniel Haynes kill Henry? Then again, what could the two of them do without risking serious injury or worse?

But just as they started forward, Daniel Haynes turned the sword in their direction. "Stay back. We're going to settle this once and for all."

Ted and Chaz stopped where they were.

In the brief distraction, Henry reached behind him and pulled a black umbrella from the umbrella stand.

"En garde." He lunged at Haynes, who whirled about and just managed to deflect the umbrella with the sword blade.

And suddenly they were really going at it like the swashbucklers they were not. It was so frightening and ludicrous at the same time that no one could do anything but watch.

"I give up," Chaz said, looking around and sitting in a chair to view the entertainment.

"Confess before it's too late," Hayes sputtered. He was already winded. As a lawyer, he probably didn't get much fencing in.

"Confess?" Henry sneered. "Confess to what? To actually thinking you were an honorable man?"

"I'll show you honorable." Haynes feinted to the right.

But Henry was there with his umbrella to parry the attack.

"Tell me where you hid that document."

"Never. It's safe; that's all you need to know." Henry lashed out with his umbrella. The tip of Haynes's sword stuck in the fabric. There was a brief tussle, then Haynes ripped the sword away, leaving a piece of black fabric fluttering from the frame. Henry looked down at his torn weapon. "Now you've made me angry." He feinted with the umbrella, fabric whipping in the air.

Ted sat down, crossed his arms, seemingly content to wait for them to tire themselves out.

"You killed Rundle to protect your family's reputation. I won't let you get away with it." Haynes lunged.

Sword struck umbrella, parried, struck again.

"I know it all," Haynes huffed. "Rundle came to me, said he had found the chest, and he would sell it to me for an exorbitant price." *Whack, whack.* "It would prove Henry Gallantine's guilt. But I refused to buy it. It was despicable to me. I thought at last you would tell the truth. Instead you killed the man. Betrayal must run in your family's blood." *Slash, whack.*

"My family?" Henry looked genuinely nonplused and dropped the tip of his umbrella.

"Yes. I have you now." Haynes lunged again, but Henry jumped onto the couch, ran along the cushions, and jumped down on the other side.

Liv started getting some not-very-happy ideas. Henry Gallantine was in terrific shape.

"Lies. It wasn't my family. It was yours."

Haynes almost dropped his sword. "My family? General Haynes was a hero."

"Not according to the document I have. You fool. Rundle

found the document during one of the few times he actually did any work around here. He would have taken it if I hadn't caught him. He never had the chest in his possession. I took it. I hid it. I would never have betrayed your ancestor."

"My ancestor?" Haynes repeated, bewildered.

"His ancestor?" Grossman jumped from the chair. "No. It proved Henry Gallantine to be the real traitor—" He broke off.

"Why is it so important to defile my family's name?" Henry asked.

Grossman didn't answer, just sank onto the chair and hid his face in his hands.

"Because his ancestor was the real traitor," Chaz said.

Everyone looked at him, including Liv. When had he discovered that? While she was asleep? Damn the man.

"He wasn't," Grossman cried. "He was framed by one of them." He pointed to the two combatants, then turned his attention to the remaining sword on the wall. Fortunately, he was too short to reach it.

"You mean you never intended to buy the property for the museum?" Henry asked. "You were here to uncover what you thought were lies about your own family?"

"Who are you?" Haynes asked, his sword still pointed at Henry Gallantine.

"I'm George Grossman, great-grandson of Hezekiah Jenkins."

"Who the hell is that?" Henry asked, his umbrella at the ready.

"You probably haven't heard of him. He was the man who was accused when Gallantine was exonerated. Your families prospered; mine lost everything."

"That's preposterous," Haynes said. "I've never heard of anybody named Hezekiah Jenkins in the war."

"It's public record," Chaz said. "The man was tried and convicted. Whether because of additional evidence or as a scapegoat. He managed to escape before his execution, but he lived in poverty and exile for the rest of his life. His family never heard from him again, but he left a son. And the rest is history."

"He wasn't guilty," Grossman repeated.

"Guilty or not, I think George here came to get revenge."

"I did. But not by killing anyone. I found the hollow wainscoting the afternoon I was here taking inventory. I was sure the proof of Hezekiah's innocence must be in there. But Ms. Montgomery never left me alone long enough to get it out. So I came back. I took the chest out and placed it on the table, but before I could open it, someone hit me over the head. And when I woke up, the chest was open and the document was gone."

He turned on Henry. "Unless you hit me and took it."

"I didn't hit you. I didn't take anything out of the chest. It was never in that chest; just some old play money and plastic junk. That chest is a reproduction of the pirate chest from *Treasure Island*, the film I made back in 1962. I put it in the false panel because. . . well . . . it just seemed like a perfect place for a pirate chest."

"I would have found it." Leo, all but forgotten in the skirmish, pushed Whiskey from his lap and stood.

Henry spread his hands. "It was a fun game we played. Not a real treasure, is it, Leo?"

Leo looked confused. "Not the real treasure, just our treasure."

Henry looked up abruptly. "Leo, you didn't think—you didn't—no, you wouldn't."

"Or course he didn't, but somebody did," Chaz said.

Suddenly Leo shambled toward Henry. "Mr. Henry, you're bleeding."

Henry looked down at the sleeve of his smoking jacket. "Well, Leo, I believe you're right."

Daniel Haynes jerked around, his sword unintentionally slicing the air.

Everyone ducked.

"Oh my God, did I do that?"

"Just a lucky hit," Henry assured him. "I'm usually not so maladroit with an umbrella. Isn't that right, Leo?"

"Mr. Henry's real good with an umbrella. We fight with them when we look for the treasure. Sometimes he lets me win, though." They smiled at each other, comrades at arms, playmates in fantasy. Liv wasn't sure it was a good thing for Leo. She knew it couldn't be healthy for a man past middle age.

"You mean this thing is real?" Haynes asked, incredulously.

"Of course it's real."

"I thought it was a prop."

"It was, but it's a real sword."

"Good Lord, I could have killed you." Haynes dropped the sword and sank into the nearest chair.

"Isn't that what you wanted?" Henry asked.

"Of course not. I just wanted you to tell the truth."

"Ah, but what is truth, really?"

"I have half a mind to run him through myself," Ted said sotto voce.

Liv cut him a look.

"I'll toss you for it," Chaz said. "I'm not altogether maladroit with an umbrella myself. What a nutcase."

"Now to the real problem at hand," Henry said.

"What's that?" Grossman asked.

"Who killed Jacob Rundle?"

"The gardener?" Grossman shook his head.

"Yes. In my absence, someone killed Jacob Rundle, who was standing in for me at the reenactment. That's why I asked you all here tonight."

Hildy descended on him. "Why didn't you tell me what you were doing? I was scared out of my wits. I thought you and Mr. Haynes were going to kill each other. I even got Ms. Montgomery to come hieing over here to help me save you.

"How dare you!" Hildy reached behind her back and, before Liv could scream, "Watch out!" Hildy yanked at the back of her apron. The apron slid off; she wrapped it in a ball and threw it at her employer.

"I quit. You're a selfish man. You don't care about what your shenanigans do to other people. Leo's had a bad time of it 'cause you had to go traipsing off to Hollywood. Well, they didn't want you, did they? Did they?"

Slowly, Henry shook his head.

"It's about time you stopped living in your glorious past and came down to earth with the rest of us."

She turned on her heel and stormed out of the room. Leaving everyone openmouthed.

"Hildy?" Henry asked—mainly to himself, Liv thought. As if enlightenment had finally dawned. She hoped it had, because his actions had caused a lot of trouble and they still hadn't caught the killer.

She looked around the room. He had assembled all the probable suspects, just like a detective in an old movie. But maybe for once he'd done something useful.

With Henry being able to prove he was in LA, and Grossman in the bleachers, Haynes on his horse, the only other invited guest was the nephew. And . . .

"Mr. Grossman, when you met Frank down by the lake the afternoon we were here, was that a planned meeting?"

"What?"

"Did you plan to meet him after you'd finished work that day?"

"No, I just, uh, wanted to look around the property."

"Mr. Grossman," Chaz interrupted: "There are laws against misrepresentation."

"I didn't plan to meet him."

"But you saw him out by the boathouse when you were looking out the window, didn't you?" Liv asked.

"Well, yes. And to tell you the truth, I was curious. I'd seen him take an object off the table when he left."

"The figurine."

Grossman's eyebrows raised. "Yes."

"You little thief," Henry said, but without much surprise or anger. "I wondered what happened to that. I was afraid Hildy had broken it."

"He's lying," the nephew said. "He's just trying to keep the attention off himself. He probably killed old Jacob."

"I am not. And I did not. When I confronted you, you offered to cut me in."

"That's a lie," Frank said.

Grossman turned on him, stretching up to his full height. "Did you really think that once I was in possession of Gallantine House I would steal from the museum for some paltry commission to help a common thief?"

Slowly, they all turned toward the nephew, who had been gradually edging toward the door.

"That's total bull. I only came here in the first place because you were missing and mother was frantic with worry. I'll tell her you're alive and well. And I thought maybe you could lend me some more money to tide me over."

"Lend you money? I've never *lent* you any money. When you loan money you have an expectation of getting it back. I knew you would never pay me. I gave you that money. The more fool me. Because in spite of all your promises, I knew I would never see any of it again. But you've seen your last penny from me. And your last stolen artifact. Get out."

The sounds of sirens rose faintly in the distance.

"Perhaps we should all wait for the sheriff," Ted said.

"You can't keep me here." Frank Gallantine made a dash for the door, but Henry, in his own inimitable style, grabbed his arm. Frank knocked him to the ground and ran.

Whiskey started barking. Leo jumped in front of Frank, blocking his way to the door.

"Get away from me."

Leo stood his ground. "You hurt Mr. Henry."

"Bo-oo-oo! Crazy boy! Out of my way!" Frank raised

his arms at Leo as if to strike. No, not to strike but to scare. *Like a big bear on its hind legs.*

Leo stumbled back and fell on his butt. Whiskey jumped in front of him, barking like crazy.

A bear on its hind legs, thought Liv. *Or a ghost disappearing. Presto!*

"It's the ghost!" Leo cried.

"Good Lord," Ted said.

"Chaz!" Liv yelled. "He's yours."

"Don't mind if I do." Chaz jumped from his chair.

Frank swung around, making for the door. But before he got two steps, Chaz's fist slammed into his nose.

Blood gushed everywhere, just as Hildy returned with Bill Gunnison, three officers, and Phillip Schorr.

"Sorry, Hildy," Chaz said, shaking his hand.

"Don't you worry none, Charlie. This is one mess I won't mind cleaning up."

The officers handcuffed and Mirandized Frank and led him out to a squad car.

Bill looked around the room. "Would anyone like to tell me what just went on here?"

"You just hold your horses, Bill Gunnison." Hildy bustled out of the room; she returned seconds later with a tray of gauze, Band-Aids, and iodine.

She marched over to Henry. "Sit."

Henry sat and held out his arm. "Does this mean you're not quitting?"

"Who would take care of you if I did? But there are going to be some changes made."

Leo knelt by Henry's chair carefully watching Hildy clean the wound.

"I don't envy Henry," Ted said. "That woman is formidable."

Henry waved his other hand. "Daniel, get everyone drinks in my stead. Leo, you can go on back to the kitchen and get yourself a soda."

But Leo wasn't about to leave his side.

Daniel made drinks just like it was an evening soiree instead of the wrap-up of a murder investigation.

And Liv thought that there wasn't so much difference between a faded movie star and a lawyer who portrayed his ancestor in a summer pageant. Both of these men had a streak of fantasy at odds with reality.

When Hildy finished, Henry began his presentation. For presentation it was. Down to "the plot thickens."

"But it's Leo here who is the real hero. He recognized the killer, didn't you son?"

"He acted just like the ghost," Leo said.

"Yes, he did, and you solved the case," Henry said.

Liv had to force herself not to tell Henry to stop filling Leo's head with any more flights of fancy. She'd have to make sure Phillip Schorr explained to Leo that he wasn't to do any more case solving in the future. That was all they needed.

The pastor and Leo were the first to leave. "Leo does have school tomorrow, and then he starts his new job at the Woofery."

"Well, don't be a stranger, Leo," Henry said.

"I won't, Mr. Henry."

"I'll join you," Daniel said. "If that's okay with you, Bill."

"Yes, we're pretty much finished here."

George Grossman, with a quick apology to Henry, followed the others out.

"Well," Henry said, "it's been quite a night."

"Yes," said Bill. "And it happened to work this time, but don't ever pull something like that again, Henry. This is not the movies."

Henry laughed, a full, round baritone. "No, Hollywood is a bit more dangerous. All that backstabbing, you know."

Bill's mouth tightened, but he refrained from answering.

Henry saw them all to the door.

"Just one thing," Liv asked. "Do you mind if I ask. Is there a document?"

Henry shrugged.

"You'd be holding out on primary source material, if there is," Chaz said.

It was the first time she'd heard him speak like a serious journalist.

"My dears, this country has lived two centuries without knowing whether it was truth or not. I think it can survive a few more without knowing for sure." He winked at Liv.

"Good night all," he said, and closed the door.

Chapter Twenty-five

....

It was Friday before Bill showed up at the Events Office, bringing Chaz with him. "Figured I might as well tell it once and get it over with."

"Hell, I thought he was arresting me." The smirk was back in Chaz's expression.

"And I might yet if you keep up this tendency to deck people."

"Hey, the last time I was aiding an arrest."

"Uh-huh." Bill lowered himself into a straight-backed chair Ted had brought in from the outer office.

"Is your sciatica flaring up again?" Liv asked.

"A bit, but with any luck things will quiet down around here, including my back." He narrowed his eyes at her. "You don't have anything special planned for the next month or so?"

"Nothing major. Besides, Ted and I are going on vacation. Not at the same time. There will always be someone in the office if we're needed."

"And I'm booked with a bunch of fishing groups," Chaz

said. "The only thing I'll be fighting are bass and lake trout. A-a-ah. Peace and quiet."

"And mosquitoes," Liv said under her breath.

"Nah, those I'll be swatting, not fighting." Chaz grinned. His face had turned from black and purple to yellow and green. Not pretty.

"Bill, can you tell us anything about what happened to Jacob Rundle?" Liv asked.

"Pretty cut and dried. It goes something like this: Rundle and Frank were both helping themselves to portable loot out of Gallantine House. Frank found out and suggested they join forces. Rundle had more access to the inside of the house. Frank had better places to fence what they stole.

"But as usually happens with the good, the bad, and the ugly . . ." Bill grinned. "Notice the allusion to the movies?"

"We noticed," Ted said. "Get on with it."

"Well, Rundle got greedy, according to Frank anyway. Though, consider the source. Rundle started holding out on him, dealing on the side. Then he found the 'treasure chest' when he was cleaning out one of the storerooms in the mansion."

"And Henry caught him," Liv said. "I bet that's why he told him not to come back in the house."

"Got it in one," Chaz said.

"How did you know?" Liv asked.

"I asked Henry."

"Anyway," said Bill, "it was just around the time that everybody was preparing for the reenactment. But according to Frank, Rundle was two-timing him, and approached Daniel Haynes on his own.

"And I surmise, mainly from what Daniel said, that Daniel sent him packing. Somehow Frank heard about Grossman offering to buy Gallantine House and rushed into town to see what was going on. Read: to see what he could steal before the sale went through.

"My words, not his. He's talking, but I'm not sure how

much of it is truth and how much wishful thinking. There's a streak of theatricality in that family that didn't stop with Henry.

"Anyway, Henry leaves town. Frank goes to confront Rundle. Rundle is getting ready for the reenactment. Puts Frank off. So Frank follows him up the tower stairs to have it out with him.

"They're arguing away. When it comes time to give the signal, Rundle puts the musket down and picks up the lantern. Frank picks up the musket. He swears he just meant to scare him, but Rundle turned around and fell into the bayonet."

"Really," Ted said. "He expects to get off with self-defense?"

"He's an idiot," Chaz added.

"Oh, he won't get off completely. But we cut him a deal."

"Why?" Liv asked. "He killed that man."

"Yeah, and we might prove it someday. But the case pretty much rests on his account and circumstantial evidence. Better ten to twenty than back on the streets and ripping off other people or putting Leo through a court case."

Chaz gave Liv a look, and Liv knew he was reminding her about the reason he got in fights, because the law didn't always work.

"But what about the cape Leo said he was wearing? Did you find it? And wouldn't that mean it was premeditated? Frank wasn't in the reenactment."

"Yeah, it does. But we don't have a cape and Frank isn't talking."

"It's better than nothing," she said as much to Chaz as to Bill.

"It is. Besides, he's seriously in debt to some not-very-nice people."

"Priceless," Chaz said. "He won't be able to pay if he's in jail."

"Obviously," Liv said.

"He can't get to them, but they can get to him."

"And probably will," Ted said. "Save the taxpayers a bundle."

"A bundle," Bill agreed.

"You're shocking Liv," Chaz said.

Ted and Bill both turned toward her.

"Liv, he's scum. He'll get what he deserves." Bill shifted to ease his back. "He might get off. Depends on what kind of lawyer he can come up with."

Chaz barked out a laugh. "They'll get to him whether he's in jail or not."

"Who?" asked Liv.

All three men gave her their versions of a don't-be-dense look.

"Oh, the people who loaned him money. So can we get back to what happened?"

"Sure, what do you want to know?"

"Did he tell you how he got away?"

"More or less. He would have gone back down through the tower and out the side gate if Leo hadn't come blundering up the stairs and blocked off his escape. He had to play the old falling-over-the-parapet trick. It worked with Leo because he didn't know about it."

Liv blushed. She'd fallen for it, too.

"Anyway he had to sit on the ledge waiting for the battle to start so he could get away. And then, miraculously, the general left his horse and went into the woods, and Frank jumped down from roof to roof like he'd probably done all his life. Took his place with the volunteers, and when they ran to the shore he went into the boathouse and deposited the loot he'd taken from the house. Then rowed away with the rest of them. The perfect getaway. He seemed very pleased with himself.

"The man can think on his feet, I gotta say that about him," Bill said.

"Too bad for him he didn't keep going," Ted said.

"That's about it. Henry and Daniel have made up. Grossman has returned to his historical research, which I hope keeps him in another part of the country for a long time. And I have work to do."

Bill stood.

Chaz stood, too. "I'll come with you. You can give me a ride home. I've got to put up my Gone Fishing sign and start tying some lures. A case of beer and some beef jerky. See you in September, maybe."

He strolled toward the door, turned back. "So have a nice vacation, Ms. Event Planner. Try to relax a little bit. Where are you going?"

Liv shrugged.

"Let me guess. Manhattan. Bright lights, big city, trendy bars."

"No."

"The islands? Nice sweet drinks with umbrellas in them. Cabana boys with ripped abs?"

"Nuh-uh."

"You gotta do something. You can't just work. At least take a weekend at the spa, mani-pedi and all that."

"Actually," Liv said. "I'm going to stay right here. I think it's about time I learned to fish."

NATIONAL BESTSELLING AUTHOR
CAROLYN HART

Dead, White, and Blue

A DEATH ON DEMAND MYSTERY

Summer is a hectic time of the year for Annie Darling,
bringing swarms of tourists to her mystery bookstore, Death
on Demand, for the latest beach reads. But Annie still finds
time to enjoy herself. The Broward's Rock Fourth of July
dance is just around the corner, and the island is buzzing
with excitement—Shell Hurst included . . .

Shell is the kind of woman wives hate—for good reason—
and most of them wish she would just disappear. But when
she does, and a teenage girl is the only one who seems to
notice, Annie can't help but feel like someone should be looking for her.

The residents of Broward's Rock grow uneasy when a second
islander mysteriously disappears. Annie and her husband,
Max, know something dangerous is brewing. They soon find
themselves following a twisted trail marked by blackmail,
betrayal, and adultery.

carolynhart.com
facebook.com/AuthorCarolynHart
facebook.com/TheCrimeSceneBooks
penguin.com

M1230T1212